BLOOD, SNOW, & CLASSIC CARS

ALSO BY JOSEPH HANSEN

BLOOD, SNOW, & CLASSIC CARS

MYSTERY STORIES

□

Joseph Hansen

Leyland Publications
San Francisco

1st edition.
The book *Blood, Snow, & Classic Cars* is copyright © 2001 by Joseph Hansen.
Front cover photo of model on left by Kristen Bjorn.
Cover collage by Stevee Postman.

These stories first appeared as follows, and are reprinted by permission:

"Surf" *Playguy* (London) 1976
"Molly's Aim" *Ellery Queen's Mystery Magazine* June 1989
"An Excuse for Shooting Earl" *Alfred Hitchcock's
Mystery Magazine* September 1992
"Home Is the Place" *Ellery Queen's Mystery Magazine* January 2000
"Blood, Snow, and Classic Cars"
Alfred Hitchcock's Mystery Magazine (pending)
"Son of the Morning" is printed here for the first time.

Library of Congress Cataloging-in-Publication Data

Hansen, Joseph, 1923–
  Blood, snow, & classic cars : mystery stories / Joseph Hansen.
  189 p. ; 22 cm.
  Contents: Blood, snow, & classic cars—An excuse for shooting Earl—Molly's aim—Home is the place—Surf—Son of the morning.
  ISBN 0-943595-83-5 (alk. paper)
    1. Detective and mystery stories, American.   I. Title.

PS3558.A513 B57 2000
813'.54—dc 21   CIP
                                                         00-58773

Leyland Publications
PO Box 410690
San Francisco, CA 94141
Complete catalogue of books is available for $1 ppd.

CONTENTS

BLOOD, SNOW, & CLASSIC CARS

TALBOT HAD LET Hovis drive the Maserati tonight. Not to Madison, no, but to Randall Falls, the nearest town not too dinky for there to be some action. It was February. It had begun to snow, and while he'd showered and shaved, Hovis had dreamed of driving back here at midnight with somebody new from the bars, in this fantastic car, snow blown into high drifts beside the cleared highway, and gleaming in the moonlight on the branches of the pines.

He was driving home alone. No one he wanted was in the bars. That was okay. He was still young. He could take his time. And even alone, he loved the snow. It was beautiful, like in some painting. Hovis sometimes daydreamed of going to art school to learn how to paint. But there was no hurry about that, either. This setup, living in Talbot's guest house, rent free, was too good to leave. About all he had to do was keep the cars shiny.

The Maserati was built for speed, and since he'd met only one rattly pickup truck on this highway tonight, he let his foot weigh on the gas pedal, and ate the thirty-five miles from Randall Falls to Talbot's sprawling ranch house in thirteen minutes. He geared down, swung the rumbling, low-slung classic off the highway past the dozen, snow-covered not-so-classic cars Talbot displayed down here, and his headlights flicked across a bundle of rags beside the drive.

He braked. People threw trash everywhere. Talbot hated that. Hovis would pick it up now and get rid of it before Talbot ever saw it. In foot-deep snow, he bent over the bundle. And it groaned. He jerked his hand back. It was no bundle. It was a man. A leg kicked feebly, an arm tried to reach out. Hovis began to shake. And not from the cold. He bent closer, narrowing his eyes, trying to see. His mouth was dry. He moistened his lips. His own voice sounded alien to him.

"Gene?"

Heart thumping, finding it hard to breathe, Hovis crouched and folded back a sheepskin coat collar that hid the man's face. The wool crackled because ice crystals had formed on it. This was Talbot, all right. The moonlight made the blood look black. His hair was matted with blood. His hands were slashed. Blood was all over the back of the sheepskin jacket. Hovis ran for the Maserati, fumbled with the gear shift, killed the engine, began to whimper, got the engine started again, and careened up the long, curved driveway to the house.

Lemke was new. That was why he was on nights from ten to six Monday through Thursday. Nothing much happened then. But something had happened tonight, and he was in charge so he handled it. The first thing he did when he got to the Talbot place was to look at the victim, radio in for an ambulance, and take polaroids. The second thing was to talk to Bobby Hovis, who had discovered the crime and dialled 911. Hovis bunked in Gene Talbot's guest house, had no visible means of support, and had been driving one of Talbot's expensive cars. He had alcohol on his breath and blood stains on his clothes and on his hands. He was pacing up and down Talbot's long living room, looking as if he was about to cry, but he didn't cry, and he didn't stop pacing even when Lemke told him to sit.

"I had his permission to drive the Maserati," Hovis said.

"I don't think so," Lemke said. "I think you took it without his permission, and when you got home, he was waiting down there for you and raised hell with you about it, and you're drunk and you shot him."

"That's crazy," Hovis said. "He's my friend. He's good to me. I wouldn't hurt him. I wish I'd gotten here sooner. I'd have helped him fight them off, whoever did it." He stopped and gazed wide-eyed at Lemke, holding his hands out. "Who would do such a horrible thing? Why?"

"Nobody liked him," Lemke said. "That's why. He was a degenerate, a drug dealer, jewel smuggler, child molester, pornographer, homosexual. If you don't know how this town felt about him, then you're the only one."

"Then arrest them, for Christ sake," Hovis said. "Why me? Two perverts with one stone, is that it?"

Lemke blinked. "You want to explain the blood all over you?"

"He was alive. He groaned. He reached out. He moved his legs.

I thought—I don't know. I thought he wanted me to help him up."

"Robert Hovis"—Lemke detached the never-before-used hand-cuffs from the back of his belt—"you are under arrest for aggravated assault against the person of Eugene Squires Talbot."

"I had three beers," Hovis said. "Three lousy draft beers."

"Turn around," Lemke said. "You have the right to remain silent." He yanked Hovis's arms behind him. The handcuffs clicked. "Anything you say can and will be used against you in a court of law. . . ."

Shattuck came in at six because he hated being home alone. Mornings were the worst. The two kids were off at college. And his wife was dead. Breast cancer. Only ten weeks ago. A house should be full of life first thing in the morning, excited voices, coffee smells, bacon sizzling. He showered, dressed, entered the kitchen only to cross it to the garage door. He drove along streets of tall old frame houses, under big, winter-naked trees standing in snow, to eat breakfast at Mom's Diner on Main street—for the talk and laughter, not the greasy food. The old joke was right: *Never eat at a place called Mom's.*

Then he drove straight to the sand-colored stucco building marked *Randall County Sheriff's Department*, the Percival sub-station of which he, a lieutenant, age forty-eight, was in charge. He pushed in through thick glass doors out of the cold, a massive man, six foot four, two hundred fifty pounds, and hung up his jacket and fur hat. Lanky Deputy Lemke was watching him from his desk like a kid. Was that pride on his farmboy face? Or fright?

"Something to tell me, Avery?" Shattuck said.

And Lemke came eagerly into his office to tell him. He was so excited, he couldn't sit down. He talked in a breathless rush, waving the papers in his hand. The arrest report. He'd been writing it for hours. He needed hours. He was slow on a keyboard. When he ran out of speech, he laid the report in its folder on the desk. Shattuck put on reading glasses and began turning the pages.

"Why didn't you phone me when the call came in?" he said.

"Middle of the night. I didn't want to wake you up," Lemke said. "I mean a man was down. It didn't sound like something all that big and important. I figured I could handle it." He straightened with pride. "I did handle it. Caught the perpetrator red-handed."

"And the weapon?" Shattuck said. "You have the weapon?"

"I don't. But Talbot keeps guns around, lots of guns. Whole town knows that. Why wouldn't Hovis carry one of those?"

"Well, did he? Did you find it on him?"

Lemke shifted from foot to foot. "It must be someplace out there in the snow. Couldn't see it in the dark."

"Yup," Shattuck sighed, and picked up the telephone. "You did make sure the injured man got to the hospital, right?"

"First thing," Lemke said.

"Good." Shattuck punched the hospital number. Not in Percival. In Randall Falls. He had to wait, and while he waited he read more of Lemke's report. After a while, not a recording but a human being spoke to him, he asked questions, got answers, said thanks, and hung up. "Sit down, Avery."

Lemke peered at him, scared. Shattuck did not have a poker face. His disgust was showing, even to as dense a subject as Lemke. "That man was shot six times at close range with a .22. Then his skull and hands and back were hacked with a hatchet. Or maybe it happened the other way around."

"He did look pretty awful," Lemke said.

"You don't say," Shattuck said. "All right, you didn't find the gun. So tell me, did you find a bloody hatchet?"

"Hovis had blood on him," Lemke said stubbornly.

Shattuck tapped the report. "But it shows here that you dragged poor Miz Durwood out into the cold from home to check the internet"—craggy Edna Durwood was the oldest employee here, and the only one on the payroll who could use the internet—"and Hovis has no criminal record."

"He was drunk," Lemke said. "Talbot chewed him out. He lost it. You know how hysterical they get."

Shattuck grunted. "So you booked him and fingerprinted him."

Lemke brightened. "Yes, sir. You bet. And locked him in a cell."

"And faxed your report over to Randall Falls?"

"Oh, no, sir." Lemke was shocked at the thought. "I wouldn't send it without you signed off on it, sir."

Shattuck handed it to him. "Good. Then you can just put it in the shredder, now. All copies, Avery. And we'll forget it ever happened."

Lemke was dumbfounded. "The shredder? Why?"

"Because you made a mistake, and unless we destroy all record of it, and humbly beg Hovis's pardon, odds are ten to one that Talbot's tireless defenders at the Civil Liberties Union will sue your ass, my ass, the whole County's ass, for false arrest and illegal detention."

Lemke said, "But he did it, Lieutenant. It had to be him. He was the only one there."

"He was the only one there, Avery," Shattuck explained, "because the assailant ran off. Hovis phoned 911 and waited around for you. That didn't suggest to you that maybe he wasn't the assailant? That's what it suggests to me. Load two shovels in the trunk of a patrol car, pick up deputy Schneider at his house, and the pair of you drive back to the Talbot place and search for those weapons. Let nobody near the house or the grounds, and do not say one word to anybody. I don't care how many TV cameras and microphones they have. Not one word, understand?"

Shattuck drove Hovis home so he could change into clothes that weren't bloodstained. Lemke and Schneider had strung between tree trunks broad yellow ribbons that said *Crime Scene* on them, and were turning the snow over around the cars down by the road. He lifted a hand to them in passing. While Hovis changed, Shattuck went into the main house and looked at the engagement calendar on Gene Talbot's dusty desk. Whoever came up here and maimed him didn't have an appointment. He roved through the sprawling house, looking for the fabled gun collection. Paintings, figurines, cut glass, but no guns. Talbot was a reader. Shattuck ran his gaze over the shelves. Brazil. Sunken treasure. Lost mines. Jewels and gems. Horse breeding. *The Male Nude in Art*. And of course classic cars. He stepped out into the cold sunshine and pulled the door shut so it locked.

Next he needed to get Hovis off the absorbing subject of himself. Driving up here from the sub-station, Shattuck had learned about Hovis's strait-laced parents, his boyhood, high school years, single year of college, his 7-11 store and Wal-Mart jobs. All in

Madison. And how, after he came out to his folks, and they changed the locks on the doors, he began staying nights with strangers picked up in parks, coffee shops, bus stations, and how this had led him out of Madison to other towns, and at last to Percival, where he met the legendary Gene Talbot.

Now Hovis sat beside Shattuck again, smelling of soap, and Shattuck was driving him to the hospital to see his friend, benefactor, lover. Shattuck still winced at that word in this context. But the long, clean-swept highway curving through pine-grown hills to Randall Falls offered more time for talk. And Hovis talked. If he was sore at what Lemke had done to him, he didn't seem to mind opening up to Shattuck. He was either guileless or a damn good actor.

"Sometimes he wants company in the evenings, and I stay with him and we"—Hovis was blond and blushed easily—"like, watch, um, videos."

Shattuck laughed without amusement. "I know all about those videos. Hauled a truckload of 'em out of there a few years back. There was a trial about it. He has a Constitutional right to keep them. We hauled 'em all back."

Hovis was quiet for a while, watching the snowy landscape out the car window. Then he went on, "Usually, if I want to go out, he doesn't mind. I can take any car I want, as long as he says okay. I don't like to take the really rare ones in case I have an accident. But last night I took the Maserati because I wanted to score, and it makes an impression, all right?"

"But it didn't," Shattuck said. "You came back alone."

Hovis shrugged. "Snow kept people home. The bars were half empty."

"The doctors say he hadn't been lying out there long when you found him," Shattuck said. "Try to remember. Did you see anybody around?"

"Nobody," Hovis said. "I mean, even this highway was empty. Once I got out of Randall Falls, I didn't meet but one car all the way back."

"What kind of car?" Shattuck said. "Where, exactly?"

"Old white pickup," Hovis said. "Just before I crossed the bridge, okay?"

"Notice who was in it?"

Hovis thought for a second. "Some high school kid," he said.

"Get a good look at him?"

Hovis turned red. "I was seeing how fast the Maserati would go."

"We had a teen-age witness once, claimed Talbot threw parties with high school boys. Wild, naked parties? Drink and dope?"

Hovis marveled. "What? Get serious! He swore this in court?"

"His parents wouldn't let him. County Attorney had to drop the case."

"Shit, I never saw any boys. Sure, friends come now and then. From out of town. Weekends, mostly. Sometimes they party. But they're Gene's age."

"Make me a list." Shattuck stopped at the hospital entrance, and Hovis got out, but before he closed the door, he bent down to add:

"One thing was a little weird. The kid driving that truck—he didn't have any jacket. And I mean, it was cold last night."

Shattuck parked in the hospital lot under a leaning, snow-clad pine tree. In a slot marked with some doctor's name. Nice thing about driving a Sheriff's car. You could park any damned place you chose. He had to ask a few busy people, but he at last found out where Eugene Squires Talbot was. And here came Hovis carrying a big bunch of plastic-wrapped flowers, and looking stormy. "Whoa," Shattuck said, and took his arm. "What's the matter?"

"They won't let me see him." Hovis pointed with the bouquet back down the corridor. Gathered outside double doors marked *Intensive Care Unit* stood a middle-aged woman, a young woman, and a young man. "Claim they're his damn family," Hovis said. "Flew in from Chicago. Say if I don't stop trying to see him, they'll call security and have me thrown out. Why?"

"This way." Shattuck led him to chairs clustered around a low table in an alcove. "Sit down. Cool off." And Hovis sat, clutching the flowers so hard his knuckles were white. Shattuck sat facing him. "That's his ex-wife," he said. "And his daughter. I don't know the man. Maybe the daughter's husband. Time flies."

"He never told me he was married," Hovis said.

"It was a long time ago," Shattuck said.

Hovis laid the flowers on his knees. "Yeah, well. 'Ex-wife,' isn't that what you said? They're divorced. So what gives her the right to shut me out?"

"I'm not sure she has the right," Shattuck said. "Maybe the daughter has. She didn't divorce him. There's no such thing as an ex-daughter."

"It's because I'm gay, isn't it? Well, so is Gene Talbot gay. They think if I don't see him that's gonna change him back? I want to see him." Hovis stood up, dumped the flowers, picked them up. He peered down the hall to those double doors. "Hold his hand, tell him I'm here, tell him I'm sorry I wasn't around when he needed me." He looked at Shattuck. "What the hell are they to him? He never talks about them. I'm here. I'm his goddamn friend." Tears came into his eyes. "I love him. Not sometime years back. Now. And he loves me."

"Yes, all right," Shattuck said. "Wait here. I'll see what I can do."

He went down the corridor, past the pale-faced family, and pushed into the unit where the glaring air was filled with antiseptic smells and voices and the beeping of monitors. Green-clad, white masked, harried staff moved grimly purposeful among beds hidden or half hidden by curtains. For a second, he got a glimpse of Talbot. He'd never seen anybody hooked up to so many wires, tubes, machines. A nurse carrying a clip-board noticed him. "Sheriff?"

"How's Gene Talbot doing?"

"His heart is strong. It's senseless, since the rest of him is broken beyond repair, but it keeps pumping away." She was a worn-looking woman who had perhaps only a year or two ago been pretty. Her laugh was brief and dry. "But whoever said the human heart made sense?"

Shattuck said, "Robert Hovis is here, the friend who found him last night, and he's very upset. They were close. Lived together. He wants to see him, speak to him. Family's digging in their heels. Can you—?"

She shook her head, her smile regretful. "I can't change hospital rules, Sheriff. You're here only because of your badge. And I'm afraid you can't stay. Whatever you need to know officially, you can learn at the desk."

Shattuck blinked. "So the family can't come in, either?"

"No one but medical personnel," she said.

"All right. Thank you." Shattuck turned away. "I'll tell him."

She touched his sleeve. "Oh, and Sheriff—no flowers."

Edna Durwood didn't have to read and clip the local papers, the daily Randall Falls *Reporter*, the weekly *Percival Press*, but she did. It was no part of her job description. But often there wasn't a lot of action in this office, and it helped to pass the time. So it cheered her up when Shattuck laid on her desk the flowers Hovis hadn't known what to do with, and asked her:

"Have you got a file on Gene Talbot?"

Steel-rimmed glasses with thick lenses perched on her witchy nose. She glared at him through them. But he'd surprised her, and she smiled, a rarity. He couldn't recall when he'd last seen Edna Durwood do that. She sniffed, "Do you know anybody in this town who's been in the papers more?" She took off her mouth-piece-earpiece rig, got up and marched off to fetch the folders. She laid them on his desk, and went to put the flowers in water.

Shattuck went through the clippings briskly because he remembered much of the fact and fancy they detailed. The paper of the oldest was brittle. It was a dozen years back when Gene Talbot jumped into print. At that time he lived in Randall Falls, where he owned a thriving new car dealership. He had driven his wife and two girls to Madison to catch a flight to Chicago, to visit her parents.

Then he had stopped off at a gay bar, where he'd picked up a fair young stranger and taken him home to Randall Falls for the weekend. This youth was not what he seemed to be. He had a gun and, poking it into Talbot's ribs, had ordered him to drive to his bank and withdraw all his savings in cash, and make the blue-eyed boy a present of them. Talbot as instructed walked into the bank with the youth close at his side, but when he got to the teller he told her what was going on. The youth didn't shoot Talbot dead as he had threatened. Instead, he tried to run away, but a security guard caught him.

Unluckily, he told the police, public defender, judge and whoever else would listen, exactly how and why he happened to be with Gene Talbot that day. Talbot's wife left him, taking along the kids. The good folk of Randall Falls decided to buy their new cars from someone better-behaved. And Talbot sold the dealership, bought the ranch house outside Percival, and settled here to live, surrounded by his collection of classic cars. He wanted to breed race horses, but Percival's zoning laws wouldn't let him.

This didn't slow him down. He raced through town in Bugatis, Aston Martins, Ferraris, even a 1933 Auburn for a while. He always wore flashy clothes the like of which Percival had only glimpsed in magazines. And on weekends he threw parties. Percival knew this because of all the expensive if not classic cars—not one of them carrying a woman—that went tooling out the highway to Talbot's place. The place was so isolated anything at all could have gone on there and nobody not invited would have seen or heard.

Percival didn't need to see and hear. Gossip filled in for lack of witnesses. It wasn't good-hearted gossip. It was mean-spirited and squalid. Shattuck came to hate the talk, and to avoid it if he could. But he wished Talbot would tone down his behavior and buy his liquor out of town. He bought a lot of booze, Wild Turkey, Glenlivet, Tanqueray. And champagne. Taittinger's, Cliquot, God knew. By the case. Art Gillespie at Economy Liquor had never seen anything like it. He didn't complain, but he sure as hell did tell everybody.

Then the foreigners started coming. Easily spotted by their chauffeur-driven stretch limousines and the costumes of the passengers. Indians in turbans, Egyptians and Arabs in flowing robes, Africans in khaftans. Japanese. South Americans. And the legendary cars that had stood around Talbot's low-roofed, rangy house on its hill, like prize bulls in a feed-lot, were carried off on trucks, as many as six masterpieces at a time.

It would figure, said the fellas at the barber shop, the gals at the beauty parlor, that if Talbot had been rich before, and everyone was certain he had, then by now he must be a billionaire. Then he added to the excitement and speculation by leaving town for a time. A travel agent in Madison had a sister in Percival, and she said Talbot had flown to Brazil, to buy land there, and raise thoroughbreds.

The FBI thought different. They thought he had flown down there to pick up cocaine in exchange for some of the cars he had shipped out earlier. Shattuck of course was told what they thought. It turned out they were wrong. Talbot had been flattered to have their attention, and while denying he was ever a courier, pretended to know a lot of Latino drug dealers. The FBI had investigated his leads. They were all brag, no substance. Talbot told one investigator that while he never dealt drugs, he occasionally used them. Recreationally.

"I doubt it," the agent in charge had told Shattuck in disgust. "Yeah, he's got ten thousand acres of land in Brazil. Wasteland. No water. You couldn't raise lizards there, let alone horses. And those cars of his—half of them are put together out of junked parts, slicked up, and sold as untouched originals." He wagged his head over the farewell beer Shattuck had bought him at the Hoffbrau on Main street. "But what a con-man he is. Jesus. What a sweet-talker. And you know, I think he believes his own lies. He doesn't live in the world we live in. He dreams it up and thinks it's real."

How true this was came out when later Talbot bought a 1953 Cadillac Eldorado Convertible from its owner, gave him $50,000 in cash and the rest, $30,000, in diamonds. The seller sued. Experts testified the diamonds were trash. The court agreed. Talbot claimed he'd been deceived about the diamonds. And he still wanted the car, so he mortgaged his house to make up the shortfall. Percival raised its eyebrows. Talbot wasn't a billionaire, after all. Still, Shattuck thought, he probably had a buyer in some far corner of the world willing to pay him more than the market price.

He stayed afloat and the town kept gossiping about him, and he was back in court a few more times, most notably when some kid told a teacher that Talbot was taping sex among high school boys at his home, and selling the videos over the internet. Shattuck, since the Sheriff needed to be re-elected about that time, was ordered to turn the ranch house upside down. He found a lot of videos that surprised him. Stuff those boys were doing he'd never even heard of at their age. Some of it not till now. But Talbot denied he'd made the videos, said he'd bought them from other sources. And the people couldn't prove he hadn't. The defense could prove the claims about the internet were false. The Civil Liberties lawyers had a gleeful time establishing Talbot's first amendment right to own and enjoy the videos. And the Sheriff was elected again, anyway.

Shattuck lifted his head and looked at the clock. He'd wasted an hour on this stuff. And learned nothing. He turned over the rest of the clippings, only glancing at them. All stuff he knew. But what was this final one? Datelined last week. A funeral writeup. From the Percival *Press*, with the usual typos and misspellings. *JURGEN JENSEN BURIED AT 34*. Shattuck frowned down the room at Edna who was fielding a phone call. She hung up, and he asked, "What's this Jensen funeral thing doing in the Talbot file?"

"I didn't know where else to put it," she said. "He's the only person ever died of AIDS in Percival. And you know who dies of AIDS well as I do. Only other gay man we've got here is Talbot."

The office was at the back of the tall white frame church. Nobody had shoveled the walk alongside the building so Shattuck kicked through snow to the five steps that climbed to the office door on which a neat sign read *Come In*. He went in. It was colder inside than outside, where a pale sun was shining. Doors stood open on three offices but nobody was in any of them. Still, maybe someone was in the building, because he heard organ music. He found the chancel, squeezed his bulk through a narrow door and climbed corkscrew stairs to the organ loft. Thirtyish, skinny, the organist wore a pony-tail, jeans, and a T-shirt stencilled with a picture of Jerry Garcia. At the sight of Shattuck, he raised his hands in mock fear. "My name is Denis Du Pre," he said. "And I didn't do it."

Shattuck said, "You didn't play for Jurgen Jensen's funeral?"

Du Pre's cheerfulness died. "Not what he would have wanted. I played groany old Calvinist hymn tunes. What his parents wanted. They sat there, stiff as wood, with their white-bread daughter and her son. They were uncomfortable. Church full of gays and lesbians. But the boy was broken up. Big kid, hockey player, straight-A student, class president. Crying like a four-year-old."

"Over an uncle? Any idea why?"

"He'd been kind to him. Years ago. When the parents broke up."

Shattuck gazed down at the rows of empty pews. "Jurgen your friend?"

"Last couple years, yes. After he got HIV. We have to help each other."

"So you know his other friends," Shattuck said.

Du Pre grew wary. "Some. Why? What's this all about?"

"Gene Talbot is in the hospital. Intensive care. He was assaulted last night. With a hatchet, among other things. He obviously had an enemy. Did he have any friends? Was Jurgen one of them? Was Talbot at his funeral?"

"No way. Jurgen knew him, but they didn't socialize. Jurgen didn't like him." Du Pre's laugh was brief and humorless. "Does anyone?"

Shattuck cocked an eyebrow. "Are you adding to my problem?"

Du Pre was appalled. "Oh, no. Forget I said that. Talbot is the kind who makes us all look bad, and he was resented for that. But no gay did this, Sheriff. A hatchet? That is pure bigotry, pure hate crime. Is he going to live?"

"I doubt it," Shattuck said.

Du Pre's mouth twisted. "And when you catch the one who did it, his lawyers will plead him not guilty by reason of mental defect. He'll be a victim, not a killer. All he needs is medication, not punishment. No one will remember poor awful old Gene Talbot."

Shattuck dug a card from his pocket. "As soon as the news is out, there'll be talk." Thin fingers took the card. Sad eyes studied it. Shattuck said, "In your crowd, you may hear things I wouldn't." He started down the twisted stairs, feet too big for the narrow treads. "If you do, phone me, all right?"

Du Pre sounded panicky. "What do you expect me to report?"

"Shouts and murmurs, especially murmurs." Shattuck edged himself out the tiny doorway into the chancel, took a step, then stopped and called up to the organ loft, "What's that nephew's name?"

"French. He'd come to the hospital to see Jurgen. Sulky. Wouldn't shake my hand. But that's the name he gave. Larry French."

*   *   *

"I left Avery, uh, deputy Lemke, off at home," Brun Schneider told Shattuck. "It was a long shift for him. He was real tired." The red-haired, pop-eyed young deputy stood holding a blue fleece-lined windbreaker jacket. Cheap. You could buy them anywhere, and millions did. "Digging up all that snow didn't turn up anything. But this was in the river. You know. By the bridge there? Avery spotted it when we was driving across. Caught in the reeds. Frozen there." He turned it over in his hands. It was still a little bit stiff. "Looks like blood here. Inside."

"Take it to the washroom," Shattuck said.

In the washroom he laid it on a hand basin and peered at it closely while it dripped on the vinyl floor. It did look like blood. Washed to a thin pink by the river, but maybe the lab in Randall Falls could make something of it. He sent Schneider after a plastic bag. When he came back, Shattuck had him hold open the bag, and he dropped the jacket into it. He said, "I don't suppose in your excitement, you and Lemke remembered the hatchet, did you? You didn't wade in up to your ass in frozen slush and poke around for the hatchet, did you?"

"You think the assailant wrapped it in the jacket?"

"I think that's how the blood got on it," Shattuck said.

"Yeah, right. Well, I guess I can go back with hip boots."

"And a rake." Shattuck took the sack away from him. "You do that."

Schneider pushed glumly out of the washroom, and Shattuck followed and said, "At a guess, how many beat-up white pickup trucks would you say there are in Percival and vicinity?"

Schneider stopped, turned, grinned at him. "You're kiddin', right?"

Shattuck sighed and nodded. "I'm kiddin', Brun."

The list Bobby Hovis had made for him of men who had come to Gene Talbot's house on odd weekends was not long. After he'd dropped the jacket off for analysis at the Sheriff's station in Randall Falls, he went to find the men. None of them had heard what happened to Talbot last night, he watched them sharply as he told them, and he judged they were truly shocked. Had Talbot told them of threats to his life? Had he spoken the name of anybody he was afraid of?

"No," from the dentist, reedy, balding, pink and white, in the expected crisp white jacket. "No," from the veterinarian, stocky, with black bristly brows over bright blue eyes. In his store, dogs never let up barking, and Shattuck wondered what the man did not to be stunned by silence at home at night.

"No," from the third man, who sold men's wear in a shop that signed itself Saville Row. He looked like the image of a beautiful youth in a snapshot that sunlight had damaged. He was, Shattuck guessed, in his mid-fifties. Like the others. Like Talbot. Maybe ten years younger was the slight, nervous man in a green apron and yellow rubber gloves who with his mother operated a florist shop on a busy corner. He took Shattuck behind a tall, glassed refrigerator filled with irises and orchids and whispered his negatives, seeming worried that his mother might discover his sexual bent. Even this late in the day.

The Tool Room was open, but without customers. The bouncy bartender bubbled over with chuckles. His Elvis pompadour and long sideburns, the way he rolled up the short sleeves of his loud Hawaiian shirt to hold a pack of Marlboros, the wooden match he chewed, and the cigarette he kept ready behind his ear, only showed how time had passed him by. His arms and chest bulged, all right, but it was fat making the shirt too small for him, not muscle. Not lately, not for a long time. He stopped joking when Shattuck told him what had happened to Talbot. He staggered backward, sat down hard on a stack of beer crates.

"I told him those South American drug dealers were dangerous. I warned him. He just laughed. And now look what's happened." He began to cry.

"Those drug deals were fantasies," Shattuck said. "I wish they'd been real. Then I'd have somebody to go after for this."

The barkeep blew his nose, dried his eyes. "Fantasies?"

"The FBI proved that," Shattuck said. "Years ago."

"Well, he certainly made me believe him."

"That was his stock in trade." Shattuck started for the door. It was old-fashioned, with a big oval of glass in it. Sun glaring off the snow outside made him squint. He turned back. "Jurgen Jensen? He ever come in here?"

"All the time." The bartender stood up. "Till he got too sick. AIDS. What a waste." He lit a cigarette and bleakly watched smoke drift in a shaft of sunlight. "He was bright and funny, but he was also good and kind. Really. Everybody adored him. Funeral was only last week. I was there. So were all his friends. In Percival of all places. I thought that ugly church would fall and crush us."

"He and Gene Talbot never came in here together?"

The bartender almost reeled. "You don't know what you're saying. No way. Those two had nothing, but I mean nothing, in common."

"When Jurgen was a kid, Talbot never, uh, took him to bed?"

Headshake. "Gene likes 'em beautiful but dumb. Jurgen wasn't dumb."

It was just five, but dark and already very cold again, somewhere in the twenties. Lights were on indoors at the Paychek place. But from the sound of it, so was the television set, and Shattuck had to ring the chimes and knock a long time before a porch light went on, and Janos Paychek, a hefty, beard-stubbly man in sweats opened the door. He looked sore. Then he took in that this was a uniformed peace officer, and he looked startled. Then he looked alarmed. "What's wrong? Something happened to my kids? They only went to the—" He shut his mouth when Shattuck held up a clear plastic bag for him to see.

Shattuck asked, "You lose this? It's got your name carved into the haft."

Paychek scowled, squinted at the hatchet, reached out.

"Uh-uh." Shattuck stepped back. "Don't touch."

Paychek said, "Yeah, it's mine. Where'd you get it?"

"Somebody threw it in the river," Shattuck said. "Last night. Just after a bloody crime out at the Talbot house."

"Oh, shit." Paychek was a pale man to start with. Now he turned paler. "It was on the news. You think I did that?"

"I don't know what to think," Shattuck said. "You know Mr. Talbot?"

Paychek shrugged. "Buys gas from me sometimes. But I don't

know him. Not how you mean. I mean, he's a drug dealer, keeps guns around, he's a pervert. Everybody knows that. Hell, no, I don't know him."

"What kind of car do you drive, Mr. Paychek?"

"A 1989 GM pickup," Paychek was shivering, rubbing his hands. He looked behind him into the glowing warmth of his living room. But he decided against inviting Shattuck in. "It's freezing. Let me get a coat, okay?"

Shattuck said. "What color is your pickup?"

"Used to be cherry red," Paychek said. "Kind of rust color, now. Look, I wasn't even in town last night. Me and the wife was clear over to Appleton. Her folks' place."

"I'll need to check on that," Shattuck said. "What's their name?"

"Henrickson. Hank and Sophie." Paychek gave a street address. "Old man's got prostate cancer. Do I get my hatchet back now?"

"It has to go to the police lab, first," Shattuck said. "To see whose blood is on it. And whose fingerprints. If any. I doubt even an ax murderer would forget to wear gloves in this weather."

"It wasn't me," Paychek said. "Somebody stole it, didn't they?"

"Maybe," Shattuck said. "Thanks for your time."

He trudged back out to the patrol car. As he started to get into it, a rust-color pickup truck with sacks of groceries in the back jounced squeakily in at the Paychek driveway. A pair of girls about ten or twelve were riding in the cab. They wore red and yellow striped stocking-caps. The driver was a long-haired teen-age boy with Paychek's pale skin. He was trying to grow a Mark McGwire beard. As he sat waiting for the garage door to go up, he stared at Shattuck. Out of curiosity or fear? Hard to tell. Shattuck motioned to him.

The kid switched off the engine, but not the lights. He got down out of the truck and came at a slouchy walk. The girls gave glad cries and followed him. They stood in front of Shattuck in a bunch. The girls didn't exactly stand. They wiggled. And giggled. Their cheeks were rosy with the cold. The boy scratched his scraggly beard. "What do you want?"

"The answer to a question," Shattuck said. "Where were you last night?"

"Right here," the boy said. "Baby-sitting them."

"We rented 'The Lion King,'" the smallest girl said.

"Yeah, for the forty-zillionth time." The boy nodded at the bagged hatchet in Shattuck's hand. "What's that?"

"Someone tried to kill a citizen with it last night. It belongs to your father. But he was in Appleton. That's why I wanted to know where you were."

"Pizza Hut," the boy said. "Video store. And here. That's all."

"You want to tell me your name?"

"Ernie." The boy gave a sour laugh. "My folks claim they didn't mean it that way, but it's some kind of joke. Ernie Paychek, right?"

"If you say so," Shattuck said. "Thank you. Good night."

Ernie slouching, his sisters skipping, they went off across the brown, snow-patchy lawn to the red pickup. Shattuck opened the trunk of the patrol car and dropped the hatchet into it and slammed the lid down. The pickup rolled into the garage and the garage door closed. Shattuck got into the patrol car and drove off.

When he got up in the dark at five, he could see out the window that it was snowing again. The streetlamp showed him that. He flapped into a bathrobe and went to the kitchen. He brewed a pot of coffee, and switched on the radio for news. The Talbot murder was in there, among storm warnings, lame jokes, and raving commercials. ". . . lies in a coma. Lieutenant Ben Shattuck stated yesterday that the Sheriff's department is using all its resources to find the person or persons responsible for the cold-blooded gunning-down and brutal beating of the wealthy classic car collector."

Shattuck showered, shaved, put on a fresh uniform, boots, sheepskin jacket, fur hat, and went out not through the garage this morning, but through the front door. This was because he'd driven the patrol car to Randall Falls last night, to leave the hatchet at the lab and to stop at the hospital for an update on Talbot. He was still alive. The ICU staff told Shattuck it was a miracle. Bobby Hovis was sitting in a waiting area. Stained plastic coffee cups were stacked one inside the other on the low table in front of him. A magazine was open in his lap. He wasn't reading it. He was staring straight ahead at nothing. He looked drained. Shattuck sat down facing him.

"You've been here too long," he said. "You need sleep."

It took Hovis a moment to recognize him. "Did you find out who did it?"

"Not yet. Tell me something. The boy in the white pickup— did he have long hair and a beard?"

"A beard?" Hovis peered. "Hey, he was blond, sixteen, seventeen."

"Why don't you let me drive you home, now?" Shattuck said.

Hovis shook his head. "He could wake up. I have to be here for that."

"They'll call me," Shattuck said, "and I'll call you. I promise."

"Yeah. Well, look, truth is I don't want to be out there alone. I don't know who this monster is. He could come back." He glanced down the hall. "If they throw me out, there's motels across the street. That way I can be here as soon as the doors open in the morning."

"You all right for money?" Shattuck reached for his wallet.

"Gene never let me run out." Tears came to Hovis's eyes. He blinked them back, made an effort to smile. "Thanks anyway. I'll be okay."

Once he'd reached Percival, Shattuck felt too damned tired to bother fetching his own car from the station parking lot, too tired even to park the patrol car in his garage. He'd left it on the street. Now he stepped out into the falling snow, pulled the door shut behind him, and scuffled along the white-blanketed front walk to the brown car. It looked oddly slumped. This was because its tires were flat. He crouched to see why. Slashed. He smiled. Hell, he must be closer to solving this case than he'd thought.

When Lemke brought him his car, Shattuck headed for Mom's Diner. But the bright windows of the place that normally cheered him up sent him on past this morning. He didn't want to hear the gloating of the breakfast crowd over the Talbot beating. And he didn't want to field their prying questions. Not even if he had answers, and he didn't. He picked up two Eggs McMuffin and an apple turnover at the drive-by window of McDonald's, and brought them here to his desk. Faxes lay on the desk. They were from the police lab in Randall Falls. The blood on the jacket and hatchet was AB Negative, an uncommon type that matched Talbot's. Good. But there were no fingerprints on the hatchet. The maniac had been mindful of the cold. He'd worn gloves.

Edna Durwood brought Shattuck a mug of coffee. The mug had *Boss* stencilled on it. "Thank you," he said, and blew at the steam.

"Welcome. The Appleton police canvassed the Henrikson's neighbors, and they say the Paycheks were there the way they claim." She started off, then turned back. "Oh, and Captain Baer wants you to call him right away."

"Will do." But Shattuck was a big man and needed nourishment to get moving, so first he ate the two little egg, cheese, and ham sandwiches and the apple turnover, washed them down with coffee, and wiped his mouth and fingers on tiny paper napkins. Then he picked up the receiver and punched Baer's number. "Ben Shattuck," he said. "What's up?"

"What kind of citizens you producing over there in Percival?" Baer said. "Two A.M., one of 'em started roaring around in circles in the hospital parking lot, yelling and firing an automatic rifle at the moon. Whoopie! So, as you can imagine, all the hospital people ran to see. Or ran to hide. Or ran outdoors to up their chance of getting shot. Just one cool character remembered to get on the phone to us. But time we got there, the fun was over."

"Anybody get a look at the driver?"

"He was wearing a ski mask," Baer said.

"Anybody write down a license number?" Shattuck said.

"Now, what do you think? But they did agree on the vee-hickle. It was a beat-up white pickup truck."

"I'm so pleased to hear that," Shattuck said.

"You'll be even more pleased to hear that another individual in a ski mask ran into Intensive Care the minute the hoo-rah began in the parking lot, while the medics were all spinning their wheels or bumping into each other. And shot off a pistol. Six times. In the general direction of Eugene Talbot."

"Oh, my God," Shattuck said.

"Can you believe?" Baer said. "Not one bullet hit him. Twenty-twos, like night before last. But these didn't go into his skull. They went into the wall, the ceiling, the floor. Oh, and one blew the valve off an oxygen tank."

"So he's still alive?" Shattuck said.

"Probably outlive us both."

"And ski-mask got away?"

"And ski-mask got away. The ICU people were focused on that oxygen tank nobody could turn off. And I don't like to say it, Ben, but my night troops—they're not too swift. Both ski-masks got away."

"In their goddam white pickup," Shattuck said.

"Cheer up," Baer said. "Only a few hundred of those in Randall County."

Shattuck grunted. "And one more firearm than we needed."

The one more firearm, it turned out, was from the collection of Herb Many Horses. Herb was important in Indian affairs hereabouts, and had all his life liked hunting deer, and had more than once been chairman, or whatever they called it, of the Randall County branch of the National Rifle Association. At one time or another he and Ben Shattuck had sat on committees together. Or had butted heads on TV and in the public prints over gun issues. Now he came through the front doors, a broad-faced, broad-shouldered, big bellied, brown-skinned man, wearing a mackinaw and a matching hat with ear flaps. He didn't stop at the reception counter where deputy Schneider presided, but pushed the little wooden gate and came direct to Shattuck. He didn't say good morning. With a disgusted look, he laid creased papers on the desk.

"There are the registration papers for an AK-47 I owned."

"Past tense?" Shattuck said. "What happened to it?"

"Some son of a bitch stole it. Got in through a basement window. Not worth locking. It's too small for a man. Had to be a kid. Screen's just laying there in the snow. What would a kid want with a weapon like that? Kick would knock him on his ass first try."

"Maybe the kid let some grownup in through the front door."

Many Horses took off his hat. "Busted the glass out of the cabinet and reached in and took it. Naw, only one set of wet footprints. Little ones." His brows knitted. "Must've happened when I was over to Randall Falls. Them Ojibwas. They get a problem, I never knew them to solve it theirself yet. Got to drag every Indian in the U.S. and Canada into it."

"Sit down," Shattuck said. "I've got a story to tell you." He sketched in words what had happened at the hospital last night. "Descriptions made it sound to Captain Baer like an AK-47. To me too. Maybe it was yours. Who knew about it, Herb? Who knew you owned one?"

"Family, is all," Many Horses said. "My oldest son, George—he give it to me for Christmas. So that's what, six weeks? No strangers in that time."

"Kids?" Shattuck wondered. "Small enough to get through that window?"

Many Horses frowned, flipping the ear-flaps of the hat on his knees. "Just my grandkids. But if they want something from me, all they got to do is ask. They know that."

"I guess not an AK-47, though."

"They wouldn't want it," Many Horses said. "They'll get their own guns when they get the right age. They know that. I taught 'em. Taught 'em everything about guns. How to clean 'em, how to carry 'em safe, how to shoot. I know you don't believe in that. But it's my way, the Indian way, the American way."

"And stealing what you can't pay for is the human way. Herb, you have to protect that collection of yours better. A glass front cabinet? Seriously?"

"Nobody ever stoled none of 'em before," Many Horses said. "This ain't no high crime area, Ben. This ain't Milwaukee, this ain't Chicago."

"Not yet." Shattuck stood up. "Ask Miz Durwood to copy these. You can take the originals back home. Deputy Schneider will take your report and you can sign off on it. Only take a few minutes."

"Yellin'? Shootin' in the air from a pickup truck?" Many Horses rose, put the hat on, picked up the papers. "Sounds like teenagers on a beer bust."

"That white pickup," Shattuck said, "doesn't suggest anybody to you?"

"Shit," Many Horses said, "suggests half the town. Used to drive one myself." And he went off, bandy-legged, in round-heeled cowboy boots.

* * *

Kevin Ralph was thirteen but still small enough to crawl through that basement window at his grandfather's. His mother brought him into the station at three thirty. It was snowing again, and the boy wore a parka and floppy galoshes. He was pale and shaken and kept repeating, "I'm sorry, I'm sorry." His young mother, in a white fake fur jacket and white shiny boots, was slim, big-busted, hawk-faced. Her expression was grim. She didn't answer the kid. Likely she'd heard his apologies all the way over here in the car and was tired of them.

Shattuck sat the two of them down. "What are you sorry about?" he said.

"I shouldn't have done it," the boy said. "But yesterday, after school, Ernie comes to me at my locker, and he goes is it true my grandpa has a gun collection, and I go it's true. And he goes, does he have a Uzi? And I go, no, but he's got a AK-47. And he gets real excited, and he goes, will I help him? Because he has to have it to capture this drug dealer he knows about. There's a big re-ward. And if I get him the gun, he'll split it with me."

"Ernie?" Shattuck frowned. "Ernie Paychek?"

"A big kid," Lorena Ralph said wryly. "A hero."

Kevin went on: "But today I heard what happened last night. In Randall Falls. At the hospital where that queer guy is dying that somebody tried to kill. And how this truck drove around firing off this automatic rifle, and I thought, Jesus, it must be Ernie that chopped the queer guy with the ax, and"—Kevin's voice broke, his mouth trembled, tears ran down his face—"and I got scared he lied to me, there wasn't no drug dealer. No reward. He got that off TV. He's just tryin' to murder this queer guy. And then he'll kill me too, because I know."

"And so then, too late, he comes and tells his mother." Lorena Ralph scowled down at the weeping boy as if he were past sav-ing. "Like he shoulda done in the first place, before he ever broke in at his grandpa's." She grabbed his shoulder and gave him a shake. "Big kids are bad news, Kevin. How many times I gotta tell you—keep away from big kids?"

"I'm sorry," Kevin said again, hanging his head. "I'm sorry."

Shattuck caught the mother's eye. He lifted his chin, and stood. She stood too, a little uncertain. Shattuck touched the boy's shoulder. "We'll be back in a minute," he said, and led Lorena Ralph to the coffee room. She went in ahead of him, and he closed the door. "I want you to take him out of town. You have relatives anyplace that can put you up for a few days?"

Fear widened her eyes. "You think this Ernie would hurt him?"

"He might try," Shattuck said.

"Eau Clair?" she said. "I have a sister in Eau Clair."

"That's fine," Shattuck said. "Don't wait. Take him now."

* * *

In the biting cold, the early-closing dark, Shattuck knocked at the door of the Paychek house again, the back door this time, and didn't have to wait long at all before a woman opened it. She was fortyish, plain. Graying blond braids wrapped her head. Her hands and apron were floury. She held a glass measuring cup. She blinked. "Sheriff?" she said. "You bringing back Janos's hatchet?"

"Not yet," Shattuck said. "It's got Gene Talbot's blood on it, Mrs. Paychek. We have to hold it for evidence. Is Ernie home?"

She turned to look at a white kitchen wall clock. "He oughta be. Truck in the driveway?"

"Not yet," Shattuck said. "Look, I can see you're busy, but"—he took a folded paper out of a pocket—"I've got a search warrant here. I need to look around inside."

Her mouth dropped open. "Search warrant? What for?"

"A gun, an automatic rifle. It was stolen yesterday. And the boy who stole it says he gave it to Ernie. I believe it was used in a crime last night. And I need to find it."

"Oh, Lordy," she said. "Now it's guns, is it?"

Shattuck edged her a little smile. "Let's hope not. If I can look around, we'll see, won't we?"

"Ernie's a good boy," she said, not stepping aside to let Shattuck in. "Looks after his little sisters real nice. Even cooks breakfast for me sometimes. Sundays. Oh, I know he brags a lot to the other kids about bad stuff he supposedly does. But it's not true. It's just to make them, like, admire him, you know?"

"I know how that is," Shattuck said. "Can I come in, please?"

She set the measuring cup aside and jerkily wiped her hands on the apron. "Well, Sheriff, I'd rather Janos was here. My husband.

I don't know . . ."

Shattuck stepped inside. It was gratefully warm, and the cooking smells were wonderful. Lots of paprika. A Dutch oven bubbled on the stove. Bread dough lay on a floured board. "It'll be all right," he assured her. "I won't take long. Just show me Ernie's room, now, will you?"

A white telephone was fixed to the end of a cupboard. She went to it. "I want Janos here." She took down the receiver. She was flushed and defiant. "I think I've got that right." She began pushing buttons. Her hand trembled.

"Absolutely," Shattuck said. "I'll just go ahead and search."

He went ahead, clumped through to Ernie's room, opened some drawers, peered under the bed and into a closet that smelled of sweaty socks. But after he stepped on something, and picked it up, and it turned out to be a painty-headed screw, he knew where the gun was. Kevin Ralph's small-boy voice said in his head, *He got that off TV.* Shattuck stood on a chair that creaked ominously under his weight, and peered through the slightly tilted grill of an air-conditioning vent. Sure enough. He got down off the chair just as the woman came to stand scowling in the doorway of her son's room, and Shattuck's search became all show. Leaving the gun was dangerous, but that's what he did. And inside five minutes, with thanks and apologies, he was out of the house into the cold again.

He drove under the big winter-stripped trees to the next block and parked. The street curved just right, so he could see the Paychek place from here. If it didn't commence to snow again. He talked to Edna Durwood on the radio, hung it up. This weather was wrong for a stake-out. He grew colder as the dark came down. But in twenty minutes the rust-red truck swung into the driveway, both men in it. Maybe the kid worked for his dad at the filling station after school. The truck rolled into the garage and the door came down.

He checked his watch and turned on the heater. Just long enough to take the edge off the cold. He didn't want to exhaust the battery. He switched off the heater, turned up his collar, pulled down the ear flaps of his fur hat, and waited. Another fifteen minutes passed. The garage stayed closed. Paycheks, father and son, were taking the news of his visit calmly, looked like. Or had she even told them? Maybe she'd wanted them to eat in peace first. Thinking how good that kitchen smelled made Shattuck hungry. Had he misjudged her? Wasn't she going to tell them at all? If not, why not?

He hadn't time to worry about it. Light glared off the rearview mirrors, making him squint. A patrol car pulled in behind him and parked. Its lights went off. A door slammed. And skinny, horse-faced Fritz Baer walked up beside him—hooded jacket, turtleneck sweater. Shattuck opened the window.

"You bring any food with you?" he asked.

Baer gave his head a wondering shake. "You always hungry?"

"I'll pick up a pizza." Shattuck started his engine. "Won't take me long. That's the place to watch." He pointed. "Number five two two. The cowboy who staged the wild west show in the hospital parking lot lives there. Ernie Paychek. Seventeen, long hair, little nothing beard. Drives a rust-red 1989 GM pickup."

"The one at the hospital was—" Baer began.

"White, I know. But what I believe is, sooner or later, maybe not till the family is asleep, Ernie will come out and drive off in the red one, and lead us to the white one. And whoever that belongs to is who tried to kill Gene Talbot. Twice." Shattuck had halfway closed the window when he remembered. "Be careful, Fritz. I searched the house. He's still got that AK-47. I left it where he hid it, so he'd think he's smarter than I am."

"I hope he isn't." Baer stepped back. "Anchovies, right?"

Shattuck touched his hat. "You're the Captain," he said, and drove off.

By the time he got back to the Paychek's street, snow had begun to fall again. He pulled up behind Baer's patrol car, switched everything off, lifted the warm pizza box off the passenger seat, opened the door, and got out. He didn't close the door. There wasn't time. A white pickup truck with its lights off came roaring up the street toward him. Someone fair-haired hung out the window on the passenger side. That someone had an automatic rifle. The rifle began to stutter and spit fire. Bullets banged into the metal and glass of the patrol car. Shattuck dropped the pizza box, crouched behind the open door of his car, and yanked his

9mm from its holster. With crazily squealing rubber, the white pickup careened past him. Bullets shattered glass over his head and the fragments struck his fur cap, his collar, his shoulders. He pivoted and fired at the rear tires of the pickup. It held the street for a heart-stopping second, then tilted, jumped a curb, fell on its side, and crashed into a tree. Shattuck ran to the patrol car. Baer was bunched on the floor under the steering wheel. All angular elbows and knees, he pulled himself awkwardly onto the seat. He hadn't been hit.

"Sorry," he said. "He must have sneaked out the back way. On foot."

"You want to radio for an ambulance?" Shattuck said.

Doors began to open up and down the block, yellow light streamed out into the snowfall. Householders appeared, shrugging into coats, calling "What happened?" to each other.

"Everything's okay," Shattuck shouted. "Sheriff's already here."

Baer was talking on the two-way radio. Shattuck, to reassure the citizens, reached in front of Baer and switched on the bar of winking colored lights on the roof of the patrol car. Then, shaking splinters of glass out of his fur hat, he trudged up the snowy street to see who was in that silent white pickup truck.

By ten-thirty Larry French, the big fair-haired hockey-playing A student who had fired the AK-47 tonight lay in the Intensive Care Unit of the Randall Falls hospital in a coma, in a bed only six feet from Gene Talbot's. The smash-up of the white truck had fractured the boy's skull. His thin, washed-out mother, probably a nervous wreck anyway, sat in the waiting alcove in the hall, across from a sour-looking man in a cheap suit, who must be her husband. She chain-smoked cigarettes. He worked a crossword puzzle.

Ernie Paychek, whose turn to fire the AK-47 had come last night, had broken an arm, a few ribs, and a good many teeth, but he was in a regular room. His mother and father were with him. They sat side by side on stiff steel chairs, staring numbly at their son. His face was bruised and swollen. His mouth was puffy. He was drugged for pain. But the doctors had told Shattuck that he could talk. And he did talk. What he said was:

"Go fuck yourself, Sheriff."

Three hours later, a broad, white, many-buttoned telephone yodeled on Fritz Baer's desk, where he and Shattuck were drinking coffee and writing up a report on a computer. Baer lifted the receiver, said his name, listened, and hung up. He looked at his watch. He stared at Shattuck. The expression on his long, lantern-jawed face Shattuck couldn't read.

"You're not going to believe this," Baer said.

"Try me," Shattuck said.

"Gene Talbot died at one-oh-five."

Shattuck frowned. "That surprises you?"

"What surprises me," Baer said, "is that Larry French died seven minutes later." He watched Shattuck stand up and head for the coat rack at the end of the room. "Where you going?"

"Ernie Paychek will talk to us now," Shattuck said. "You coming?"

"He came over around eight," the boy said in the room where Shattuck and Baer stood like a pair of shadow monoliths beside his bed. They had not turned on the lights. The only illumination came through a window. Landscape lighting reflected off snow. "He wanted me to go with him, but I couldn't. I had to babysit my sisters. He had ski masks for us. Gloves so we wouldn't leave fingerprints. A twenty-two was stuck in his pants. He said we'd break into the house. Talbot had all kinds of guns. Larry said he had to have an Uzi.

"I said, 'What for?' and he said you can rule with one of those.

"And then I went outside with him, and he saw this hatchet by the wood pile and took and threw it in the truck. 'What's that for?' I said, and he said it was in case the house was hard to break into. Then he got in the truck. 'See you after,' he said, and drove off. Look, can I go to sleep now?"

"Soon," Shattuck said. "Did he come back?"

"Sure. I was surprised how soon. Like he'd been to the store or something. He said Talbot had been home. So Larry rang the doorbell, and pretended he wanted to buy one of those junkers Talbot keeps down by the road. A Mustang. But it needed a lot of work. And Larry said thanks but no thanks and got in his truck and came back. So it was a big nothing.

"But I could see he wasn't telling me the whole story. He was pale and jittery and kept jumping up and walking around, grinning to himself. We were in the kitchen, right, and my sisters were in the family room watching 'The Lion Yawn,' but it's not all that far, they could see and hear us, and finally he grabbed me up and yanked me into the garage and said:

" 'I killed him, Ernie. I killed the rotten pervert. He kept talking all the way down the hill, joking, being charming, right? That voice. The lah-di-dah way they talk. It drives me crazy. And when he bent to unlock the Mustang I pulled out the twenty-two and shot him in the back of the head. Filthy faggot. He was the one who gave Jurgen AIDS. My uncle. He was the one who killed him.

" 'He fell down in the snow. He was all bloody but he wasn't dead. He was reaching out. "Help me," he kept saying. "Something's happened to me. I need your help." And I just kept pulling the trigger till all the bullets were gone. "Die, you creep," I said. "Why won't you die?" But he wasn't dead. So I started kicking him. But he just grunted. He didn't die.

" 'And then I remembered the hatchet. And I ran and got it and I chopped him. Like chopping firewood. Just chopping at his head. And he put up his hands and I chopped his hands. His shirt pulled up from his belt and I saw his back and I chopped his spine. And finally he stopped moving. He didn't say anything more, didn't make a sound. He was dead. Christ, I'm glad. That son of a bitch. I'm so fucking happy.' He stretched his arms up. 'Thank you, Jesus,' he said."

"What was so special about this Jurgen?" Baer said.

"When Larry's dad walked out when he was like nine or something, Jurgen, like, I don't know, filled in for him, right? He was Larry's mother's brother. And he was always around. He took Larry to hockey games, ice fishing, the Brewers. Then, when his mother married again, the husband didn't like a queer hanging around and told Jurgen to get lost. But Larry never forgot, and when he turned sixteen, and his new so-called dad wouldn't buy him a car, he went to Jurgen, and Jurgen bought it for him. The white pickup. Who from? Had to be Gene Talbot, right?" In the aseptic darkness, Ernie Paychek laughed. "Isn't that what friends are for?"

"Talbot didn't sell pickup trucks," Shattuck said. "And he and Jurgen were never friends. Larry was mistaken, Ernie. His beloved uncle didn't get AIDS from Talbot. He couldn't have."

"Why not?" Paychek said. "They were the only two faggots in town."

"We've seen his medical records," Baer said. "Talbot was HIV negative."

AN EXCUSE FOR SHOOTING EARL

RIVERA WAS UP at the seminary on the ridge, a full-fledged priest now, secretary to the Monsignor, and not always free to help out Bohannon. Old George Stubbs was suffering in his joints from the dampness of the winter as he commonly did. At Bohannon's insistence, he lay in bed in his white-washed plank room at the end of the long stable building, alternately dozing and cussing the pain.

So when the day's last two riders came through the gate at sundown, the job of unsaddling Seashell and Geranium, watering them, rubbing their coats down, cleaning their hoofs—this work fell to Bohannon. It had been a long day. He wanted to put his feet up and have a drink. He closed the half door of Geranium's stall, went along past the other stalls saying good-night to the other horses, some his own, some just boarding here, and stepped out of the stable into dying daylight.

He was making wearily for the ranch house, when a young man he hadn't seen before stepped in front of him. Bohannon looked past him. He'd arrived in a new car—a Sterling, so new it still had a paper license plate. He was smartly dressed—meaning everything he wore had enough cloth in it to suit up two of him. He was thin—maybe even gaunt. How old? Hard to say. Less than thirty.

He said, "Mr. Bohannon? Can I talk to you?"

Bohannon said, "I was about to have a drink. Come inside and join me." Bohannon led the way, into the big, plank-walled kitchen where shadows had taken over. He sat the boy at the kitchen table, brought whiskey and glasses with ice in them to the table, and sat down himself. A lamp stood in the middle of the table, but he didn't switch it on. He liked sitting here in the twilight, found it restful. "What's on your mind?" He expected, with a car like that, the kid might have money enough to own a horse, and wanted Bohannon to board it for him. Wrong.

"You're the only private investigator in this area."

But what was he doing in this area? The frame on the Sterling's license plate named a Fresno dealer. Not exactly next door. And it was a good sized town, bound to have a PI, more than one. Bohannon only said, "That's right."

"Do you find people?" The boy had a coughing spell then. It racked him. And it sounded awful. He sipped some whiskey, grimaced, pushed the glass away. But he stopped coughing, and used a handkerchief to wipe his mouth and dry his eyes. "I mean —that's one of the things private detectives do, isn't it?"

"If they can." Bohannon lit a cigarette, watching the kid. "You understand, I only do investigations on the side, part-time. These stables keep me pretty busy."

"Oh, shit. You mean you won't help me?"

"I don't know," Bohannon said. "Who's missing?"

"A man called Earl Cartmell. Do you know who he is?"

"I used to know his father," Bohannon said. "You want to tell me your name?"

"My name isn't important." He put out a hand, and Bohannon shook it. It hadn't much life to it. No strength. "Uh—Taylor, uh —Cliff Taylor."

"What do you want with Earl Cartmell? How long has he been missing?"

"That's not important, either. I just want you to find him." The boy drew a wallet from those blowsy trousers of his, took money from it and spread the money on the table. "Here's a thousand dollars." His eyes, large in his wasted face, pleaded. "Like a retainer, right? I'll give you another thousand when you locate him."

"Is it your money?" Bohannon asked.

"What do you mean?" Taylor yelped. "Of course it's my money. And, oh, yes, make a—an expense sheet. I'll pay all expenses." He was reciting from instructions, wasn't he? He ticked the details off on his fingers. "Airline tickets. Hotels. Meals. Car rentals. Earl Cartmell is a gambler. That'll probably mean looking in Laughlin, Las Vegas, Reno, Gardena—the poker parlors. Santa Anita— the race track."

"Suppose I find him and he doesn't want to come back with me?" Bohannon said. "I can't force him. Not unless you give me a reason. Did he commit a crime? Is there a warrant out for him? If so, you want the Sheriff, not me."

"You don't have to bring him back. You don't even have to speak to him. Just phone me up and tell me where he is. I'll give you a number to call." When Bohannon said nothing to this, Taylor cracked open the wallet again. "Look—how about three thousand dollars?"

"Keep your money," Bohannon said.

Taylor looked ready to weep. "You won't do it?"

"I'm short-handed here. One sick old man, one part time helper. I can't travel, I can't leave the place that long."

"But you have to!" Taylor shouted in despair. Bohannon smiled a little. "Oh, I guess not. Look"—he swept up the money like loose playing cards, tamped its edges, handed it back—"Earl Cartmell's not worth the trouble. Anyway—if he's gambling, he'll lose. He always does. Then he'll come home. You know the Cartmell ranch? That's where you'll find him."

The kid sat with the packet of bills in his hand, a hand so thin and the skin so transparent blue veins showed. His head hung. Bohannon wondered if he was crying. But he was dry-eyed when he looked up. Still, he didn't say anything. Bohannon asked, "What do you need with Earl Cartmell? What does anybody need with him?"

The boy drew breath to speak but didn't speak. He was sweating as if he'd run a long way, and when he stood up it was like his legs were too tired to bear him. He put the money back into the wallet, put the wallet away, and moved toward the door. Bohannon followed and pushed open the screen for him to go out. He took a few slow steps along the roofed plank walkway, then turned back. "I heard you were a kind man," he said, reproachfully. "Always helping people."

"They trust me," Bohannon said. "You don't trust me."

"I'll pay you more. How much? You name it."

Bohannon said gently, "Just tell me what it's all about." The boy only looked at him bleakly. Bohannon said, "Or don't you know? That's it, isn't it? You don't know."

Without a word, Cliff Taylor, or whatever his name was, turned and went off through the twilight. To do what—search for Earl Cartmell himself? He looked too sick.

Bohannon had almost forgotten him when Earl's name came up again. Bohannon had got three giggly and slightly scared college girls safely aboard Ruby, Buck, and Twilight, and sent them on the dependable old mounts out the gate and up the canyon road, and was trudging back to the kitchen to catch up on his bookkeeping, when he heard a car turn in at the gate, and checked his stride. The faded yellow pickup truck he saw used to roll in here every week or two. And he'd felt good when he saw it. But that was past. Hubert Cartmell was dead. And this could only be that empty-headed high school girl he'd married when he was old enough to know better. After that, Cartmell had stopped coming around for rides in the canyons, card games, companionable talk over drinks. And Bohannon had seen him again only in his dying days, when Cartmell sent for him.

The yellow truck halted beside Bohannon's green one, the door opened and, as he'd feared, a young woman got out of it. It surprised him mildly that she wore jeans, a plaid shirt, boots, like a working rancher. The little he knew of her, she'd preferred flounces. Nobody thought much of her, but they'd never said anything against her looks, that trim figure, the hair that glinted gold and fell to her shoulders. She might be a TV star in Western duds, Bohannon thought. Maybe the dark glasses made him think that.

"Mr. Bohannon?" She held out a hand. He shook the hand.

"Mrs. Cartmell?"

"Ruthann, please." She looked around at the green-trimmed white buildings, the towering eucalyptus trees, the flower beds, the rail-fenced corral and the oval of hardpan where children of all ages learned to ride, jump, barrel race. They were learning now—Rivera was leading four little ones slowly around and around. He wasn't in black suit and turned collar: the newly-minted priest was a cowboy for the day—flannel shirt, Levis, boots. Ruthann Cartmell asked, "Are you busy? I need a minute of your time."

Bohannon said, "I was just going inside for a coffee break. Why don't you join me?" She came along, limping a little, silent, preoccupied. She didn't take off the dark glasses when Bohannon opened the screen door and ushered her into the kitchen. She kept them on when he held a chair for her at the round table, poured coffee from the tall, white-specked blue enamel pot, brought mugs of coffee to the table, and sat down opposite her.

She said, "Hubert told me if ever I was in trouble to come to you. He said you were the finest man he'd ever known. The straightest. And the wisest."

"He was a good friend." Bohannon lit a cigarette. "I'm sorry he's gone." She laughed ruefully. "Not as sorry as I am."

"Something wrong at the ranch?"

"There's no income," she said. "When Hubert got so sick he sold off the cattle to pay the medical bills." Hubert had been fifty when he married her. Then in only six or seven years had come cancer, the fast-acting kind. It was shocking to see the big, robust rancher, with his long stride, loud laughing voice, his youthful eagerness for living every day to the hilt, reduced in a few miserable months to a skeletal, sunken-eyed wreck, scarcely able to whisper.

"I don't know how I'm going to hang onto the place." She sipped some coffee, reached across for Bohannon's cigarettes and took one from the pack. He lit it for her. "And I have to. I can't let it go, Mr. Bohannon. I gave Hubie my solemn word." Bohannon winced at the nickname, but he kept quiet. She went on, "It's the Cartmell ranch. He put his whole life into it. It's his monument."

Bohannon said, "What about a bank loan?" She laughed bleakly. "Those silver-haired old dudes put a fatherly (I don't think) hand on my knee and croon that cattle'll only ruin me. On what I'd earn from beef, I could barely pay my running expenses. I could never repay a loan, not one big enough to get the ranch back to what it was."

"So what do they advise?"

She shrugged and blew smoke away. "That I let them put the land up for sale. To real estate developers. The Central Coast is the coming place. Everybody wants to live here. I'll be rich." Her laugh was sad. "Where? Why?"

"Didn't Hubert own stocks, bonds, shares?"

"Not a whole lot. Earl sold his half right off, of course. And gambled the money away." Earl was Hubert's son by his first marriage. Hubert had been so proud to have a big, strapping son like himself, he'd let the boy run wild. Earl had inherited only his father's size and strength—he'd missed out when it came to character. "From my half, the dividends keep food on the table, gas in the truck, and a few horses in the barn."

Bohannon said, "Life's no good without horses."

"Hubie taught me that. But now I'm faced with taxes."

"So . . . what will you do? Sell the stocks?"

She said miserably, "That's all I can do. Unless—"

Bohannon swallowed coffee and watched her with his eyebrows raised. She took a breath and blurted, "There's a man, Jeremy Essex. He's in the music business. Promotion. He wants the ranch for a week-long summer rock festival. Like"—she wrinkled her brow—"what did they call it?"

"Woodstock?" Bohannon said.

"That's the one. Years ago."

Bohannon smiled because he couldn't help it. "Ancient history." He wondered to himself how old she was by now. Thirty? Not quite. "A Woodstock by the sea?" he said.

"Jeremy wants it halfway between LA and San Francisco. Monterey County won't hear of it but our board of supervisors don't seem to mind. And the Cartmell ranch would be perfect, he says. A natural whatchacallit—amphitheatre to set up the stage in, the lights, the sound system, all the space in the world for parking. Plenty of motel rooms and restaurants in the area." She put out her cigarette. "He'd pay me ten percent of the take. And the take would be millions." Bohannon noted that she used the promoter's first name. Young and goodlooking, wasn't he? "You believe him?"

"Should I? You tell me." She took a card from her shirt pocket and held it out.

"Looks impressive," he said. "But I'd check up on him if I were you."

"Will you do it for me?" she said. "For Hubie?"

"All right." He nodded, put the card into his wallet, sat down. "What if it doesn't draw—nobody comes?"

"He can get Bruce Springsteen," she said, "the Grateful Dead, Morrisey, a whole list of stars. People will come."

He tilted his head, studying her. "So why are you here? You already know you're going to do it."

"Earl's dead set against it," she said. "He wants to sell the ranch for housing tracts."

Bohannon drank. "And neither one of you can sell it unless the other one agrees?"

"Mr. Fitzmaurice says it's a terrible will," she said. "He tried to get Hubie to set up trust funds for each of us till we're older. No way. I got half, Earl got half, and that's that." She repeated her bitter little laugh. "On his deathbed, he made Earl swear to stop gambling and whoring around, patch things up with Trish, go back to his kids. Course Earl promised. But what's that worth?"

"You can still keep him from selling off the place."

"And he'll do his damndest to stop the rock festival."

Bohannon scratched an ear. "Maybe he's right. There was only one Woodstock. This would be a one-time thing."

"But if the money is as much as Jeremy—Mr. Essex says, I could buy livestock again, hire hands, start the ranch over. I wouldn't need another rock festival."

Bohannon worried. "Times change. In the sixties the kids wanted to sleep naked in muddy fields, wanted to hear the music in the pouring rain, wanted to be little children forever. They're not like that anymore."

"They still go to rock concerts," she said. "I did until I married Hubie. My whole crowd did."

"I'll check out Essex, see if he's real." He reached quickly across and lifted the dark glasses from her face.

She grabbed for them. "What are you doing?"

"That's quite a shiner. Who gave it to you?"

"It was an accident," she said.

"You came for help," he said. "Let me help."

She sighed glumly. "You know Earl." She put the glasses on again. "He's not too bright. When it comes to a difference of opinion, his fists are his only argument." She stood up. "I have to go. Thanks for your help."

Bohannon stood up too. "You'd better not go back there alone. I'll trail along and straighten him out."

"This happened three days ago. He packed up and stormed off. He had a bundle of money. God knows where he got it. But he won't come home till it's gone."

"Home from where?" Bohannon asked.

"He didn't confide in me. Why?"

"Two nights back, someone came asking me to find him."

"Probably somebody he owes money to," Ruthann said.

"A skinny kid in expensive clothes, driving a brand new high priced car. From Fresno. He claimed his name was Cliff Taylor. Mean anything to you?"

"Earl never talks about his friends." She smiled and laid a hand on Bohannon's arm. "I'll be all right." She headed for the door. He followed her. She limped past flower-beds. "Hubie's guns are still racked up there in his den. And he taught me how to use them." She opened the pickup's cab, and climbed aboard. "It would be nice to have an excuse for shooting Earl." She slammed the door, started the engine, and smiled down at Bohannon. "Now wouldn't it?"

It was still dark when Bohannon went out to the stables to do the morning chores. By the time he'd finished, the sun had topped the eastern ridge, and dew sparkled on everything—rooftops, pickup and stake trucks, horse trailers, fence rails, stretches of mowed grass. He showered, shaved, and dressed. And when he walked into the kitchen, carrying his best boots, stocky old Stubbs was at the cookstove fixing breakfast. The smells in the air were good ones of coffee, bacon, cornmeal mush frying in butter. Bohannon sat down at the table and pulled on the boots.

"You're supposed to be in bed," he said.

"So you can have women running in and out of here at all hours?" Stubbs poured coffee and brought a mug to the table for Bohannon. "What would Father say?" He meant Rivera, who was half Bohannon's age and a quarter Stubbs's. "She's a client," Bohannon said. "Strictly business."

"Hah," Stubbs said. "That pom-pom girl Hubert Cartmell went crazy over, wasn't she?" He hobbled back to the stove. "Any reason you couldn't go crazy too?"

"I'm not old enough," Bohannon said.

"You're getting there." Stubbs laid the fried bacon on a brown paper grocery sack to drain, and set out golden brown slices of fried mush next to them. Now he cracked eggs into the bacon grease. "What are you all dressed up about? Who'd you swipe the suit and tie from?"

"They've been in my closet." Bohannon tried the coffee. Too hot. "Can't you smell the mothballs?"

"She's sending you to the wicked city, ain't she?"

"Hollywood," Bohannon said. "The music business."

"I figured as much." Stubbs hovered over the eggs. The hand that held the spatula was warped, the joints swollen. But he managed, and he was tetchy about offers of help. "Talk is there's gonna be a big rock and roll thing at the Cartmell ranch, end of August."

Bohannon was surprised. "Talk is—where?"

"At the drugstore." Stubbs laid the eggs neatly on plates, sunny side up. "Seems to me I'm always in there. Pills. Capsules. Rubs. Haven't found one yet that works." He put bacon and mush on the plates and brought them to the table. "To hear the ads on the radio"—he sat down with a grunt of discomfort, and tucked a napkin in at the neck of his shirt—"you'd think every one of them had discovered the final cure for pain at last."

"Nobody wants the final cure." Bohannon poured a lick of maple syrup on the crusty chunks of mush, and picked up his fork. "Who at the drugstore, George?"

"Gawky kid that works there," Stubbs said. "Hair done up all spiky. He's all on fire about it. Rattled off a lot a names, singers and bands I never heard of. Outlandish."

Bohannon spotted Sharon Webb lined up with other earlybirds outside the bank, waiting for it to open. He liked Sharon Webb, a staunch, pug-nosed little widow, the local watchdog for the save-the-earth types, of whom there were a good many in Madrone and Settler's Cove. Retired people, mostly, keen on country living, wanting the landscape and the wildlife left as it was. They were in friendly territory. There was a seabird sanctuary not far from Morrow Bay. And the Fish and Wildlife service kept an eye out for the safety of the sea otters along this rugged coastline.

He asked her, "Have you heard about a summer rock festival at the Cartmell ranch?"

She snorted. "Earl Cartmell came to alert me soon as that nitwit stepmother of his told him. Next thing, I hear it from Celia Van Slyke, all smiles."

"Figures," Bohannon said. "She owns a motel."

"And there's twenty more like her," Sharon Webb grumbled.

"And fifty Sloppy Joes, with a license to poison people with fat, cholesterol, whiskey and gin."

"It's not a done thing," Bohannon said.

"No, and if I've got anything to say about it, it never will be. You know why I cried at Hubert's funeral? Because I could see this kind of thing coming. That trashy little—"

"She's all right," Bohannon said. "She's just trying to save the ranch."

"Save it, my foot. They'll chop up his oaks for fire-wood, scatter trash ten feet deep, pollute the creeks. Hack, think of the environmental impact. Otto Tylson and I are taking a delegation over to San Luis for the next supervisor's meeting, and if they won't listen, we'll go to the Coastal Commission in Sacramento. We'll get up a—"

He didn't hear what she and Otto, a wealthy real estate agent, were going to get up. The bank doors clattered open, and everybody hurried inside. Including Bohannon, who had a week's checks to deposit and, mournfully, a cashier's check to buy for the mental home over the mountains where they looked after his wife Linda, who had retreated again into silent withdrawal from life. As to putting anything into savings—he wasn't managing that these days. Owning horses and paying for their board was a luxury some people were finding lately they couldn't afford. Business was falling off. Two years ago he'd have been able to lend Ruthann Cartmell the money to pay her taxes. This year, he'd be lucky to pay his own. He sealed the hospital check in an envelope already addressed and stamped, crossed the sleepy street to the little post-office, poked the envelope through a slot, then got into the green pickup and headed south on Highway One. He had nothing to lend Hubert Cartmell's widow, but maybe he could at least keep her from being swindled.

"What I'm sorry about," he told Rivera that afternoon, as he helped him muck out stalls, "is that I didn't get to see Jeremy Essex. He was out of town." Rivera shoveled wet straw and manure into a wheelbarrow. "But the people you did see—recording executives, musicians, journalists—they assured you he is what he claims to be? He is not lying to Señora Cartmell?"

"He's not lying." With a grunt, Bohannon heaved up on the handles of the wheelbarrow, and got it rolling along the passageway between the stalls. The wheel jarred over the planks. "He's put on some of the biggest concerts with some of the biggest names in the business, Elton John, Don Henley, Paul Simon, I don't know who-all. Not just in the U.S.A. Overseas. Japan. Australia. Even Russia." Outside, Bohannon dumped the wheelbarrow, and checked the sky. A few wisps of cloud to the west. Mare's tails. He judged them harmless, and he'd heard no storm warnings on the truck radio. So most of the horses out grazing on the fresh winter grass of the canyon slopes could stay the night. A few, high-strung or sneaky, he'd ride out and bring in now. It was growing late. He'd take Bearcat—the old bay gelding knew the drill. Back in the stable, Rivera was clipping the wire bindings on a bale of fresh straw for the clean stalls.

He said, "And now for his greatest triumph, this Jeremy Essex will bring rock to the Central Coast of California."

"Ah, but not for just one night, and not just one band." To Bearcat Bohannon murmured, "Come on, old man," opened the stall door, and led him out, hoofs thudding slow and solid on the planks. Bohannon bridled him, threw a blanket across his broad back, took down a saddle. "For a whole week, a different show with a different headliner each day."

"You don't have to sell me, Hack." Rivera's voice came from one of the box stalls, where he was laying down straw. "I will be the first in line for tickets. I will bring the entire student body from the seminary."

"Ruthann Cartmell will kiss you for that." Bohannon hoisted the saddle, but the old horse shifted ground a little, just for the hell of it, so as not to make things too easy for the man. He tossed his head and blew through his nose, pretending to be spooked. He was a great kidder. "Stop clowning around," Bohannon told him. "This is serious business. Work to do." He put the saddle on.

Rivera said, "Will a handshake be all right?"

"Maybe for you." Bohannon bent to cinch the saddle girth. "But she'll feel she hasn't thanked you enough." He gathered an armload of lead straps, and led the bay toward the bright doorway. "She may never smile again."

Rivera groaned. "I will give you the money, okay?" he çalled. "You buy the tickets for me."

On his way to Madrone next day, he detoured through green hills and cool canyons to have a look at the Cartmell ranch. The last leg entailed a long uphill drive between rolling pastures from the main roadway. When the ranch buildings hove in sight through their grove of oaks, he let go the breath he'd been holding, and his heartbeat slowed. Earl hadn't come home. There was no sign of the boy's beloved monster Buick convertible from the gas-guzzling years before he was born. Only the yellow pickup, and beside it a flashy red European sports car. Bohannon pulled his green GM up next to them, switched off the engine, jumped down, and stretched. It was quiet. Chickens clucked. In reeds down by the creek, redwings piped. He climbed porch steps and knocked. The sports car said she had company, so Ruthann ought to be stirring, but no one came. He hiked around the sprawling house to the rear. A lone horse in the paddock swished flies with its tail. He knocked on the frame of the back door, and fat little Maria Cortez came waddling. "Señor Hack." She smiled, and unhooked the screendoor. The smile was unexpected. Back before Hubert Cartmell had married Ruthann, Maria had always been cheerful. Not since. She'd never desert Cartmell. But she meant to sulk until that upstart girl left this house forever. He touched his hatbrim. "Where's Mrs. Cartmell?" "Out riding." Maria seemed charmed by the idea. "With that nice Englishman." She gaily waved Bohannon to the breakfast nook. "Sit down, Señor Hack. It has been a long time since you came to this house." From the stove, she brushed away whatever answer he might have tried for. "I know why, but you were wrong. And you have come back at a happy time." She brought him coffee and slices of *pan dulce*, a lemony sweet Mexican bread whose taste, wherever he met it, brought him back to this house in memory. He was a little startled. "A happy time?"

"Si. I am ashamed to say that for all these years, I did not like or trust Señora Ruthann. God forgive me, I hated her. I believed she had only married Señor Hubert for his money. What else could a young girl like that want with a man old enough to be her father?

She was waiting for him to die, no? Then she would sell this rancho and go off with the money."

Bohannon buttered a slice of pan dulce. "You weren't the only one who believed that." He began to eat.

"Ah, but I was mistaken. When Señor Hubert died, I thought that I alone was left to defend this rancho and its memories. He had provided for me in his will, and had implored me to stay on. It was not necessary. This is my home. I have no other. It was his mother who hired me, when I was still a girl, when this house was new. I was here when he married Señora Dorothy, when Earl was born. I nursed La Vieja through her last illness, then years later Señora Dorothy, when she died so young. And last the Señor himself. Who else remained to save this rancho from the evil designs of that grasping girl?"

Bohannon drank some of Maria's rich coffee. "But now you know you had her wrong. We all did. She's told me. She feels the same way you do about the ranch."

Maria nodded so hard two tortoiseshell combs fell out of her hair and rattled on the floor. "I know, I know." She touched her bosom. "And my heart is glad."

"It's to raise money to pay the taxes and get some beef stock back on the place that she's going to let this man Essex put on his rock festival."

"Si." Maria bent, picked up the combs, stuck them back in place, and leaned close to Bohannon, smiling, voice low and trembling. "And do you know? I think they are in love."

Bohannon pushed back his hat. "Is that so?"

"Si, I have seen them kiss when they did not know I was nearby." Her face shadowed. "He was furious at what Señor Earl did to her. He said he could kill him for that."

Bohannon said, "Earl brings out the best in folks."

Maria was thinking her own thoughts. "She is young, and she has been alone too long. She needs a husband. And Señor Jeremy—he is very handsome. But will such a man be content to live in this—this wilderness?"

"I wouldn't count on it," Bohannon said. "But they don't have to get married for him to help her save the ranch." Bohannon tilted his head. "That beating Earl gave Ruthann—did you see that?"

She nodded. "Earl does not want this—this *fiesta*."

"No. He wants to sell the place outright."

"Si." Maria looked grim. "This is how he respects his father's dying wish." She heaved a sigh. "I pray to the Virgin daily that this place will be spared, that I may grow old under this roof, and die in peace here when my time comes, but . . ." She broke that off. "Anyway, you want to know what happened on Tuesday. He took from his pocket a bundle of money. Ten thousand dollars, he said. He would give it to her, if she would agree to sell the ranch."

"A downpayment on her half of the sale price?"

"No, no. She would still receive her entire half. He said this again and again. The ten thousand would be extra, a—a—" She waved her little fat hands. "—a bonus?"

"A bribe," Bohannon said. "What did she say?"

"She asked where the money came from—it could not be his. 'What do you care?' he said, and tried to push it into her hands. She pulled away from him, shaking her head, putting her hands behind her back. She would not touch that money. When I saw how determined she was about this, I realized how I had misjudged her all these years. He followed her, shouting from room to room, and finally he struck her. This temper of his—he had it even as a child, but never like this. He knocked her down. He kicked her. I was terrified." She crossed herself quickly at the memory. "I thought he was going to kill her. I am only a woman, but I could not stand by and see this happen. I ran into Señor Hubert's den to get a gun. But when I came back, Señor Earl he had gone off and slammed the door of his room. I ran to her. She was bleeding and hardly conscious. Somehow I got her to her bed. She would not let me call a doctor. She did not want the gossip to spread. So I nursed her. I owed her this, for how coldly I have treated her all this time." She gave her head a glum shake. "You have seen only her face, but she has many bruises hidden by her clothes."

"She told me Earl packed up and left," Bohannon said. "Any idea where he went, Maria?"

"No." She rattled pans at the stove. "But that money was not his. So he will be found, Señor Hack. Do not worry. The one whose money it is—he will find him."

Now a ruckus started outside. Dogs barked, chickens squawked, children laughed and shrieked. A woman yelled for order. A horse neighed and Bohannon heard hoofbeats. He made for the kitchen door, slammed it behind him, ran down the backporch steps. A pair of small dogs chased the chickens. Feathers flew. He grabbed one of the dogs up, then the second one. They wriggled happily in his arms, and licked his face. A woman came running to take the dogs and pop them through the door of a camper truck parked under an oak beside the ranch house. At the corral fence, three young kids were yelling at the panicked horse. The oldest, a yellow-haired girl in ragged jeans, was throwing stones at the horse. Bohannon ran to her, picked her up the same way he'd picked up the dogs, and turned to carry her, yelling and kicking, to her mother.

He set her on her feet. "You've got a mean one here."

Her mother slapped the girl. "Shut up, Deb."

Deb staggered backward, a hand to her face, dazed, amazed. "You hit me. You're a vicious bitch. I'll tell Daddy. He'll make you sorry." "I'll vicious bitch you," her mother lunged for her. But the skinny little girl dodged, and ran across the yard and around the corner of the barn, shrieking, "Daddy, Daddy, Daddy," all the way.

The smaller kids, two boys, Bohannon guessed, stood at the paddock fence and stared as the woman stumbled a few steps after Deb and then gave up. The youngest one, maybe four, had his thumb in his mouth. Behind them, the horse stood in a corner of the paddock, sweating, trembling. Bohannon eyed him, concluded he'd settle down by himself given time, went and took the boys by the hand and led them to their mother.

"It's Mr. Bohannon, isn't it?" she said.

"Trish?" He scarcely knew her. She'd been a peaches-and-cream schoolgirl when he saw her married at this house eight, nine years ago. At the time, knowing Earl, he'd worried for her future. Earl was a mean sulky nineteen when she turned up pregnant, a simple sixteen. She looked hard-bitten now, all signs of innocence vanished.

She pushed at her straw-dry, straw-color hair, and tried to smile as she shook his hand. She'd lost some teeth. Earl had punched her around, hadn't he? "I guess I've changed. You haven't. You still look the same."

"I live an easy life," Bohannon said.

Her expression soured. "I don't."

"I didn't expect you would," Bohannon said. "But at a wedding, everybody hopes for the best. You here for Earl?"

"This is where he lives." She turned toward the house. "The lying bastard promised me a year's back child support payments two weeks ago. Swore to it in a magistrate's courtroom. But has he sent the money? Hell, no." She started toward the house. "So I came to get it. That's how it always is with Earl and promises. You want him to keep them, you have to catch him first."

"He's not here," Bohannon said.

She whirled around, white-faced. "What? Where is he?"

"He took off a couple days ago. I don't know where, Maria doesn't know."

"What about Ruthann? Did she go with him?"

"She's out riding," Bohannon said. "Maybe she can tell you when she gets back."

" 'Out riding.' What a tough life she married into."

Bohannon saw out of the corner of his eye that Deb was coming at a drag-foot walk from behind the barn. He didn't want her tormenting the horse again. Which she might do—since her mother probably wouldn't put up with having stones thrown at her. But Deb came on without a glance at the paddock. She squinted up at her mother, "Can I have a soda?"

"Sure, honey," Trish said, hugged her, and stroked her hair. "You boys go drink a soda with Debbie."

"And leave that horse alone," Bohannon said. "Okay?"

They stared at him, as if they'd never heard a man speak before. Then they trailed off toward the Winnebago. "They're just restless from the trip," Trish said.

"Teach them to be kind to animals," Bohannon said.

He had left the ranch house out of sight behind him when he saw two riders coming up the road through the pasturelands. He pulled the pickup off into brush beside a barbwire fence and waited. Insects buzzed in the dry weeds. A meadowlark sang. As the riders neared, he could see that Ruthann sat her palomino gingerly, and he thought of those bruises Maria had mentioned. *He knocked her down and kicked her.* Essex was in his late thirties, small and wiry, handsome and aware of it. His Levi outfit was manufactured to look worn and faded, but it was new. So were his hat and boots. The riders reined up. "Mr. Bohannon," Ruthann said.

Bohannon jumped down from the truck. "Just passing. Stopped in to see if you were all right."

"Hack Bohannon," she said, "Jeremy Essex."

"Bohannon?" Essex scowled at Ruthann. "Hack Bohannon is a friend of yours?"

"An old family friend," she said. "Jeremy? What is it?"

"He was in LA yesterday, checking up on me." He glared at Bohannon. "I phoned my office—routine when I'm out of town. They told me you'd been poking around. A writer friend from *Downbeat* left word for me at my motel." He turned again to Ruthann. "I assumed he'd been hired by the Sierra Club, or the estate agents." He laughed wryly. "And now I find it was you." He shook his head. "Bit of a shock. Proves you never know people."

Ruthann looked stricken, and Bohannon lied for her. "You're wrong about that. Hubert Cartmell was one of my best friends. We went back a long way. When I heard about this proposition you'd made Ruthann, I thought I'd better be sure you were legitimate."

"And am I?" Essex said coldly.

"I'm satisfied," Bohannon said. "Don't blame Ruthann. I was the one who was out of line. Hubert never told me to watch over her, but she's young, and I didn't want her to make a mistake if I could prevent it."

Essex reached out to press Ruthann's hands that were folded on her saddle horn. "Forgive me?" He swung down from his mount, and shook Bohannon's hand. "I've been bloody rude. Sorry. It makes me edgy to be checked up on." "Why?" Bohannon said. "You passed inspection."

"You think like a policeman," Essex said.

"Maybe because I used to be one," Bohannon said.

"Everyone's guilty until proven innocent?"

"If some of us didn't think like that"—Bohannon climbed back into the pickup—"what would become of the innocent?" He closed the door and started the engine.

"Follow us back to the house," Ruthann called. "Maria's fixing lunch. There'll be more than enough."

"Thanks—I've got a lunch date in Madrone." He let go the parking brake. "Anyway, there won't be more than enough. Not this time. A crowd has arrived." Essex had swung into the saddle, and he and Ruthann had started to ride on. She reined up the palomino.

"What do you mean? What crowd?"

"Trish and the kids from hell."

"Oh, no," Ruthann wailed. "What in the world for?"

"Seems a court ordered Earl to come through with his overdue child support payments. She's here to collect them. With blood in her eye. How can she afford a Winnebago?"

Ruthann walked the horse back to him. "That's their home—Trish's and the kids. They live in it year round."

"You don't mean it."

She nodded. "Earl won it in a poker game. It's the only thing he ever gave her he didn't later take back."

"Where is Earl, Ruthann?" Bohannon said.

"I don't know. He had a lot of money. He could have bought a plane ticket to anywhere in the world." She frowned to herself. "When he beat me up, Maria screamed at him that he'd killed me. Maybe he believed her. Maybe he'll never be back." And now she smiled that wicked smile again. "Wouldn't that be nice?"

T. Hodges had bowed her head and was looking at her watch when the screendoor banged behind Bohannon at the luncheonette in Madrone. T. Hodges wore her deputy's uniform, looked as always trim and fetching, and she gave him one of those smiles of hers that tried to conceal her upper teeth that stuck out a little and embarrassed her. The smile was mostly in her eyes. They were beautiful eyes, large and brown and limpid. Her smiles had a way of weakening his knees. He sat down at the gingham table and laid a gingham napkin across his knees. "Am I very late?"

"Only seven minutes," she said. "That's a record."

He told her about his stop at the Cartmell ranch. "Where would Earl Cartmell get ten thousand dollars?"

"Nobody's reported it stolen. Not to us."

"Can you check with Morro Bay and San Luis?"

"I will." Their table was on the screened porch. She peered through the main room of the eatery toward the kitchen. "Who's cooking today, do you think?"

"Not the one who burns everything," Bohannon said. "He or she only works the lunch shift one day a week."

"God pity the dinner customers," T. Hodges said.

A plump jokey young woman in a Raiders sweatshirt took their orders. When she'd gone, Bohannon said, "What does the Sheriff's department think about the rock celebration?"

"That the roads can't handle the traffic," T. Hodges said. "That telephone complaints from citizens will jam our switchboard. That car crashes will keep the highway patrol hopping around the clock. That the jail won't hold all the beer-swilling, pot-smoking, coke-snorting teenagers. That there'll be bonfires up and down the beach all night every night. That the trash cleanup will take a month and cost half the county budget." She busied herself popping the can of soda the plump girl had brought, pouring from it into a glass of shaved ice. "Other than that, we think it's a wonderful idea. Lieutenant Gerard says the town council should give Ruthann Cartmell a medal for community betterment." She eyed Bohannon, who was tasting his beer. "And you're siding with her."

"She wants to hang onto the ranch," Bohannon said. "I can understand that. Hubert would be proud of her."

"Not if he knew the way she was going about it. Hack, I'm surprised. And disappointed. That little blonde airhead has made a fool of you."

He shrugged. "The thing hasn't happened yet. Sharon Webb and Otto Tylson are agin it. They're on the move, and you know Sharon. She'll never give up."

"Mmm." The plump girl brought bacon and avocado hamburgers for both of them. T. Hodges tilted up the bun to inspect the meat. "You were wrong," she said. "The phantom scorcher has struck again."

"Damn," Bohannon said, but he was hungry and bit into his

hamburger anyway. So did she, hopeless. And in a minute, asked:

"Don't Otto Tylson and Sharon Webb make funny allies? I know he's all for recycling, saving the ozone, and so on, but isn't what he really wants the Cartmell property? Isn't it really Earl Cartmell he's siding with—not Sharon?"

Bohannon blinked. "Maybe I'd better ask him."

"Sharon will just die if he helps her stop the rock festival, only to turn around and buy the ranch from Ruthann. In the long run, a subdivision there would do a lot more environmental damage than any rock festival."

"Sharon's heart is in the right place," Bohannon said, "but she suffers from terminal innocence."

No one was in the reception room at Otto Tylson's plush offices, but beyond the door marked PRIVATE he heard a sound that suggested somebody was here. He opened the door and looked into a big, handsome office with a picture window that gave a fine view of the mountains. No one was in here, either, but there was a side door that wasn't fully closed, and the sound was coming through that door. He said, "Excuse me," and poked his head into another room. It had been fixed up as a gym, with weights, bench, a rowing machine, and an Exercycle. It was the whirr of the Exercycle he'd heard. And Otto Tylson was pedaling it, studying a blue-backed contract as he did so.

He blinked at Bohannon, startled, then smiled a professional smile, got off the machine, laid the papers aside. He came in white tennis shorts, a T-shirt, a towel around his neck, and shook Bohannon's hand. His eyes were intensely, almost unreally blue. His beautifully capped teeth gleamed in a crinkly smile. He was well-tanned, trim in body, stood straight, moved young. But he was past fifty. Hack wondered who the realtor went to all the trouble for. Not Enid, his sensible wife, who looked her age, and didn't mind it. Heiress of an old local family, it had been Enid's wealth that had set Otto up in business.

"Sorry to break in on you," Bohannon said.

"Always glad to see you, Hack. What can I do for you?" Wiping his face with the towel, Tylson went to a small icebox and brought out Gatorade. He held up the green bottle. "Care for a glass? Restore those minerals?"

Bohannon shook his head. "I'll pass. I hate rattling when I walk. Reason I don't wear rowels."

Tylson laughed and poured a glass of the stuff for himself and put the bottle away. "Come in here, sit down. Let's be comfortable." Bohannon did as he was told. Tylson tilted back in a leather executive chair behind a desk heaped with work. He'd made good on his wife's investment. He never stopped. The lights often burned late here. "You aren't thinking of putting your place on the market at last?"

"I'm not quite broke enough," Bohannon said. "Anyway, if you buy the Cartmell ranch, that will tie up all your available funds for a while, won't it?" "The Cartmell ranch?" Tylson's eyebrows shot up. "Somebody tell you I'm buying the Cartmell ranch? They're blowing smoke, Hack. It's not for sale. That former child bride of his is going to hang onto it if she has to ruin the whole Central Coast to do it. Haven't you heard about—?"

"The rock festival? I've heard about it, sure. Even met Jeremy Essex, the fellow who's going to stage it. Ruthann asked me to check up on him, see if he was legitimate. I did that. He's big time."

Otto Tylson said, "Yes. That's what makes this thing so scary. There's money there, and power. Essex has already got the local Rotary, Kiwanis, the JCs on his side, the motel owners, the restaurateurs. We're fighting back, but show business types like Essex can run roughshod over anything in their path—forget about who's right or wrong."

Bohannon gave him a thin smile. "Over you, Otto? I wonder. Ruthann is only part owner of that ranch. The other half is Earl's, and Earl wants to sell the place."

Tylson grew guarded. "So Sharon Webb says."

"Earl didn't tell you himself? He didn't come to you and ask your help in changing Ruthann's mind?"

"How could I help Earl Cartmell? To change Ruthann's mind? Has she got a mind?" Now it was Tylson's turn for a wry smile. "That's news to me."

"How could you help Earl Cartmell?" Bohannon shrugged. "By helping yourself."

Tylson frowned. "What do you mean?"

"Earl turned up a couple of days ago with ten thousand dollars. It wasn't his. What his father left him, he'd gambled away months ago."

"I know that. Everybody knows that. Turned up with ten thousand dollars where?"

"At the ranch. Offered it free and clear to Ruthann if she'd agree to sell out."

"And did she take it?"

"No. You mean Earl didn't report back to you?"

"Report back to me!" Tylson blinked, bewildered. "Hack, what are you talking about?"

"You didn't advance him that money to help you corner the Cartmell ranch?"

"You're kidding. Hand money to Earl Cartmell?"

"The stakes are high, Otto. That ranch is beautifully situated. Whoever develops it will make millions. A man of your experience might think ten thousand was a small sum to risk. After all, every realtor around here started sniffing the wind the minute Hubert Cartmell died. Why not put up ten thousand to secure Earl's promise to sell to you and no one else? Wasn't that the deal?" Tylson squinted at him. "You really mean this?"

"I'm asking. For Ruthann. When Hubert was dying, he told her to come to me for help in case of trouble. And she'd naturally like to know what in hell's going on. No, she didn't get straight A's in school, but she's bright enough to know Earl got that money from somebody else. And I figure that person had a lot to gain."

Tylson laughed annoyance. "Why choose me? Why not Hickman and Macaulay, why not Sunny Beach, why not—?"

"Because you're the only one fighting alongside Sharon Webb to block Ruthann's plan to save the Cartmell ranch."

"Oh, come on, Hack. You're overplaying the private detective bit. This is life, not junk television." Tylson laughed again but good-naturedly now, and shook his head in gentle toleration. Bohannon had to hand it to him. If he was guilty, he was covering it masterfully. Getting to his feet, grinning, he reached across the desk to shake Bohannon's hand. "Nice try, old friend, but no, sorry—Earl Cartmell never got any money from me."

Stuart Fitzmaurice was tall, fleshy, florid-faced, and though his family had been in America for centuries, he favored rough high-land tweeds, gold caps, tattersal vests, and carried a gnarled walking stick. On ceremonial occasions he'd been known to wear kilts and a tamoshanter. He climbed out of his right-hand-drive 1930's Morris and marched as if to the sound of bagpipes to where Bohannon was saddling Twilight and Ruby. For a young woman and her ten year old daughter who stood by, the mother resigned, the child bright-eyed and so eager she couldn't stop fidgeting.

"Isn't it early for lawyers to be out?" Bohannon asked.

"Ruthann Cartmell," Fitzmaurice said, "is in trouble. She asked me to tell you."

"Give me a minute, please." Bohannon cinched the girth on Ruby, and led the two horses to the customers, saw them into the saddles, gave some words of caution and instruction, and turned back. "What kind of trouble?"

Fitzmaurice watched the woman and girl ride out the gate and start up the canyon road through the long tree shadows cast by the morning sun. "Earl is dead," he said. "Shot to death."

"I can't say I'm surprised," Bohannon said, "but it seems to me that should mean an end to Ruthann's troubles."

Fitzmaurice didn't see the humor. He shook his head. "She's been arrested. On suspicion of murder."

"No." Bohannon frowned. "Tell me about it."

"The sheriff's version? Right. Earl arrived home at midnight, she was waiting for him in the dark, and when he turned off the lights and climbed out his car in front of the house, she shot him through the chest with one of Hubert Cartmell's rifles. His children discovered the body"—Fitzmaurice took out a pocket watch and studied it for a moment—"scarcely two hours ago. The cook, Maria, had shooed them out of the kitchen, and they'd run around to the front of the house to play." He tucked the watch away.

Bohannon said, "Everybody in that house hated Earl—his ex-wife Trish, even Maria. Why arrest Ruthann?"

"Only one rifle had been fired," Fitzmaurice said. "Maria cleans and shines all of them up regularly. Only the one had any finger-prints on it. And those fingerprints, unhappily, were Ruthann's."

Bohannon led the lawyer to a white slat bench near a flowerbed.

"What's Ruthann's explanation?"

"That the sound of a shot woke her." A bee buzzed at Fitzmaurice's ear. He absentmindedly waved it away. "She ran to the den for a gun. She went to the front door, but she was too frightened to open it." The bee buzzed at his nose. He made a slow gesture like a priestly sign of the cross. "She looked out a window, but there was no moon, it was too dark to see anything. She waited for a time, and when nothing more happened, she decided it must have been a truck backfiring down on the main road. She put the gun back in the rack, and returned to bed."

"She didn't fire the gun?"

"She says absolutely not."

"No one else heard the shot that killed Earl?"

"According to the sheriff's report—no."

"Not even Jeremy Essex?"

Fitzmaurice squinted against the bright morning sunlight. "Who's Jeremy Essex?"

Bohannon told him. "She's taken a fancy to him. I thought he might have slept over."

Fitzmaurice said, "His name isn't in the report."

Bohannon pushed up off the bench and walked across to the white fence of the paddock. Some horse had been at the top rail with its teeth. Probably Buck, back to bad old habits. He fingered the splintery place, but not thinking about it, thinking about Ruthann locked up at the sheriff station. "They sure the bullet came from that rifle?"

"The bullet went clean through him." Fitzmaurice used the walking stick to help him to his feet. Or pretended to. He wasn't an old man, nor a cripple. "And they can't find it. They messed up the evidence in several ways. For one thing, they didn't look for tire tracks until they'd run three County vehicles up and down the access road and all over the ground in front of the house."

"Tire tracks?" Bohannon cocked an eyebrow.

"Someone shot the man. Lieutenant Gerard is satisfied it wasn't Trish or Maria, and you and I are equally sure it wasn't Ruthann —that leaves an outsider, doesn't it?" He peered into Bohannon's face that was shadowed by his sweaty old Stetson. "Someone who arrived in a car and left in a car. Perhaps this Jeremy Essex of yours?"

"Come to think of it," Bohannon said, "he mentioned having a motel room around here. Probably on the beach." Fitzmaurice cracked a slight smile. "Where else?"

"I know, there's a dozen," Bohannon acknowledged, "but he has a distinctive car. Italian. Red. Probably cost a hundred thousand. I'll spot it from the road."

"Unless after shooting Earl Cartmell, he left the area."

"Unless that." Bohannon nodded.

Bohannon drove the service road along the beach, slowly, studying the cars parked at each of the motels, even the cheapest. No sign of the red roadster. He hadn't time to check the motel registers. The horses wouldn't understand. He drove back up Rodd canyon to his chores. But at the supper table, he learned what he'd feared. Rivera, who had come in the afternoon to make the beds and clean the ranch house, shook his head. "No, Hack. I'm afraid not."

With a mouthful of Stubbs's turkey stew, Bohannon blinked at him. "What do you know about it?" Rivera didn't often smile, but now he actually grinned.

"What's up your sleeve?" Stubbs asked.

"Only what's up the sleeves of say, fifty million other inhabitants of this great land today."

"Something on television?" Stubbs said. "You know we can't get television up here."

"This is no time for games, Manuel," Bohannon said. "A woman's life is at stake."

"Forgive me." Rivera sobered at once. "Monsignor and I had dinner last night with generous donors at their beautiful home in Santa Barbara. Mr. Lorenzin has investments in the entertainment industry. And after dinner they asked us to indulge them while they watched a television program."

Bohannon eyed him narrowly. "Which one?"

"The Grammy awards." Rivera looked questioningly at him, plainly wondering if Bohannon knew what he was talking about. Bohannon knew. "Don't tell me," he said. "Jeremy Essex was there?"

Rivera nodded. "And not just as a spectator. He was on the stage. In front of the TV cameras. He presented several of the awards." "And the show went on till how late?" "Eleven," Rivera said, "though it seemed later to the poor Monsignor. He kept nodding off."

"Hack, it takes four hours to drive up here from LA," Stubbs pointed out. "There's no way Jeremy Essex could have shot Earl Cartmell, now is there?"

"He could have flown up, chartered a plane."

"Sorry, Hack." The *Times* lay in a dishevelled stack at Rivera's elbow. He pushed it over to Bohannon. "There was a big party afterward. In Malibu. It lasted into the early hours of the morning. Essex was there. Dancing with many celebrated women. Look inside. There is a photograph."

"Forget it," Bohannon said glumly. "Essex never really figured. He wouldn't murder somebody where he planned to put on a show. Bad for business."

Bohannon drove to Fresno the next morning. The automobile showroom was deserted beyond its plate glass. Only one car stood in the wide driveway to the garage. Inside the dealership, a lone man in a business suit sat at a desk, sorting papers into a cardboard carton. The door at the side was open. Bohannon stepped in. "Excuse me?"

"Out of business," the man said without looking up.

"I didn't come for a car. I came for information."

"Sterling has folded up," the man said. "Damn good car. The Brits make great cars. But everybody wants Japanese, don't they? Shows all the good wars do."

Bohannon went to the desk. "A young fellow, very thin, very trendy clothes, bought a Sterling here in the last few days." Bohannon took out his wallet, laid his license on the desk. "I need to find him." The man bent his head to read the license. He had a bald spot. He looked up. "I thought the only private eyes were on TV. And you look more like you belong in Westerns."

"Can you tell me the young man's name?"

The man gave back the license. "What's happened to him?"

"Something's happened to somebody he knows." Bohannon put the license away. "I need to ask him about it."

"Well," the car dealer said, smiling, rocking back in the chair, "he wouldn't be hard to remember. My last customer. Even if he hadn't paid cash."

"Whoa," Bohannon said. "That's a lot of cash, right?"

"It surprised hell out of me," the dealer said. "And if you want to know the truth, I didn't think it was his. Still—there's funny money around, you know. For big ticket items like luxury cars. Drug money, right?" He snorted. "Even in Fresno, the raisin capital of the world."

"Drug dealers are all over. And they get younger and younger. What's his name? Where can I find him?"

"I had to do a couple things to the car to get it ready," the dealer said, "so I delivered it, so I know where he lives." He gave an address. "New condominiums."

"I don't know this town," Bohannon said. "How do I go?"

Dumping the last of the letters, receipts, computer spreadsheets into the carton, the man told him how to find the quarters of the boy whose name was not Cliff Taylor.

No one answered the doorbell. He tried the door. It opened. He went inside and closed the door. The place was handsome, still smelling of new paint, new carpeting and drapes. And something else. Unpleasant. It took Bohannon a moment to place the smell. Bleach. He went from room to room. Good furniture. Lavish electronics—forty inch TV, VCR, stereo receiver, compact disk player, enormous speakers. But there were signs of neglect. Videos, albums, books, magazines strewn around carelessly. A plate with a half-finished meal on it on a coffee table. A blanket tousled on the couch. And in the kitchen, what looked like a half-assed chemical laboratory. He picked up vials, bottles, jars, and set them down. A book lay open. He closed it. The cover said it contained formulae for drugs you couldn't get in the US, that weren't approved yet. Drugs to help you fight AIDS. He laid the book down on the counter, turned, and a wasted bald young man with a skimpy beard was looking at him hollow-eyed from the kitchen doorway.

He said, "Are you one of Dougie's friends? He never mentioned a cowboy."

"Where is he?" Bohannon said.

"The hospital," the wasted boy said, and tears began to run down his face. "He's not going to make it this time."

"Which hospital?" Bohannon asked. And the wasted boy told him.

It was a two-bed room, and serious trouble had drawn half a dozen white-dressed nurses and green gowned medics to one of the beds, and Bohannon waited out in the corridor. He waited standing. Down the hall was an alcove with two chairs and a sofa, but a middle-aged couple sat in the chairs, faces stiff with anxiety. Prine's parents? Four young people overflowed the sofa. A plump rosebud of a boy, another one too thin, and a pair of manly girls, one of them in a grape-picker's straw hat. Friends of Douglas Prine? Bohannon turned his gaze from them to the room. Its door stood open. There'd be no point in closing it. Staff came and went too often and too urgently. So did equipment. The faces of the nurses, doctors, orderlies were blank, but what they felt showed in how they hurried. They were in a skirmish with an enemy that never loses. It was wonderful how they all seemed bent on winning, just the same. The elevator doors at the corridor's end opened. Five people stepped out. One of them, looking taut and pale, a bunch of plastic-wrapped flowers in his hand, was Otto Tylson. Bohannon had never seen Tylson wearing eyeglasses before; he was too vain for that. Thoughtfully, Bohannon went to meet him.

Jeremy Essex had never come to bail her out, or for any other reason. So late that afternoon, it was Bohannon who drove Ruthann Cartmell back to the ranch from the sheriff's, after the charges against her were dropped. While they rode, he talked. "Otto gave Earl that ten thousand dollars, all right. But not to secure the Cartmell ranch. It was a blackmail payoff. Earl went to Fresno now and then to play outlaw poker in some back room. He sighted Otto on the street one night with Douglas Prine, got curious, spied out what was going on, took photos, asked Otto to pay him—a couple thousand, no more. Otto paid him, but in a few weeks Earl was back, for five thousand this time. And Otto paid him again. The third time, he demanded ten thousand. Otto argued he didn't have that kind of money, but in the end he caved in, and handed it over."

"And realized Earl would never stop?"

"Unless he stopped him. He couldn't get away to track Earl down, so he asked Prine to do it and then call him, when he would go wherever Earl was and kill him—though he never told Prine that part. Prine said he was too sick, so Otto sent him to hire me. I told him there was no point in looking—that Earl would go broke and come home sooner or later."

"And he did," Ruthann said wryly, "didn't he?"

"That night, Otto had worked late closing a deal, and was eating at a cafe on the highway when he saw Earl's car heading for home. No mistaking that car. He followed it." They drove in silence for a time. Then Ruthann sighed and said, "Poor boy," not meaning Earl.

"Otto loved him," Bohannon said. "Had for three years. Paid the rent, the bills. But while he was busy being a model citizen here by the sea, Prine was bed-hopping in the Valley. Otto knew it. He says it didn't matter. For eighteen months, Prine lied to Otto about what was wrong with him. He got away with it because Otto could only get to Fresno now and then, and never caught him at a bad time. When he finally admitted he was dying, Otto bought him a posh place to live, a fancy car, a monster television set—"

"Not life," Ruthann said. "He couldn't buy him life."

Bohannon turned off onto the access road to the ranch, and here came little Deb Cartmell, riding the horse she'd thrown stones at the other morning. He pulled the green pickup to a halt. "Howdy, cowgirl," he called.

She reined up and looked down at him. "Oh, it's you."

"You sit that horse very well," he said. "Do you have any other skills?"

She screwed her face up. "What kind of skills?"

"Ranch-hand skills, roping, shooting? Ever shoot a gun? Just for practice?"

She was wary. "What makes you think that?"

"Somebody took one of your grandfather's guns out of the rack the other day and fired it. I thought it might have been you. Just for practice." He grinned. "Hit anything?"

"A tin can on a fence post," she bragged, "first time."

"Some people are born crack shots."

"I wiped it off afterwards," she said, "like Maria keeps them. I didn't think anybody'd ever find out I borrowed it."

"Don't worry." He studied her, frowning. "Where'd you get the blue eye? One brown, one blue, that's unusual."

"It's a contact lens," she said. "I found it."

"Near where your father was shot?" Bohannon asked.

"How'd you know?" she said.

"It belonged to the man who killed him," Bohannon said. "Did you find anything else around there?"

She looked at him doubtfully. "Such as?"

"A bullet, maybe? In the dust?"

She complained, "How'd you get to be such a good guesser?" She sighed noisily, dug into a pocket, and tossed him a little ugly chunk of lead.

He snatched it out of the air, touched his hat brim, said, "Thank you, miss," and drove on.

"You're fantastic," Ruthann said.

Bohannon shook his head. "I haven't saved the ranch."

"You've saved my life, and where there's life there's hope." She turned him a grave smile, but they both knew she'd have to sell. In a year or two, a housing tract would cover these rolling hills. With luck, maybe some of the oaks would stay, as reminders of the way things used to be.

MOLLY'S AIM

THE TOWN OF Poinsettia waits among brown rolling hills under a high, wide, blue California sky, for something to happen. And it never will. That's how Molly feels. It never will. Time stands still here. Poised on a corner now, waiting for one of the little town's two stoplights to change—main street is a State Highway, and strangers can come speeding out of the hills, and around the curve, and be surprised by the town—she looks up and down the street and sees the same dowdy one and two story brick store buildings she's seen her whole life long here—all thirty years of it.

Two cars streak past, filled with kids bound for the Consolidated High School. They shriek and laugh. Arms wave out of windows. A soda pop can goes flying. Molly aches for a moment at the sight, the sounds. She wishes she were back in high school. Those were the good times.

The light changes, and she crosses the street. The Sleep EZ motel is tucked back among old eucalyptus with thick, twisted trunks, at the south end of town. She has worked here ten years already. And she can't see how she'll ever leave. The door to the office is plate glass. She pushes inside. A bald head is visible behind the woodgrain plastic counter. Molly says cheerily:

"Good morning, Mr. Gobineau."

He wakes with a snort, blinks at her, pushes to his feet. It must take effort. He is a big-bellied man. "Imagine. Ten o'clock already?" He winces at the daylight pouring in through the glass door. "Another fine day, I see."

"The ranchers want rain." Molly studies the registration cards in a loose leaf contraption on the counter to learn the numbers of the occupied units. From the automobiles on the weedy tarmac of the parking area, she knows how many. Five. It's been a quiet night.

She glances at the vinyl tile floor of the office. A quick damp mopping will do for it. Checking for dust and disorder, she eyes the fake leather chairs, the woodgrain plastic coffee table with its vase of plastic flowers, ragged travel magazines, ashtray. Some dog has streaked the glass door with its nose. After she changes from her jeans and sweater into white smock and trousers, she will take spray cleaner and paper towels to the door. She wants to keep busy until checkout time at eleven, when she can get into the units, clean up after the guests, change the bedding and towels.

But now she frowns. Has she really seen that name? She turns back to the registration cards. Her small hands flip them over swiftly. There. Is she right about that name? She traces the letters with a finger. She never really got the hang of reading. She must be wrong. *Hugh Henderson?* She makes a little sound. She is dizzy. Her knees feel weak. She catches the edge of the counter to steady herself.

Mr. Gobineau's brows rise. He tilts his head. "What's the matter? You're pale. Are you sick?"

She gives him what she knows must be a wan smile. "I'm just a little dizzy."

What shall she do? She isn't ready. For twelve years she's wished for this to happen, wished so fiercely she sometimes thought she would die from wanting it—that Hugh Henderson would return to Poinsettia. Now it has happened, and she has no plans.

"You're trembling," Mr. Gobineau says. "Sit down. I'll call Mrs. Gobineau. Here"—the big green Arrowhead bottle back of the counter gurgles, and he passes her a paper cup of water—"drink this." He lumbers away, panicked, calling, "Marie, come quickly. Molly's sick."

Molly doesn't drink the water, doesn't sit down. She stands at the counter, her heart beating heavily, thickly. Her voice sounds strange and high to her and trembly, as she asks Mr. Gobineau's worried old face, "Hugh Henderson—why did he stop here? Why not at his mother's house? His house. Where he grew up?"

"Henderson?" Gobineau squints at the registry card. "Ah, that young man. Well, it was late when he arrived. Perhaps he didn't want to awaken his mother."

"She died," Molly says. "Day before yesterday."

"Ah, then he's here for the funeral," Mr. Gobineau says. He peers at her. "You know him?"

Molly must be careful. She's already said too much. She stammers quickly, "No—not really. We—we went to high school together, is all."

Mr. Gobineau cocks a sly eyebrow. "You are blushing. He was your childhood sweetheart, no?"

She laughs. She can't help it. Little scrawny Hugh, with his big, brown eyes in a face that, even when he was a high school senior looked like a ten year old girl's? What a silly idea. It was tall, strapping, fair haired Carl Wynant who was Molly Byrne's sweetheart. For a dreamy moment now, she glows with remembered pride in that, then the old, black rage rises in her, so strongly that she feels dizzy again.

Motherly little Mrs. Gobineau hurries in, and Molly gives her a wan smile. "I—I'm sorry. I didn't have such a good night. The pizza I ate or something." She turns for the door, acting weaker than she really feels. "I'd better—better go home and rest today." Hand on the door, she turns back. "Can you manage without me?" Mrs. Gobineau waddles to her, gives her a hug with her soft fat arm, her pillowy old face wrinkled with concern. "Yes, yes. I'll manage, *ma petite*. You stop at the doctor. Telephone us. Tell us how you are."

"Thank you," Molly says, and pushes out into the warm sunshine. She is frightened at having left work. She never did this to the Gobineaus before. She mustn't lose her job. Who else would hire her? Not Snyder's Luncheonette. Mrs. Snyder died, and the cafe's been sold. The Snyders and the Gobineaus didn't care that Molly can't read and write and figure, and has to have things explained to her so often. When the Gobineaus are gone, who else will be so patient and kind? What will become of Molly if she loses the friendship of the Gobineaus?

She stops at her corner, and stands breathing quickly, excited, frightened, watching for speeding cars. It can't be helped. She needs time to think and plan. Anyway, at the motel, Hugh might see her. And that could ruin everything. She crosses the street and padding along quickly in her soft-soled shoes makes for the haven of her rooms where she can be alone and decide what to do.

Her mind has never been quick. As a girl, it had hurt her when other girls said so, made fun of her, called her Molly the Moron. Time has taught her that though cruel they were right. She is not clever. If she'd been clever, Carl would never have been able to trick her as he did. But—she sets her jaw and she works the latch of the wire-mesh gate to the yard of old grapefruit trees—she can get even with him now. The knowledge makes her dizzy with excitement.

She closes the gate and walks up the cement strip beside an old white frame house to a side door at the rear and her little apartment. Inside, in her tiny kitchen, she takes a Coke from the shivery old fridge, sits down at the paint-faded table, lights a cigarette. She pops the top of the dewy can, swallows some of the cold, sweet, tingly drink. If she takes her time now, she can make a plan. She has no choice. Her chance has come at last, and it may be the only one she ever gets. She frowns, trying to concentrate.

But her thinking is all a jumble. She jumps up impatiently, goes to the window over the chipped sink, stares out at the only view, the side of the neighbor's paint-scaly garage. If she can't think, she can remember. Sometimes she wishes she couldn't. But remember she can and does. If she's lucky, her memories are of the happy high school times. There had been boys. They never mocked her as the girls did. They bought her beers and fried chicken, and took her to drive-in movies in their cars, and out into the hills or sometimes even to the far-off beach, to make love afterwards. And if this one didn't ask her a second time, there'd soon be another, and another. She loved high school.

Her childhood had been a nightmare. After her mother died, her father snarled at her sober and hit her when he was drunk. She didn't want to anger him, but she couldn't understand what he wanted. His temper made her jumpy, and she kept breaking things and breaking rules and not living up to her mother. Not in looks, not in brains, not in anything. Except her aim with a gun. He was proud of that. When he remembered it—less and less often as time went by. Molly was worst of all at cooking. The meals she fixed on her own her father pushed away. Sometimes he threw the plate at her. She took to heating TV dinners. And grew grateful for the times, more and more common as the years passed, when he snored unshaven, mouth hanging open, unconscious from whiskey in his chair facing the television set, or felt too awful even to get out of his bed, sometimes for days at a time.

But this meant he couldn't get work. He was good and quick

and sure at fixing up whatever needed mending—plumbing, wiring, roofing—on ranches and in town. But he got so unreliable, promising to show up, and not showing up until days later, that finally the phone stopped ringing.

A trickle of money came every month from a tiny trust fund of her mother's, but it wasn't enough, so Molly had to take work to bring in extra. A half crippled old widower, Morgan Dowd, had her in for a couple of hours after school every other day to dust and vacuum his big empty old house, do the laundry, wash up the dishes, scrub the bathrooms, shop for groceries, pick up his prescriptions from the drug store.

She had one dream in those grim years. To escape. First she'd escaped into heavy makeup, flashy costume jewelry from Woolworth's, into dresses too old for her, into smoking, flirting, drinking beer and wine, talking sexy with the boys. Into having sex with the boys, when she learned that was what drew them. Other girls were prettier, other girls had better families, nicer houses, more money, even cars of their own, other girls got better grades. But the boys liked Molly and she liked the boys.

Still, she hadn't been prepared for Carl Wynant. Carl was the star of the football team, captain of the basketball team, a four hundred hitter in baseball. On the big campus of the Consolidated High School, among a thousand kids from all over this side of the county, he was the best known. He could have the company of pretty girls, rich girls, girls who got all A's. But it was Molly Byrne he picked.

In the cafeteria at lunch one day when it was raining so hard no one had gone off campus to get decent food—pizza or burritos or Big Macs—she asked him why. She knew it was dumb of her, even as the question came out of her mouth between bites of meatloaf and mashed potatoes. A girl should be grateful for a miracle like hunky Carl and not mess with his head. But not knowing was driving her wild. She had to ask him. He stared at her for a minute, surprised, and then he laughed. She felt cold. Was he laughing at her?

He swallowed the food in his mouth, gulped milk, and grinned at her. "They don't really want me, Molly. They just want to show the other girls they can corner the big man on campus. I'm a trophy. They're hunters."

"I think you're great," Molly said. "The greatest."

"I'm not. I'm good at sports, that's all. And what is this?" He gestures to take in not just the wide, chattery, clattery cafeteria, but the whole campus and all its buildings. "High school, in the boonies. I'm a star here, but I wouldn't be nothing at a school with real competition."

"You could be anything you want, Carl," she said.

He wiped his mouth with a paper napkin, and crumpled this into a ball. He tossed the ball at the head of a boy seated across the room. It hit its mark, and the boy looked around to see where it came from, and couldn't see. Carl snorted laughter, turned to Molly, soberly again. "None of those girls would dream of marrying me, Molly."

"Why not—of course they would."

He counted on his strong fingers. "I'm poor, I got no background, no future."

Molly took his hand, squeezed it, looked into his blue, blue eyes. "I don't think that's true, but even if it is, I still love you."

He nodded and stood. "We're two of a kind." He picked up his dishes, piled them on her tray, picked up her tray. "Come on," he said. "I need you, Molly. Right now."

She scurried after. "But the rain, Carl."

"I've got the truck today," he said.

It was a rattly old truck with fading red paint and a scaling sign on its doors WYNANT'S EGGS. It smelled of chickens. She knew where he was taking her. Copenhagen, a long-deserted ranch whose house had burned down but whose barn still stood, bearing on one side a weather-bleached advertisement for Copenhagen snuff. She didn't know what snuff was or Copenhagen either, but Copenhagen was what they called the place. Carl wasn't the only one who knew about it—it was whispered about among the older students, giggled about, but she knew of no one else who ever actually used it. Carl called it his place, and she went along with his make believe. It made her feel warm inside.

It wasn't warm inside the barn. It was cold and damp. They climbed to the haymow up a splintery ladder. The rain pattered softly on the shingles. Carl crossed deep straw and dug the rolled-up sleeping bag from its corner. It was the kind with zippers all around so it could be spread out. Its black satiny lining always felt luscious on her skin. They undressed each other, stopping for long kisses, long fondlings, shivering in the weather but not noticing that they were shivering, warmed from within themselves by the heat of their blood. They dropped, already joined where they both craved wildly to be joined, onto the padded, satiny bed on the deep springy straw.

Afterward, Carl turned away for an instant, and stretched an arm to get cigarettes from his castoff jacket, lighted one for himself, one for her, and lay naked, blond, shining, hair in his eyes, leaning up on an elbow, looking down at her thoughtfully. She didn't use words to ask what he was thinking. She just raised her eyebrows a little, smiling up at him. "You really like it," he said. "You like doing all the different things, don't you?"

"All of them." She pushed up to kiss his smoky mouth, lay back. "Don't you?"

"Hell, yes, but that's different. Boys are horny, girls aren't supposed to be horny—you know?"

"Who says?" she scoffed. Then she was grave again. "I love doing all the things with you. I love how strong and smooth and hard you are. I love you, Carl."

"You know how I feel?" He got up off the opened out sleeping bag and stood looking down at her. "I feel as if we're one person. That's crazy, isn't it? When we're doing it. Any of it, all of it. As if you were me, and I was you, and we were both the same." He blew out his breath in a self-mocking laugh, and wagged his head. "Crazy."

She sat up, clutching her knees. "No," she said soberly. "It's not crazy. That's how I feel too. It's as if you felt what I felt, needed what I need just when I need it." She knelt up and rubbed her face against him, soft and cool now where he was so firm and hot before. She looked at him. "You're wonderful."

He turned away and, balancing on one leg, then the other, pulled on jockey shorts. "What do you think?" he said, and drew a T shirt on over his head. "Do you want us to be together forever?" He smoothed the shirt down.

"Can we?" She could hardly believe what he was asking. Her heart thudded. Her mouth was dry. "Do you mean it?"

"Hell, yes." He kicked into his jeans. "Only not like this. Not here, Molly. Not in Poinsettia. Not with your father, the drunk. Not with my mother and her damn ten thousand chickens and nothing ahead but eggs and more eggs forever." He zipped up the jeans. "With maybe ten dollars between us for a Friday night Chinese supper in Atascadero and a movie afterwards." He flapped into his checkered flannel shirt, and poked the tails down into his pants. "I'm sick of being poor. I'm sick of working my ass off for nothing." He sat down to pull on thick white gym socks, and then those short, strapped, motorcycle boots he always wore. "Aren't you sick of being poor?"

"Yes." She nodded. "Only what can we do about it? I can't get a good job. I don't know anything. There's no money to send me to college. And if there was, I couldn't go. I'm a very poor student."

He laughed that grim laugh of his again. "Yeah, that's another way we're just alike." He gathered up his jacket, and walked to the ladder, the planks of the loft creaking under his weight. "Come on. Get dressed." He looked at the watch they gave him after last year's football season. "It's after three. My mom will chew me out. And you'll be late to old man Dowd's." He started down the ladder. "You know what they say? He's got money hidden all over that house." Carl makes a heavy thump when he lands on the barn floor below. "Is it true, Molly?"

"People make up stories," she said.

"Maybe not," he called up to her. "Why don't you nose around, and find out?"

Molly now almost believes she did eat tainted pizza last night. She feels a little nauseated, and goes and lies on her bed. It makes up into a sofa if she wants it to, but ordinarily she doesn't do the stowing of pillows and heavy lifting needed to make the bed part disappear. She gets enough of that kind of work at the EZ Rest, and she's often tired when she comes home. At the motel, when she's cleaning the rooms, she ordinarily switches on the television sets. She could switch her own set on now. But she doesn't. She just pries off her shoes, lies down, in her jeans and sweater, puts two pillows under her head, and gazes at the leaf-shadowed open window, where a hot breeze moves the half-drawn roller shade so it ticks, ticks against the frame.

And she thinks of Hugh Henderson, who has come home to bury his mother. It never came to Molly that Mrs. Henderson would die. Why not? Everybody dies, at last. And mostly when they do, their relations, certainly their sons and daughters, come home. But maybe because nothing good ever happens to her, she's settled in her mind that Hugh Henderson would not. True, what happened was a long time ago—but because so little ever does happen here, when there's a scandal people remember, and Hugh would know that. Yet come home he has. She can't believe her luck.

But how is she going to take advantage of it? She scowls. It's back to planning again, isn't it? And her mind shies from the assignment. The thought of it wears her out before she can begin. Instead she slides once more into remembering—this time how it came about that little Hugh Henderson, who had adored big Carl Wynant, came to hate him.

For a long while, that spring term of 1977, he tagged Carl around, in the school hallways, across the campus under the oaks and pepper trees, was always there sitting alone, a frail figure on the forsaken bleachers snapping picture after picture of Carl at afternoon batting practice, footracing, jumping hurdles on the gravel truck—even, Molly was told, in the locker room, hanging around among the big, shower-sleek bodies of the athletes. That camera around his neck seemed part of Hugh. He wore it everywhere, all day.

Toward the end, he and Carl began to eat lunch together, to drive together in Carl's truck to movies in Paso Robles or Santa Maria on Friday and Saturday nights. At least once, they traveled to the coast on Sundays—they were seen sailing at Morro Bay. Then somebody started the rumor that they were gay. Flowers appeared in Carl's locker with a card signed *To Carl with all my love—Hugh*. The girls all chattered and giggled about it. Then someone stole the white stuff they used to draw lines on the football field and printed out there in letters four feet high CARL

WYNANT LOVES HUGH HENDERSON together with a heart with an arrow through it. The coaches pretended to make a big fuss about this, but they never caught who did it. They tried to rub out the words, wash them out with hoses, but the words stayed till next fall's football games scuffed them away. And the coaches grinned. They thought it was funny too. Anyone could see that.

Carl didn't grin. He hated being laughed at. He hated being called queer. The next Saturday night, he filled the truck with his best jock friends, and picked up Hugh, and they took him out in the hills and stripped his clothes and made him do things to them, and did things to him, and then brought him back and dumped him, kicked, beaten, bleeding, and stark naked in the center of town, in front of the post office and the lighted stores, and drove off. A lot of people were still awake, and they saw little Hugh stumbling miserably home through the streets. They weren't scandalized at what had happened to him. They were scandalized because he didn't have any clothes on.

The sheriff questioned Carl and the other boys, but they wouldn't tell on each other, and no one was arrested. But at Snyder's Luncheonette, where Molly, even though she couldn't write down the orders or add up the checks, sometimes helped out if Wilma Snyder was sick, the breakfasters agreed it was Carl and his friends who'd done it. And Carl himself told Molly about it the next year, one of those good times when they lay naked, close together in the dark. At first it frightened her to know Carl could do such a thing. But she soon forgot about it. He wasn't cruel. He was only protecting his reputation. He wasn't gay. Those other boys forced him to prove it.

And Hugh wasn't killed, after all, only bruised and shamed. He left town, not even waiting for the semester to end. His mother claimed not to know where he had gone. So no one could ask him how he felt. But Molly knew. He hated Carl, with the same betrayed fury Molly later came to feel, and still feels. She's had to keep her hatred secret. But everyone, including the sheriff, knows Hugh has to be Carl's enemy. And now Hugh is back, and Molly can have her revenge on Carl at last—if only she can figure out how to make the sheriff pin the blame on Hugh.

An hour later she is back in the little kitchen, seated at the table, drinking another Coke, and struggling to put a plan onto paper. It's old, unused notebook paper from her high school days. She rarely put anything on paper then, and it is hard for her to form words now. She does it like a kindergartener, one crooked letter at a time. She thought it would help keep her mind from wandering. And maybe it has, a little. It's also given her a headache. *Carl*, she has printed, *Hugh*, *Molly*, and *Carl's Come-On-Inn*. She has drawn lines radiating out from these last words, so it will look as if they are shining like the sign on top of Carl's road-house on the highway outside town. She has rung information, and written down the telephone numbers of the nightclub and the Henderson house. But none of this gets her anyplace.

The one thing that makes her feel that somehow what she must do she is going to do, is the 30-30 rifle she's pulled out of the back of her closet, dusted off, cleaned, oiled, loaded, and that now stands leaning beside the stove, the rifle she bought quietly in San Luis Obispo, to replace her father's, which she lost on that most terrible night of all her life, twelve years ago. The new rifle cost her all her pitiful savings, and she was scared to death her father would discover it wasn't his gun, but he was so drunk most of the time she could only hope he wouldn't notice—and he didn't, or if he did, he never said so.

When she and Carl lay naked on the sleeping bag again in the loft at Copenhagen, she told him how, the day before when it turned cold in the late afternoon, she'd gone back to Mr. Dowd's house to fetch the coat she'd forgotten, and there in the dining room was the old man, down on his bony knees, a corner of the carpet folded back, and prying up a square of the parquet floor. He took out a fishing tackle box, opened it, and pushed money into it, paper money, quite a thick stack, to lie on top of stacks already in the box. Not then, they had other things to occupy them then, but when they were driving back to town in the egg truck, they planned what they would do. As she climbed down out of the truck at her front gate, Carl leaned across the seat and told her in a loud whisper, "Bring your father's gun."

She slid it from under her father's bed, when he's sprawled there in his filthy clothes, whiskery, reeking of drink, snoring like a pig.

It never occurred to her to ask what they would need with a gun. She took it because that was what Carl said to do. She had a key, of course, and when she softly unlocked the back door of Mr. Dowd's tall house on its ten acre lot that cold night and they tip-toed into the dark kitchen, Carl was carrying the gun in one gloved hand. Molly's heart pounded with fright. It made a roaring in her ears so she could hardly hear. Not that there was much to hear—crickets out in the darkness, now and then a car droning along the distant highway. The neighborhood was asleep, the town was asleep. Carl groped for her hand, and she guided him into the dining room, where the long, polished table, its erect and empty chairs, the big mirrored sideboard were no more than darker chunks of the darkness.

"Where?" Carl whispered.

Mutely, on trembling legs, Molly led him to the corner where a little side table lurked, holding a clutch of silver vessels, cof-feepot, sugarbowl, cream pitcher, on a silver tray. These things glinted in the starlight through the windows. One of Molly's duties was to polish them once a month—though they were never used. No one came to dinner at the Dowd house, not after Mrs. Dowd died.

"Show me," Carl whispered. Molly knelt, pushed his legs, so he stepped aside. She folded back the corner of the carpet. "There." She jumped up as quickly as if she'd uncovered a snake. She didn't want to touch the square of flooring. Carl did. He handed her the rifle. She cradled it in her arm, as her father had taught her. Carl knelt and felt around with his hands.

He said softly, "Ah," and the next minute she heard a little squeak, and a square hole opened at his knees. He laid the patch of flooring aside, reached down and lifted out the fishing tackle box. It wasn't locked. He opened it, pawed inside, laughed a soft laugh, straightened up. And his head struck the table. The silver pieces rattled. The coffee pot teetered and fell. It gonged on the bare floor.

"Who's there?" It was Mr. Dowd's voice. He wasn't upstairs. He was very near. She heard his slippers, scuffing across the hall-way, into the living room, only a few paces away. He walked with a cane, and couldn't get downstairs fast, so he must have been lying awake, and heard the truck arrive, heard them enter the kitchen. In bathrobe and slippers, thin gray hair mussed from sleep, he was pointing the beam of a flashlight around.

"Who's there?" he said again, in his high, trembly voice. Then the flashlight beam caught her full in the face and held her. "Molly? Is that you?"

Carl clapped a hand over her mouth, and somehow or other the gun went off. It gave a terrible kick that bruised her arm. It made a terrible noise. She dropped it. But the harm was done. Mr. Dowd lay on his back in the gaping black opening to the living room. The flashlight shone on him. A dark stain spread on his chest. He didn't make a sound.

"Jesus." Carl pushed her out of his way, ran to the old man, knelt beside him. He picked up the flashlight and shone it on the old man's face. He touched the old man's scrawny neck, grabbed a limp wrist, held it for a minute, dropped it. He turned and looked at Molly. "You've killed him." He stuffed the flashlight in a pocket of his jacket, and came striding back to Molly. He grabbed and shook her, so hard it seemed her head would snap off. "You've killed him. What the hell did you do that for?"

"I—I—I—didn't—mean to," Molly gabbled. "The gun just went off, Carl. I was scared, the light was in my eyes, and the gun just went off."

"Yeah, wonderful." Carl flung her backward. She struck the little table, and the other silver pieces fell and clattered on the floor. She stood huddled against the wallpaper, looking at him wide-eyed. He crouched, grabbed up the metal box and the rifle. "You stupid cow. I should have known you were too dumb for this."

"Carl, don't," she begged. "It was an accident."

He stepped to her, pushed his face close to hers, furious. "It was murder in the course of a robbery," he said. "You get the death penalty for that, Molly—they put you in the gas chamber."

Molly reached out to him. "No, no. I didn't mean it."

He slapped her hands away. "Don't touch me." He held up the box. "We were going to have a great life. I'll bet there's thousands in here, Molly. We could have gone anywhere, done anything."

"We still can." She turned toward the kitchen swing door. "Let's go, Carl. Let's go now. The two of us. Together. Like we planned."

"Oh, no." He caught her arm. "I don't want any part of you. I'm going alone. You worked for Dowd. You'll be the first one they suspect. You don't dare leave town."

"Wh-what?" Molly could only stare.

"They'd come straight after you, Molly. Anyway, you think I'm teaming up with a killer? You think I'd put my life in your hands?" He gestured with the gun barrel at the dead body of Mr. Dowd. "After what you did? Think again. I'd have to sleep sometimes, Molly. Who says when I'm asleep, you wouldn't murder me, and take it all for yourself? Oh, no. I'm going alone." She shook her head in horrified protest. How could he be saying what he was saying? He yanked her against him, not lovingly, threateningly. "And if you got some idea of telling the sheriff about me, just remember, I saw you kill that poor old man. And I've got the gun you did it with—your father's gun. They can match up the bullets. All I did was take the money. It was you that did the killing. You think you can remember that?"

He slammed open the swing door with a fist, dragged her with him through the kitchen, down the back steps, down the long, clod-stumbly orchard to the truck. "Come on. I'll drop you home." He yanked open the door, pushed her roughly up into the cab, slammed the door. He walked around the truck, set the cash box on the gritty floor, dropped the gun back of the seats, got in, and started the noisy engine.

"Take me with you, Carl," she begged. "You promised."

"That was before I knew you were a killer," he said.

She hiked back to Mr. Dowd's house after school the next day, because it was one of her days to go there and clean for him, and she had to act as if everything was the same as ever, didn't she? Her legs felt weak when she climbed the back steps. They trembled. She trembled all over when she stepped into the daylit kitchen and heard the silence of the house and knew the reason for the silence.

She pulled out a chair at the kitchen table and sat down. She didn't want to go any farther. But she made herself. She pushed the swing door and entered the dining room. She looked at the fallen silver pieces, the folded back corner of the rug, the square of flooring, the hole it had concealed. But she could not look at Mr. Dowd. There was no other way to get to the telephone but to pass him.

She went to the opening, looking at the table and chairs, the sideboard, the windows, the ceiling, anything but the dead body in the opening. Feeling as if she might faint, she slipped past it, edging around the door-frame, then ran through the living room, and in the hallway snatched up the receiver of the telephone on the little table there, and dialled zero.

"What was in there, Molly?" The bony sheriff tapped the edge of the hole in the floor with his boot. "Do you know?" Molly shook her head. "Hid money in there, did he?" The sheriff smiled —he had horsey teeth. His thick glasses glinted. "Old people get funny ideas sometimes. Don't trust banks. Stuff money all sorts of crazy places, you'd be surprised." He turned to watch the young men who had come in a County ambulance load the stiff body of Mr. Dowd onto a stretcher and carry him down the living room, and out of sight into the hallway. The front door opened and closed. The shoes of the men thumped across the hollow front porch, and down the steps. The doors of the ambulance slammed.

"I don't know anything about it," Molly said.

"Appears Mr. Dowd caught the robber in the act, and the robber shot him."

"I suppose so," Molly said.

"Mr. Dowd keep a gun, did he? Hunting rifle?"

"He did say sometimes he'd like to shoot the deer eating the bark off his fruit trees. Maybe he had a gun in a closet someplace, but he was old and sick. I guess he wouldn't be using it, would he?"

"Maybe when he heard the robber," the sheriff said, "he got it out of that closet, came downstairs with it, and the robber just took it away from him and shot him with it."

She looked at the floor. "That's terrible," she said.

"He should have phoned us, not tried to take care of it himself. I don't know when people will get that idea through their heads." The sheriff pushed back his flat-brimmed hat with one finger and studied her. "Old people that hide money in the house usually lock up tight at night. But we can't find any sign of a break-in. Rob-ber just walked in—front was locked, downstairs windows too. What about that, Molly? Did he usually leave the back door open?"

"It was always locked when I got here to work," she said. "He gave me a key to let myself in."

The sheriff's eyebrows went up. "Did he, now?" He tilted his head, blinking. "Have you got that key now?" She showed it to him. He took it, turned it over in his fingers. "Lend this to any-body last night?"

She shook her head. "Can I go, now?"

"In a minute." The sheriff pocketed the key. She opened her mouth to ask for it, and then realized she wouldn't need it any-more. She was out of a job. The sheriff said, "Did he have any vi-sitors lately—strangers?"

"Nobody came but Dr. Keinplatz," she said. "I used his car and did his shopping for him. Groceries, drug store. I did the laundry."

"Repair men, gas, electricity, plumber?"

"Not that I ever saw," she said.

"And you never told anyone he had money hidden here?"

"I didn't know," she said again. "Can I go now?"

"You got a boyfriend?" He showed those horsey teeth again. "Pretty girl like you must have a boyfriend."

She felt herself blush hotly. Her heart began to pound. But she said, "I don't have time. I go to school, and keep house here, and wait tables at the cafe, and look after my father. I don't have time for boyfriends."

Into his pale, vague eyes behind the thick lenses came a pitying look. He patted her shoulder kindly. "Well, don't fret. You will have. Some rich young fella will see you one day at the cafe, and decide he can't live without you, and take you off to the bright lights and the big city."

"I guess not," she said.

Mr. Dowd was buried—a very old sister-in-law from the mid-west came to see to all of that, a creaky little woman, who left straight after the funeral. She and Molly were the only ones in the pews of the big, hollow, high-raftered Presbyterian church, the only ones at the graveside.

Molly kept fearing that the sheriff would question her again. At home, she nervously peered out the front windows, expecting to see him coming up the walk, bony in his carefully pressed tan uniform. Or maybe he'd come banging in at the screen door of the cafe one morning and put handcuffs on her and drag her away to jail. She imagined him asking around the high school, and finding some girl who'd tell him Molly'd lied to him—she did have a boyfriend, and it was Carl Wynant.

And then the sheriff would go to Carl's mother's chicken ranch and find out he had left town the very night Mr. Dowd was killed. Molly would see the sheriff in his patrol car when she was out on the streets. He seemed to gaze at her long and thoughtfully. But he never said a word. If he noticed her noticing him, he'd nod and touch the brim of his hat, and just drive on. But every time she saw him, it made her jumpy. She lay awake worrying about the sheriff.

"What's the matter with you?" her father growled at her over the breakfast table. "You look half dead. If you don't stop running around all night with the boys, you'll end up pregnant. Well, when you do, don't expect any help from me."

That was a laugh. When had he ever helped her? Not since her mother died and he started drinking. After that, she was the one who did all the helping. "I don't run around with any boys," she said. "That's over with."

"Glad to hear it," he grunted. "When you going to get another job? Only one creature I know can live on air, and that's an orchid, and we ain't neither one of us orchids."

Dully she picked up his empty plate and carried it with hers to the sink. "I talked to the people at the EZ Rest motel. It's hard for them to keep maids. They're always leaving to go home to Mexico. Maybe they'll take me on. They said they'd phone."

"Don't leave it up to them." Her father pushed up from his chair. "Keep going down there and reminding them."

"I will, Daddy," she said, and ran water into the sink.

She wondered what had become of Carl. Days slid into weeks, and weeks into months, but she couldn't get him out of her mind. Was it love or hate? It made her angry to admit it, after what he did to her, but she wanted him, wanted to be with him naked again at Copenhagen. She couldn't forget him. Was he in Las Vegas, like he'd sometimes said? Wherever he was, she wanted to be with him. She dreamed of getting on the Greyhound bus and going to look for him.

One Sunday, when she had time on her hands, she walked out to the chicken ranch, and stood looking down the long, two-rut road to the small white house among walnut trees, and the long, whitewashed chicken sheds behind it. In vast pens, hundreds of white chickens pecked the dust. She touched the crusty steel latch of the gate, urging herself to push it up, swing the gate open, walk down the road, knock at the door, and when Mrs. Wynant appeared, ask if she'd heard from Carl.

But of course she couldn't do that, could she? Mrs. Wynant would wonder what business Carl was of dumb little Molly Burne's, anyway. She might get suspicious and demand to know what Molly knew about Carl and why he'd run off with the truck that night. Women weren't easy, like men, like the sheriff, women weren't soft in the head when it came to dealing with a young girl if she'd interfered with one of their menfolk. Molly was afraid of Mrs. Wynant, and after that long, hot walk out to the chicken ranch, she dropped her hand from the gate, turned, and trudged emptily back home.

At last, a thing happened she would never have believed. Carl came back to Poinsettia. She smiles wryly to herself, now. It seemed as if she was about the last person to hear of it. The one who cared the most. And no one told her, she overheard it. No one would think to tell her, she guessed. Most of her high school class had long ago left town. Those able to go to college were over to Cal Poly in San Luis, or at UC Santa Barbara, or at the agricultural college in Davis. The others had to leave too—there were no jobs in Poinsettia, not for bright people. They scattered to Los Angeles or San Francisco. Molly was about the only one who stayed.

She was working at the EZ Rest by now, but they wanted her more and more at Snyder's Luncheonette, because Wilma was sick more and more of the time, so Molly worked twelve and fourteen hours a day sometimes and got home only to fall exhausted into bed. No time to watch TV or even listen to the radio—and she never read the papers: they were too hard. So she heard it from a table of women—from the bank, from the Highway Patrol office —eating early breakfast, and gossiping about how the deserted roadhouse outside town had been sold, and guess who had bought it—Carl Wynant.

"Wynant's eggs?" one of the women said.

The other nodded. "That's the one."

"I remember him," a hatchet-faced woman said. "Big, blond boy. Football player at the high school. Got into some kind of trouble with the sheriff once."

"I never thought he'd amount to anything."

"Well, you see," the first woman said, picking at her omelette, looking for more pieces of mushroom than there were. "You never can tell about youngsters. They grow up and surprise you."

"Where did he get the money? Could his mother afford to buy him a nightclub?"

One of the bank women laughed. "I handle her account. She can't save a dime, just barely makes ends meet, poor woman, once she's paid the help. When she had a husband and son, it was different, wasn't it?"

"Ranch hands won't work for their meals and a place to sleep, anymore," the woman with the omelette said. "Those days are gone forever."

"Why should trash like that work," the hatchet-faced woman said, "when they can live on welfare?"

"Isn't that the truth," the others said.

Mr. Snyder, red-faced in his chef's hat and apron, behind a service window filled with steaming plates, called impatiently for Molly, and she wasn't able to stay and listen anymore. She had to take other people their breakfasts.

She waited in a lattice-work patio beside the newly painted roadhouse. Ferns hung up in pots, and new banana trees and flowering shrubs were stuck into corners. New redwood planks were underfoot. A jacaranda tree spread feathery shadows on the deck. Lacy white metal chairs with designs pierced in the seats surrounded round white metal tables. She sat at one of the tables. She was the only one here. It was early afternoon. But the grand opening of Carl's Come-On-Inn happened last Saturday night. She'd walked out footsore after Snyder's closed, and seen the gravel parking area beside the highway filled with cars, dressed-up people going in and out, laughing, chattering in the glow of the big new sign on the roof. So she figured Carl would be along today. Now a rattling at the side door got her attention, and in a minute the door opened, and a thin, young Asian man in kitchen whites stood there, blinking in the sunlight. He seemed surprised to see her. She got off the chair, and hurried to him.

"Please tell Mr. Wynant Molly Byrne wants to see him."

The man jerked his head. "He inside. You come in?"

"No. You tell him. I'll wait out here."

The man blinked at her, shrugged, turned, and was gone.

She went back to sit at the table again. Then Carl came out. He'd changed. His hair had been shoulder-long at school. Now it was cut short as a banker's. He wore a gold embroidered red cowboy shirt, narrow-legged beige whipcords, tooled cowboy boots dyed maroon and purple. All this seemed cheerful, but he didn't look cheerful. He looked angry. He closed the door behind him, came to her, scowling. "What the hell are you doing here?"

"Why did you come back? You hated Poinsettia."

"Until I saw other places. Molly, what do you want?"

"To remind you that half of this should be mine." She had rehearsed just what she was going to say. It surprised her that she got it out. She was terribly frightened. "You said that money from Mr. Dowd would be ours between us, together, Carl. That's what you said."

"I don't go partners with murderers," he said.

"I can tell the sheriff where your money came from," she said. "He's always watching me. He thinks I know who robbed Mr. Dowd."

Carl straightened sharply. He stepped to the latticework and peered toward the highway. In a minute, he snorted and turned back. "You're crazy, Molly. It's been years."

"He's still waiting for me to tell him," she said. "And I can, can't I? He asked if I had a boyfriend. I said no, but I can still tell him the truth. And he can check it out too, with who was in school with us then. It wasn't the big secret you thought it was. They

knew we went to Copenhagen. The sheriff will believe me when
I say you were with me at Mr. Dowd's. And if it was you that ran
off with the money, why wasn't it you that did the shooting?"

"Wasn't my gun. It was your old man's gun," Carl said. "Only
fingerprints on it are yours, Molly. It was cold—I wore gloves that
night—remember? I hung onto the gun—it's all wrapped up and
put away safe. So I've got proof. All you've got is a story, your
word against mine."

"You ran away that night," she flared. "That's proof."

"My mother never reported the truck missing," Carl said. "So
nobody knows when I left. Forget it, Molly. Get out of here and
leave me alone. If you come pestering me, it will be me that tells
the sheriff. You worked for old man Dowd, not me. You knew
about the money. You were the one had your eye on it. You were
the one killed him to get it."

"I want my half," she repeated stubbornly. "You wouldn't dare
tell. You'd lose all of this."

"This wasn't bought with old man Dowd's money, for Christ's
sake," he said. "I couldn't have bought a used car with what was
in that fishing tackle box." Molly frowned. "Then where—"

"I used it to gamble with," he said. "Las Vegas. Faro, poker,
blackjack, dice. I was stupid and I lost. Damn near every penny.
I was worse off than here—had to sleep in the truck, live on potato
chips. Finally I figured even the egg ranch was better than starving. So I headed for home."

"You didn't get home. Carl, it's been years."

"I had twenty bucks in my shoe, and I stopped at Santa Anita.
I hit a Pick Nine. You know what that is? You pick the winners
in all the races, and they practically give you the damn race track.
For a sixteen dollar bet."

"But where have you been?"

"Found a partner, lawyer, he had the brains, I had the money,
bought a broken down tavern in Azusa, fixed it up, got it going
again. Sold it for twice what I put into it, did the same with
another in Pasadena. Then I was ready to come home like any man
wants to come home." He turned and pointed at a big glossy car.
"Mercedes. Forty thousand dollars, Molly." He glanced around
again to be sure they were alone. "Not Mr. Dowd's money, not

your money. Mine. Now, clear out of here." He yanked her up off the chair, turned her, pushed her. "Back way, through the hills, so nobody sees you."

She stumbled, had to clutch the latticework to keep from falling. She glared at him. "You'll be sorry," she said.

"You can't tell the sheriff about me," he said.

"I can kill you, Carl," she said, amazed at the sound of the words in her own ears. "Just like I killed Mr. Dowd. I can and I will. You got your money and your freedom. Now I want mine. I want my half," she repeated again. "You promised. Don't make me wait."

"Get lost," he said; strode back into the building, and slammed the door.

Her father died. She found him slumped in the chair with the television going, whiskey bottle and glass on the carpet beside the chair, where they'd left rings she'd never managed to scrub out. There was a wide stain where he'd spilled the glass this time. She worried more about how she was going to clean it up than about losing him. He'd been a torment and a burden to her for years. She wouldn't miss him. She was glad to watch him buried in the cemetery plot under the live oak beside her mother.

Then she learned she had to move. The house wasn't hers. Her father had, unknown to her, transferred ownership to his brother in Montana when he couldn't make the mortgage payments, and the brother had allowed him to live on here till he died. But the brother was dead too, and the bank in Missoula that held the house under the agreement, now was free to sell it, and that was what they did. Which was how Molly ended up in these little rooms. All the same, her father's death eased things for her. There was only one mouth to feed, and no whiskey to buy. She quit waitressing at Snyder's. After cleaning up the units at the Gobineaus, she could come home, lie on her bed, watch TV—and think about killing Carl.

She is still thinking about it, when knuckles rattle the screen door. A shadow lies on the screen. A man's shadow. The sheriff? In a panic, she crumples up the paper she's written on, and jams it into the overflowing waste basket under the sink. The blank paper and pencil she hides in a drawer. She forgets all about the gun. She's in a daze. She goes to the door, stands, hand on the latch, breathless. "Who is it? What do you want?"

"It's me, Molly," the shadow says, "Hugh Henderson."

She can't believe it. "I'm—sorry your mother died," she stammers. "I'll come—to the funeral—if you want."

"It's not about that," Hugh says. "Can I come in?"

"I'm sorry." Flustered, Molly pushes the door open. Hugh Henderson surprises her. Except for those soft brown eyes of his, he's changed from the runty boy he was in school. He's almost six feet tall, broad-shouldered, nothing frail about him. He looks handsome in a suit and shirt and tie and polished shoes.

"Come in," she says.

"Thank you." He glances around at the small place. "Are you all right, Molly? Mom wrote me, your father died."

She goes to the fridge. "Hot day. You want a Coke?"

"Yes, thanks. Shall I sit here?"

"Help yourself." She closes the refrigerator, sets a can in front of him, sits down and pops the top of her can. "I've got a job at the EZ Rest motel. I get along."

"My mom wrote me about that." He opens his own Coke. "It's why I checked in there last night. I thought I'd see you. I wanted to talk to you." Molly's heart begins to hurry. "To me? What about?"

He shrugs, smiles, opens his hands. "My mom kept me up to date with everything going on in Poinsettia. She never got it through her head I hated the place, just wanted to forget it." He laughs bleakly, shakes his head. "And now she's dead. And I'm going to miss those letters." He looks at her with tears in his eyes. "Crazy, isn't it?"

Molly smiles bitterly. "I even miss my father—and you know what he was."

Hugh nods sympathetically, but his mind is back on his reason for coming here. "Mom wrote me when Mr. Dowd died, somebody robbed and shot him. She said the sheriff questioned you about it."

"Only 'cause I worked for him," Molly says. She shrugs and

drinks some Coke. "It was a long time ago."

"Same time Carl Wynant left town," Hugh says. "His mom told my mom about it—she was hurt enough Carl left, but what really burned her was he took the truck." Hugh drinks some of his Coke, holds the can for her to see, says, "Thank you." He sets the can down, frowns. "What do you think? I think it was Carl that robbed Mr. Dowd. He was always telling me the old man hid money in his house." Hugh glances at her wryly, and away again. "Back when we were friends. Carl wanted to escape from Poinsettia, that egg ranch. To live like people—that's how he put it. What good was the money to Mr. Dowd, anyway, sick as he was, dying?"

"Carl's back," she says. "He owns the road house now."

"I know." Hugh draws a breath. His gentle brown eyes find Molly's, and hold them, grave, insistent. "After he did what he did to me—Mom wrote she'd see you and Carl together driving past in the truck, on your way out of town. But not in toward Wynant's ranch. On the way to Copenhagen, right?"

"How do you know about Copenhagen?"

Poker-faced, Hugh says, "He used to take me there too."

Molly opens her mouth, but she can't find words. Hugh says, "Mom figured you two were sweethearts."

Molly blushes. "You know how this town gossips."

"Come on, Molly. He told you about the money at Dowd's too, didn't he? That was a plan he had. To have sex with you, make you think he loved you, so you'd let him in with your key, and show him where the money was hidden."

"You're lying." Molly jumps up. "Get out of here."

But he only sits looking at her quietly with those gentle brown eyes. She struggles to get her breath, to stop trembling, to find her voice. She shuts her eyes, and nods in defeat. "He did that," she whispers. "That's just what he did." She sits down again. "He said he loved me, and after we got Mr. Dowd's money, we'd go away together."

"A real sweetheart," Hugh says. "He always was."

"I wish he was dead," she says.

"That what the rifle's for?" Hugh reaches for it from his chair, lays it on the table. "Is it ready to shoot?"

"My father taught me how to clean it, oil it, load it," Molly says. "Yes. It's ready to shoot."

Hugh stands and closes the door. "Let's talk," he says.

It's a good night. A full moon shines on the smooth round dry-grass hills outside town. Hugh has a beautiful new car. It smells of newness. It purrs almost soundlessly along the highway, and when Hugh swings it onto the two lane country road that leads to Copenhagen, it scarcely notices the ruts and potholes in the neglected tarmac. Molly sits with the rifle between her knees. Her hand keeps stroking the velvety upholstery of the seat. She is so happy to be riding in this lovely car, she forgets for long minutes at a time where they are bound for and why.

In the dim glow of the elaborate instrument panel Hugh's face is set grimly. When she glances at him, it reminds her, and she takes her hands from the softness of the upholstery and puts them on the cold wood and steel of the gun. This is the night she has been waiting for all these years. She looks out at the moonlit hills, the shadows of the scattered oaks on the hills, stars above, a far off ranchhouse, lights aglow. It is beautiful. Her heart swells at the beauty of it. She turns suddenly to Hugh. And he is beautiful too. She wants to lean across and kiss him.

He glances at her. "You all right?"

She catches hold of herself, nods stiffly. "Fine."

He reads his watch. "I hope he's not early." He switches off the headlights, slows the car to a crawl. She can see why. There, to the far left, the great deserted barn that is Copenhagen looms up, the moon silvering its roof. Hugh glances into the rearview mirror. There is a mirror on Molly's door. She looks into it. The road lies dark behind them. Hugh spins the steering wheel, and gingerly eases the car bumping between the crooked fence-posts that long ago shed their gate, and up the two rut road toward the barn. It is so still, she can hear the tall weeds brush the underside of the car. "Get the gun ready," Hugh whispers.

She lifts the rifle. The space is too cramped. She hears a soft whine, and the window beside her opens. She jacks a bullet into the chamber, pokes the barrel out the window, works an arm out to balance it, her head out into the cool night to lay a cheekbone against the stock. The hardpan of the yard is rough. This jiggles the gun. But there's nothing to fire at. The yard is empty. Hugh stops the car in the middle of the yard, switches off the engine. There is just enough moonlight so when she looks at him, she can see his white teeth bared in a smile.

"We got here first," he says.

Molly draws in the gun, opens the door, gets out into the silence, the gun hanging in her hand. It's not like the other times she came here, is it? She felt wonderful, those times. Well, she feels wonderful tonight, doesn't she? It's just a different kind of wonderful, that's all. The other was foolish. This is real. She reaches into the car, and Hugh puts a flashlight into her hand.

"Good hunting," he says.

"Don't worry," she says, switches on the flashlight, and walks into the barn. It hasn't changed much. Bums have used it, so there are more cans and bottles and paper trash strewn around, but she just kicks these aside in her walk to the ladder. The loft is the same. She stands at the top of the ladder in the deep straw for a minute, wanting to go to that corner over there, where Carl spread out the sleeping bag, and they made love. A lump forms in her throat. Her eyes grow misty.

But she turns away. Over there gapes the big door used to pulley bales from trucks below up into the loft. The door looks down on the barnyard. She goes there, making the old planks creak, lays the rifle on the straw, and stretches out beside it. She turns off the flashlight and looks down on Hugh's car with the moonlight shining on it. She smiles to herself. It all seems so simple now. But she could never have done it alone. Molly Byrne could never have lured Carl out here. It took Hugh Henderson's long-lost "How are you, old buddy?" on the telephone to do that.

She watches the empty road. She reads her watch. It is still not nine o'clock. Time is standing still. What if he doesn't come? What if he sensed Hugh was lying, when Hugh told him he had brought home with him naked, grinning photographs of teenage Carl doing obscene stuff for Hugh's camera in his bedroom out at the egg ranch—and Hugh wanted five thousand dollars, or he'd show them to the Poinsettia newspaper. Hugh told Molly it wasn't true. The pictures once existed, all right, and he cherished them, but the day he left Poinsettia, he angrily burned every picture he'd ever taken of Carl, and all the negatives. He was smooth and menacing on the phone, but is Carl really so stupid as to come along to this godforsaken place to meet a man who hates him as Hugh Henderson does? Along the road, the shadows of the trees shift as the moon climbs higher in the sky. Her watch says it is now ten past nine. Hugh has got out of the car and stands leaning against it, arms crossed, gazing toward the road.

"He's not coming," Molly calls.

"Be quiet," he says, without looking up.

And soon, light flickers beyond the farthest hills. Moving light. The lights of a car. She keeps her gaze on them. They vanish and reappear, each time closer. Then the car is within sight. It comes on, following the beams of its headlights. It swings in at the entrance to Copenhagen. It is the sleek Mercedes. Its headlights jitter a little over the uneven ground of the yard. She turns, picks up the rifle, fits it against her shoulder as her father taught her, squints, sighting along the moonlight-glinting barrel. The car rocks to a halt. The sound of its engine dies in the night silence.

Hugh Henderson takes a step toward it. The headlights of the Mercedes shut off. The door opens. Carl, dressed in white, climbs out. Hugh walks toward him. He reaches into his jacket pocket, and takes out an envelope. It's nothing but a piece of junk mail from Molly's waste basket under the sink, coupons for laundry detergent, not photographs. He holds it out to Carl. And this is the moment, the split second she has been waiting for all these years. Her finger tightens on the trigger.

A plank creaks. The floor of the loft shakes under her. A voice behind her says, "Don't shoot, Molly." The rifle barrel wavers. The rifle fires. Below, in the moonlight, Hugh Henderson yelps, throws up his arms, spins drunkenly, and falls. That's all she sees. Rough hands jerk her to her feet, fling the rifle aside. It's the sheriff. He must have been here all along, hiding in the shadows. Carl must have sent him. "Didn't you hear me?" He gives her an angry shake. "I told you not to shoot."

"You spoiled my aim," she cries, "you spoiled my aim."

HOME IS THE PLACE

THE LIGHT WAS poor. It was early morning and fog hung in the pines of Settler's Cove. But as he rounded a bend in the road, Hack Bohannon saw the gray shapes of three men cross up ahead. The hats told him two were sheriff's deputies. The lumbering prisoner was Clay Gilmore, a coach at the high school. The deputies opened a rear door for him and he folded into the car. The officers got in, doors slammed, and the car came toward Bohannon and passed, heading for the Coast Highway. Lt. Phil Gerard drove. The deputy in the back seat was named Vern. Bohannon lifted a hand to them. Gerard touched his hat and looked grim.

Bohannon parked his battered green pickup in front of the Gilmore house, a hulking dark box in the fog. He climbed a slope among ferns and poison oak under trees with rags of fog caught in their branches, nodded to the bulky young deputy, Lundquist, stationed at the front door, and went along the side of the house to the rear where he found a tall plank gate half open, and stepped into a patio with a large swimming pool that was empty except for dry brown pine needles. They'd piled up. The pool hadn't held water in a long time.

There was a story to that. He knew part of the story. Everybody did. But nobody knew the end of it. Or hadn't until this morning, about three-thirty, four o'clock. One panel of a sliding glass door at the back of the house stood open, and fog had crept into the room, but he knew whose the trim figure was that stood there—deputy T. Hodges. "Morning," he said, stepped inside, twitched her a half smile and looked at what lay at her feet. If he hadn't been told different, Bohannon would have thought the body sprawled there was that of an old man.

He crouched beside it. In spite of ugly dark splotches, on forehead, cheek, jaw-line, the face was a very young man's. Bohannon touched the thin black leather of the jacket. The shoulder and arm inside were wasted like those of an old man sick and dying. A bullet had gone through the leather right at the sternum. A little blood had seeped from the entry wound, but not much. Death had been quick: when the heart stops, so does the bleeding.

He looked up at T. Hodges, who had jangled the alarm-bell phone in his stables before sun-up, as he was making the horses ready for the day, and asked him to come here. Though young, T. Hodges had been in law enforcement for years, and wasn't as a rule shaken up by murder, though it was far from common in her bailiwick, here on California's picture-postcard central coast. But her eyes glistened now with what he figured to be tears.

"Belle still not here?" He meant the wry old woman doctor who grudgingly served as district medical examiner. "It's been hours."

"Maybe she had horses to look after too." T. Hodges tried for a smile but failed. She gazed again at the boy. "His name is Charles Gilmore—Chico, his father calls him. Called him. Age twenty-six. Last known place of residence, San Francisco. He wasn't expected home."

"No?" With a grunt, Bohannon got to his feet. "Well, the shooter didn't let surprise spoil his aim. Right through the heart. Find the weapon?"

She shook her head. "We'll search the woods once it's light."

"No bullet?"

"It could be under him," she said. "Or in him."

"Right." Bohannon looked around the floor, wanting the glint of a shell casing. There was ample dust, but no shell casing. The room had a pair of ravelled green wicker chairs and a green wicker couch. An old white enamelled chest of drawers with flaking Donald Duck decals. No books, magazines, no pictures on the walls, just faded rectangles where they'd once been. No one cared about this room now, any more than they cared about the swimming pool.

The door of a closet was ajar. He looked in. A lumpy blue canvas backpack hunched on the floor. A zipper was open on one of its pouches and little white-capped amber plastic vials, the kind that hold prescription medications, had tumbled out. Bohannon didn't touch it. He had long ago quit sheriffing. He had a Private Investigator's license, but no status here. She had asked him to come. He loved her, and he had come. "Anyone search this bag?"

"I left it for you. You'll read it better. I cleared it with the Lieutenant."

With a grunt, he picked it up, set it on the bed, opened the zippers one by one and took everything out. It was pathetic. The sexy bikini briefs were ragged, the elastic gone, the bright dyes too. Same for the net skivvy shirts. All of it was very clean and smelled of Clorox. Cheap white dimestore socks. Two pairs of jeans. Three shirts. Shapeless sweaters that had cost a lot once long ago.

In one pocket of the backpack were papers that showed Charles Gilmore had sold his life insurance to a company that had then doled money out to him, on the odds that he would soon die, a company pretty sure it could not lose, a company of such compassion it made you want to weep.

There were sad receipts. He had sold his car, a late model Lexus, a pair of Mapplethorpe photographs, his sound system, his 40-inch television set, his part-ownership in a sailboat. A bundle of paycheck stubs showed he had left his job at a brokerage eight months ago. They'd given him big separation pay, but his medical bills—hospitals, laboratories, pharmacies—had been bigger.

He poked around. There was a scuffed and faded children's picture-book, *Fletcher & Zenobia*, but there were no personal letters. Stranger still, no snapshots. Not from here, not from San Francisco. He was leaving a big part of his life behind, friends, events, yet he hadn't brought reminders of any of it. Why not? Bohannon sighed, and stuffed everything back. Except the book. The book he handed to T. Hodges. "What do you make of that?"

"I'll read it," she said.

Bohannon said, "He wasn't just sick, he was broke."

T. Hodges gave him a crooked little smile. "And 'home is the place where, if you have to go there, they have to take you in.'"

"Robert Frost," Bohannon said. "Well, not even he was right all the time."

Another door showed him a dusty little bathroom with a toilet, basin, shower-stall. No towels on the racks. Nothing in the rust-flecked medicine cabinet but a long-ago toothbrush. He came out again.

Charles Gilmore's worn Nikes lay on the floor beside the couch. The faded cushions on the couch showed he had been lying there, but not at the time he was shot. When he was shot, he had been standing. That was plain from where he lay now, how he lay.

Bohannon lit a cigarette. "Gerard arrested the father, right?

Clay?"

"Did he have a choice? There were only two people in the house, Hack, the dead one and the living one. As the lieutenant sees it, if it wasn't deliberate murder, then Clay heard a noise, grabbed a gun, ran out here, and in the dark shot what he thought was an intruder."

"And what's Clay's version?"

"He didn't know Chico was here. Assumes he arrived late, very late, found the house dark, didn't want to wake his parents and just sacked out here. Clay's sleep was broken by shouts and a shot. He stumbled out of bed, ran back here, found Chico dead, went to the phone in the kitchen, and dialled nine-one-one. Didn't shoot anybody, doesn't even own a gun."

Bohannon said, "His son's been gone must be eight, nine years. What was he, seventeen? It was about swimming. The kid was going to be on the Olympic team. It was in all the papers. His father was his trainer and he was proud. Then all of a sudden the boy quit. Left town, and never came back."

T. Hodges made a brief, bleak sound. "He should have stuck with that."

Fingerprint powder was around the lock on the patio door. Bohannon squinted at the lock. "This hasn't been forced."

"Coach Gilmore says it's never locked. Anybody could just walk in."

"Could and presumably did," Bohannon said. "Who? And why? Was it a mugging? Did they take anything?"

"His wallet was in his jacket. Twenty-nine dollars in it."

"That so?" Bohannon pushed back his old Stetson and peered upward. The fog still hung in the pines. The ocean was downhill a short way through the woods. Waves thudded. A sea lion barked. Bohannon took a last drag on the cigarette, stepped outside, dropped it, ground it out under a straw-caked boot. He turned back. "And Clay claims nobody knew he was coming?"

"It could be true. We searched the house for letters. Didn't find any. And there's no computer."

"Phone records being checked?" Bohannon said.

"Here and in San Francisco," she said. "The coach also claims he didn't know anything about his son's life since he left home, how he lived, where he lived, who his friends were." She made a face. "He didn't want to know, Hack. He didn't say that, but it was obvious."

Belle Hesseltine banged in at the patio gate, tall and gaunt and grumpy, in jeans, sheepskin jacket, cowboy hat. "Sorry. Triplets. In a shack. Mexican illegals. They didn't send for help. Scared to." She marched toward them, soldier straight and grim of face. "Neighbor finally ran to the gas station and phoned."

"Triplets," T. Hodges said. "Did you drive her to the hospital?"

"Too late for that. But mother and young are doing well. Three brand new American citizens." She laughed. "I filled out the birth certificates. That made the parents happy. Whole reason they came, poor things." She stopped short and scowled down at the dead youngster. "AIDS," she said, and looked at T. Hodges. "Those lesions on his face. Kaposi's sarcoma. You didn't tell me he had AIDS."

"It's not what killed him," Bohannon said.

The old woman set down her kit. "I hope you didn't touch the body."

Bohannon ignored that, and asked T. Hodges, "Isn't there a mother? Real estate agent? Celia, that her name? Where is she in all this?"

"At her sister's in Santa Barbara. There's a sick child, and the sister is divorced, and has to work. So Celia is down there keeping things together for a few days. I've called her, told her there's been an accident. She's coming home."

"You didn't let on who the accident happened to?"

She tightened her mouth. "Hack, I didn't just fall off the turnip truck."

"Sorry," he said.

"She thought it was Clay," T. Hodges said. "She thought he was dead."

Belle Hesseltine pulled on latex gloves and dropped to her bony old knees beside the body. "Get out of here, you two," she said. "Let me do my work."

"When you roll him over," Bohannon said, "look for a bullet."

The old woman zipped open the black jacket, apologetically, as if it were an intrusion. "If it had gone through him, there'd be

blood and tissue splashed around." She unbuttoned the boy's shirt.
His chest was parchment stretched over a rack of bones. The entry wound was small and neat. The neatness made it obscene. She
touched it. "Poor child," she murmured.

Bohannon raised his eyebrows. "The doctor has a heart."

"I thought I asked you to get out of here," she snapped.

They got out and met a skinny bespectacled boy and a hefty La-
tina girl in green coveralls, coming with a gurney and a body bag.
Bohannon thought to himself, not for the first time, that he ought
to stop labeling these adults boys and girls. It was a mark of growing old, and he was only fifty-six. He said to T. Hodges, "How
long are you stuck here? When can I take you to breakfast?"

"The Lieutenant will be back with Vern to look for the gun,
now that it's daylight, but he'll want me to wait for Celia. He'll
want me to break it to her. Woman to woman. It's how he thinks."

"Right," Bohannon looked at his watch. "When did you notify
her?"

"Four, a few minutes after." T. Hodges gave a little shiver.
"Come on. The Lieutenant had me make coffee, earlier. Woman's
work, you know. Maybe there's still some left. Kitchen's this way."
The coffee pot was empty: Lt. Gerard and Clay Gilmore had sat
here a good while, talking. Bohannon threw away the grounds,
and made fresh coffee. T. Hodges sat at the table and read *Fletcher
& Zenobia*. The only sound in the room was the grumbling of the
coffee maker. Bohannon carried filled mugs to the table, and sat
down across from her. She closed the book.

"What's it about?" he asked.

"A cat and a Victorian doll who have a party with cake and bal-
loons and funny hats high up in a big old tree." She frowned, turning the book over. "I don't know what kind of child it was written
for."

"Doesn't sound like a clue," Bohannon said.

And Belle Hesseltine came in and set down her kit.

"Coffee?" Bohannon stood up.

"I'd say the bullet's lodged in a bone." The old woman took a
seat. "Rib or vertabra. It stopped his heart while he was still standing." She watched Bohannon set the mug in front of her. "We'll
get it out at the lab. Then we'll know more." With a bony, age-

spotted hand, she waved away the waxed cardboard carton of cream Bohannon offered. She saw a question in his eyes before he asked it. "No. Not a rifle. It wasn't some dim-witted deer-hunter's miss."

"Rifles are commoner than pistols in these parts," he said.

She nodded, tried the coffee, burned her mouth, but held the steaming mug instead of setting it down. She wanted the coffee. "You'll find the handgun in the woods, I expect. About the distance Clay Gilmore could throw it. He reported the shooting right away. Body temperature shows that. He didn't take time out to drive down and throw it in the ocean."

Jittery metallic rattling came past the kitchen window. They saw the heads of the ambulance pair go by. It was the wheels of the gurney with Chico Gilmore's body on it that rattled. That was below eye level. It continued on until it was out of hearing.

Belle Hesseltine tried her coffee again. "Don't mourn, you two," she said. "He hadn't much longer to live."

"Maybe that makes it even sadder," T. Hodges said.

"It was clean and quick," the old woman said. "AIDS is not. His suffering is over. Years of it, by the look of him." She drank a little more coffee. "He wasn't losing his life. Not what anybody'd want to call a life. All he had left was agony."

T. Hodges stared. "You think it was a mercy killing? You think his father did it to put him out of his misery? An act of kindness?"

The doctor didn't answer that. Her faded blue eyes were regarding Bohannon with a wry twinkle. "Go ahead, have your smoke. You've touched that pocket five times in the past two minutes. I'm leaving." She set the coffee mug down and stood up. "I have to find the bullet that's hiding in that boy." Her mouth twitched grimly, she picked up her kit, pulled open the door and stepped outside.

And not far off in the silence of the pines, a woman screamed.

"Oh, God." T. Hodges threw Bohannon a panicked look.

He laid a hand on her arm. "Take it easy." He got to his feet and told the blank-faced doctor, "That will be the victim's mother. She was out of town."

The lean old woman studied T. Hodges. "You stay here and collect yourself. I'll take care of it." And she started off at a stiff, long-legged stride. The screaming kept up, hysterical, broken by hoarse sobbing.

A young man's voice, panicky, ready to crack, yelled: "Hodges, where are you?" And Lundquist came running, dodging past Belle Hesseltine. He stopped in the kitchen doorway, red-faced, breathing hard. "Hodges, will you get out here, please? It's Mrs. Gilmore. She zipped open the body bag before I could stop her." He waved an arm toward the shrill crying. "She's going crazy."

"Right away," T. Hodges said, and went to him, and they trotted together out of Bohannon's window view, along the side of the house toward the front. Belle Hesseltine followed. Frowning to himself, Bohannon lit a cigarette, gulped some coffee, and trudged after them. He watched them run slipping down the ferny slope between pines to the crooked hilly road, and across the road, to where the green-clad youngsters were trying to slide the gurney into the rear of the County ambulance. A middle-aged woman, shouting, "No, no, no," clutched at them. "You can't take him. Don't you understand? He's my son, my son. This is where he belongs. He's just come home."

Now T. Hodges and Lundquist caught hold of the woman. She stared at them, wild-eyed for a moment, then went limp, whimpering, seeming to give up. The ambulance pair slammed shut the rear doors, ran and climbed into the cab. The doors banged, the engine roared. Celia Gilmore surprised the deputies, broke away from them, ran to the front of the ambulance and threw herself on the hood. "No, no. You can't have him, you can't have him. He's mine. He's all I have. I've waited so long."

The deputies caught her again and dragged her to the brushy far side of the road and the ambulance roared off. The woman was struggling, keening, mad with grief. She stretched her arms out after the departing ambulance. Bohannon had glimpsed her often in the town, a good looking woman, well-groomed, well-dressed, younger than her years, bright, brisk, businesslike. Not this morning. This terrible morning she was wild-haired Niobe, weeping for her child, older than a thousand centuries, as old as motherhood itself.

"Come on," Belle Hesseltine said grimly. "She's a danger to herself. Or making a damned good show of it. In either case, I'll give her a shot to knock her out." She started down the slope. Worried that she might fall, he tried to take her arm, but she wouldn't let him. The Gilmore woman began screaming and struggling again. With a short, dry laugh, Belle Hesseltine said, "Do you know what they told me when I moved here to retire?"

"Sure," Bohannon said. "'Nothing ever happens in Settler's Cove.'"

Otis Jackson had come to work for Bohannon when George Stubbs was still alive and in need of care. Jackson, a hefty, good-humored young black man, was working as a rent-a-nurse, swatting the books, and saving his money for medical school. When Stubbs died, Bohannon, desperate for help that wouldn't walk out on him after a few days, weeks, months, coaxed Otis into staying on as his stableman. The pay was minimal, all Bohannon could afford, but room and board were free and the job would leave him time to study, so Jackson had agreed. But he'd never been near a horse in his life before, and was still a little spooky around them, and Bohannon was spooky at leaving him in charge of things for long. Horses could panic over nothing, and if a horse panicked, Otis might panic.

So, once Celia Gilmore was sedated, and an ambulance had come to get her to the hospital in Los Osos, T. Hodges riding there with her, to wait there to question her when she woke up, Bohannon headed for his pickup truck. But as he opened the door, a shout stopped him. "Where you going?" He looked. Phil Gerard had just rolled up in the patrol car with Vern.

"Back to minding my own business." Bohannon ambled over to him.

"That would be a novelty," Gerard said. He opened the trunk of the patrol car. Rakes lay there. They looked fresh from the hardware store. He handed one to Vern and one to Bohannon. "But for a change, this morning I'm going to be grateful for your help." He got a rake for himself, slammed the trunk closed, and started toward the Gilmore house. "That gun is out there in back someplace. We have to find it."

Bohannon and Vern trailed after him. Bohannon said, "According to Hodges, Clay Gilmore didn't own a gun."

"Technically the truth," Gerard said, climbing through the ferns, looking at the ground as he walked, maybe thinking the gun could be out here in front. The fog had pretty well dispersed now but dampness dripped from the trees. "It wasn't his. It was his wife's. She bought it a year ago after she unlocked the front door of a property to show it to some prospective buyers and surprised housebreakers at work."

"Hah," Bohannon said. "And you think it was here in a dresser drawer?"

"People at Principal Realty say at first she kept it in her desk there, took it with her in the car when she showed houses, but nobody's seen it or heard about it for months, now."

They trailed along the side of the house. "She got a computer there?" Bohannon asked.

"Yes, and a Deputy Bruce Busby from San Luis is checking it out, looking for e-mail to or from Charles Chico Gilmore in San Francisco. To see if mom knew junior was planning to come home. Because mom could have told pop, right?" He grinned at Bohannon over his shoulder. "I'm on top of this, Hack. Been a long time since we were partners. Try not to worry about me, okay?"

Bohannon stopped at the open gate. "That swimming pool's got a lot of duff in it. Must be two feet deep. Be the handiest hiding place for the gun."

"Check that will you, Vern?" Gerard said, and took Bohannon with him into the trees. He said, "This isn't going to be a big challenge. What is it—an acre?"

"Half an acre," Bohannon said, and stepped in something sticky. "Wait. Look at this." Gunk was on his boot, and flies were buzzing around the gunk.

"Somebody threw up here," Gerard said.

"Killing takes some of us that way," Bohannon said, and scraped his boot on a tree trunk to try to clean it. "It wasn't the coach. He'd have thrown up in his own bathroom."

"Not if he came out here to get rid of the gun," Gerard said.

"He didn't." Bohannon ran his gaze along the ground. For a couple of yards footprints showed. Spaced far apart. Somebody running. He pointed at them and Gerard saw them and understood what they meant.

"It wasn't Clay Gilmore. He must wear size thirteens." The lieutenant scratched his cheek. He'd had no time to shave this morning. "Well, we'd still better try to find the gun. If the killer was so disgusted with himself he threw up, he also probably threw the gun away."

They spent forty minutes raking among the ferns and brush beneath the pines. Methodically. Marking off the areas covered one by one until they reached the side road and back road that bordered the property. Bohannon sat on a stump, lit a cigarette and, when Gerard walked across to him from where he'd finished off raking, nodded toward a dark shiny spot on the ragged paving.

"Some car with an oil leak parked here lately," he said.

"What sharp eyes you have, Grandma," Gerard said.

"He kept the gun," Bohannon said. "Drove off with it. In an old car."

"But who, for God's sake? It makes no—" Gerard's beeper sounded. "Gotta call in," he said.

Bohannon stood up, stepped on his cigarette, and went with him. As they passed the plank gate, Vern joined them. "No gun down there. Banana slugs, though. You ever see one? They're beautiful. Bright yellow. Great big. Eat decaying vegetation." He laid the rakes back and closed the trunk of the patrol car, while Gerard used the two-way radio. It crackled and buzzed and Lundquist's voice came out. "Doc Hesseltine recovered the bullet, Lieutenant. It's a thirty-two. Same as the gun Mrs. Gilmore bought."

"Ten four," Gerard said, hung the radio up, and looked at Bohannon. "I know how your mind works. Like a chainsaw. Hack, it wasn't Mrs. Gilmore."

"Because she doesn't drive a leaky old car?" Bohannon said.

"She was in Santa Barbara." Gerard peered at him, disbelieving. "You like her for it? Aw, Hack, She was heartbroken. You saw her, you heard her."

Bohannon shrugged. "After she zipped open the body bag."

"She expected it to be Clay. She didn't know the son had come home."

"Then why open the bag?" Bohannon said. "Phil, she knew he was coming. It wasn't grief that made her scream. It was rage."

"Oh, boy!" Gerard snorted, and drove away with Vern.

He kept Otis Jackson watching him, leaning on the rail fence of the oval where kids, mostly horse-crazy girls, were taught to ride, while he conducted the lessons. George Stubbs used to do this. And Manuel Rivera. Now Stubbs was dead and Rivera had long since become a priest. And Bohannon himself was losing patience with the chore. The delight and fear and joy and despair and all the other emotions so near the surface in children that accompanied the lessons gave him a happy sense of aliveness that any honest man past fifty knew full well he was slowly losing. But it was wearying too. He'd be glad when Otis got over the idea that he couldn't do it, and took over for him. Otis had bought himself a white cowboy hat. That was a good sign, Bohannon hoped.

And he had mastered saddling and unsaddling the horses, and most of the arcana of keeping their equipment and quarters clean and well-ordered, and the horses themselves curried, fed, watered, and contented. He had even got less visibly uneasy in the saddle, and would soon be out on the canyon trails leading the Saddle Seniors group on their Saturday morning outings. Most riders who rented his mounts went off on their own. Now, leading Stanton Criss around on her palomino, teaching her what to do with the reins when she wanted the pretty little filly to step over a length of telephone pole laid in the way, Bohannon suddenly had a recollection of coach Clay Gilmore coming here to ride, bringing his young son, eight, ten years old. A long time ago. The boy had been afraid of the horses, paralyzed by fear. His father had laughed at him, called him a little girl, bullied him. It was an ugly memory.

"He's still that way," T. Hodges said. She had come up to the ranch house at sundown, after her shift ended, for supper, as she often did. Tonight, though, she hadn't done the cooking. Otis had. Ham, beans and rice, collard greens, corn bread. They were all three gathered at the big round deal table in the plank-walled kitchen, while the slanting daylight turned to gold and crimson outside the windows. "Celia says he hated the boy until he learned to swim. It was the only sport he took to. And he was brilliant. His father forgave him all his earlier failings, what he regarded as failings. And Chico was so amazed to be doing something at last that his father took pride in that he doubled and redoubled his efforts to be good at it, to be the best."

"And here was a son his father could be proud of?" Otis said.

"Exactly. Until it all went sour. Very suddenly."

"Did his mother give you the particulars of that?" Bohannon asked.

She cheered, "Otis, I never liked cornbread till now. What did you do?"

He had a fine chuckle. "Just what my mama showed me."

"Isn't it great, Hack?" she said.

"If you eat it all up, how will I ever learn?" Bohannon's face sobered. "Did she give you the details on what happened between the boy and his father?"

"Only that somehow Clay found out Chico was gay. She claims not even to know how. The subject wasn't fit for women's ears. But it completely outraged him, and before he had time to come to his senses and realize that, gay or not, the boy still had the potential to fulfill his father's dream by starring on the U.S. Olympic team, he had thrown him out."

"And now, after nine years, he was coming home? Did he write to her and tell her how sick he was and how broke he was and that there was no place for him to go and begging to be allowed to come home?"

T. Hodges grimly shook her head. "She says he wouldn't have done that. Chico wouldn't dream of coming anywhere near his father. Never. His father hated him, wished he'd never been born."

"And she thinks his father killed him?" Bohannon asked.

T. Hodges looked away at the windows and the view of the steep, grassy canyon walls with their rocky outcrops, grown shadowy now in the dying light. When she looked at Bohannon again, her eyes were wide and hurting, and her voice was low, and trembled a little. "Yes. She thinks he did that. She thinks he killed his own son, the minute the boy walked into the house."

Otis Jackson murmured shock and disbelief.

Bohannon asked. "With her gun?"

T. Hodges nodded. "She told me she brought it home from the office weeks ago, and it was in a dresser drawer. And, yes, Clay did know where it was."

"If she thinks that about him, why did she stay married to him?"

T. Hodges said: "She meant to leave him. That was why she

went out and got her license and started selling real estate, to be self-supporting. Chico had filled Clay's life because he was going to be a celebrated athlete, a champion. Hers because she loved the boy. Probably too much. In the end, I guess, she found she needed Clay to fill the emptiness." She shrugged, with a wan half-smile. "Who knows? Why does the moon rise?"

Otis reached out and switched on the light in the middle of the table. It was a converted kerosene lamp with a domed red glass shade. It cast a gentle glow. They ate for a time in somber silence. Then Bohannon rose to collect the plates and take them to the sink. "What about phone calls? Chico never called home?"

"Never," T. Hodges said. "And home never called him. Not while he had a phone. Evidently he couldn't afford one, the last few months."

"I'm not surprised. Lost his apartment too, did he?"

"San Francisco PD says he doesn't live there anymore. He checked out of the hospital two-three weeks ago. Where he went from there, nobody knows. When they get too sick to look after themselves, the officer told me, sometimes friends take them in. But it's our case, Hack. They were polite, but they're not going to do our legwork for us."

Otis hove up off his chair. "Who's for pecan pie?" he said.

Rodd Canyon was unreachable by television in the old days, and even after cable came in, Bohannon didn't bother with it. His days started early, and that meant he went to bed early. Prime time was sleeping time he couldn't spare. So he learned Clay Gilmore had been indicted for the murder of Charles Chico Gilmore only when Sorenson, the tall, tow-headed fire warden, jounced into the yard in his red pickup around noon. The morning had been busy, with more than the usual number of customers wanting to ride the canyons this beautiful fall day. Bohannon was glad to take a break over coffee in the kitchen with Sorenson.

"Did they find the gun?" Bohannon said.

"Not that I heard, no."

"Then how can they indict him? There's no evidence."

Sorenson got up lankily and peered into the refrigerator. "Wife's testimony."

"What?" Bohannon stared.

Sorenson set the remainder of Otis's pecan pie on the table and went for utensils and plates and brought them back. "She says he hated the boy because he was gay, threw him out of the house, said if he ever came back, he'd kill him."

"A man will say that." Bohannon said. "Doesn't mean he'll do it."

Sorenson sat down, cut wedges of pie, eased them onto two plates, slid one across to Bohannon. "Depends on what man you're talking about."

"How's that?" Bohannon reached for a fork.

"The CA's office dug something else up. Seems back in 1972, the coach hounded an English teacher called Morton Lowry. Thought up a rotten nickname for him. Jeered it at Lowry at a basketball game in front of the whole school. The kids took to using it to his face in class." Sorenson filled his mouth with pie, wagged his head, and hummed at how good it tasted. He washed the bite down with coffee, and said, "Lowry finally went to the school administration and complained. They reprimanded the coach. But he didn't let it drop. Dug up a ten year old police record, multiple arrests, in L.A., that proved Lowry was what Gilmore claimed, and Lowry got fired. Story was all over the news. With his picture. Finished him. Man would never get another job teaching school."

"That a fact?" Bohannon forked pie into his mouth.

"Clay Gilmore's got an obsessive hatred for gays. That's how the County Attorney puts it. School administration denies it, of course. But two of the other coaches bear it out, not giving their names of course. And the kids in the locker rooms. Kids these days. Gay bashing, they call it. And it is definitely uncool."

Bohannon drank some coffee. "The indictment won't stick. Somebody else murdered Chico Gilmore."

"Another crazy? Two of them in one case?"

"I don't think there's even one." Bohannon lit a cigarette.

"The kid was dying of AIDS, Hack. Who in their right mind would murder somebody like that? Anyway, his mother said nobody knew he was in town."

"And his mother is the soul of truth, right?"

"The County Attorney thinks so," Sorenson said, and carried the plates to the sink. They clattered. "Good pie, thanks."

"Otis made it," Bohannon said. "Thank him on your way out."

Next morning, at twelve past nine, Bohannon came out the back door of the Madrone bank into the little parking lot and the long shadow of a gnarled old California oak that made parking awkward there. He headed for the green pickup with the horse head in a circle George Stubbs had painted on the door. And a siren hooted. Only for a second. He turned his head. T. Hodges in her helmet sat in a brown patrol car on the street. Bohannon cheered up—seeing her always had that effect on him. He edged between the big terra cotta pots of tough, spiky native plants that margined the parking lot, and leaned in at the window on the passenger side of the car. "Everything all right?"

"All wrong," T. Hodges said. "After her deposition to the County Attorney, Celia Gilmore went home. I know. I delivered her there."

"Don't tell me," Bohannon said, "let me guess. She's disappeared."

"In her gold Mercedes. I should have parked where I could watch without her seeing me, right? And stayed till Vern or Lundquist relieved me."

Bohannon nodded. "You know that. I know that. Gerard didn't order it because he trusts her."

"She didn't go back to her sister's in Santa Barbara. Nor into her office. Nobody saw her here in town, none of the stores. Not the service station. Not the bank, post office, laundromat. She buys her groceries at Lucky's in San Luis. No sign of her down that way. Yet she didn't pack for a trip, Hack. Closets full, dresser drawers."

Bohannon straightened up, pushed back his Stetson, stood frowning for a minute at the flag fluttering atop its pole in front of the post office, blue sky and tawny mountains beyond—then bent again. "She make any phone calls?"

"We've checked. She didn't touch the phone. That's strange in a way. You'd have thought she'd be making funeral arrangements, for one thing. And talking to relatives. Her mother lives with

Celia's brother and his family in Wisconsin. Not one call."

Bohannon opened the car door and sat inside, leaving the door open. "She had to do something, see somebody, and right away. No time for anything else."

"See somebody?" T. Hodges watched him light a cigarette. "Oh, Hack. What are you thinking?"

"That somebody threw up in the woods behind the house right after Chico was killed, and that somebody had parked a car that left a fresh oil leak on the road back there, and that this somebody was known to Celia Gilmore."

She cried impatiently, "Hack, that's all speculation."

"Then where's the gun?" Bohannon blew smoke into the clear morning air. "Somebody has it. I vote for the man who ran away through the woods. And he had it because Celia Gilmore had given it to him."

"To kill the son she adored? Please. Can we get back to reality?"

"Sure. You said an expert checked out her computer at work. He didn't find any e-mail messages to or from Chico?"

"Not a thing," T. Hodges said.

"One of you should go to San Francisco," Bohannon said. "This is not an open and shut case. Phil Gerard always settles for the obvious. I'm sure Chico's father didn't kill him, and you're sure his mother didn't. So who did? Chico Gilmore lived up there a long time, one third of his very brief life."

"It's his death we're working on," T. Hodges said. "That didn't happen in San Francisco."

Bohannon gave her a quick kiss, and got out of the car. "Let me know when you find the missing mother."

"Hack." She leaned across and peered up at him anxiously. "She wouldn't have killed herself, would she?"

"You saw her last," he said. "How did she seem?"

"Steely. She is one strong lady. When I let her off at her house, and offered to send a woman officer from San Luis to stay the night with her, she said there was no need, that she'd be all right. She'd rather be alone."

"Uh-huh." He stepped on his cigarette. "Too bad she didn't say where."

He crossed the highway into Settler's Cove and drove past the Gilmore house. Damn it, somebody ought to be posted here, keeping an eye out for the woman in case she returned. Her gold Mercedes was no place in sight. He drove up to the back road. No car. He braked and sat looking into the trees for a moment, then switched off the engine, got out, and tramped down to the house. He walked all around it, looking through the windows that weren't too high to look through. No sign of Celia Gilmore. Well, hell, it wasn't his business. Horses were his business.

And Otis wanted to bring the stable's accounts up to date today. Which meant Bohannon would have to look after the learners, the owners of horses who boarded, and the folks who came to ride. That was okay. He could handle all that. He couldn't handle paperwork worth a damn. And he counted himself lucky that Otis revelled in it. He blinked, frowning at the house again, sighed, trudged back through the woods, got into the pickup, and drove home to Rodd Canyon.

But it nagged at him the rest of the morning, the need to find out what the woman was up to, where she had gone, and why. It wasn't a trip she'd gone on, it was an errand—by his calculations an urgent errand. Maybe innocent, but then why hadn't she told anybody? Anyway, around a murder, innocence wasn't the factor you took for granted. Guilt was the factor. He kept busy until eleven thirty or so, then stepped into the kitchen. Otis, wearing big horn rim glasses, sat at the table, every inch of it covered— typewriter, calculator, ledger, ballpoints, staple gun, address card files, stacks of bills payable, and outgoing statements.

"There's no room to eat anyway," Bohannon said. "And I've got something to tend to in town. Take over out here, will you please?"

"Right away." Otis began tidying up. "But we have to talk about some of these bills."

"I'll be back." Bohannon lifted a hand and was out the door.

The pickup was parked beside the stake truck and Otis's modest compact, under tall, rustling, ragged-barked eucalyptus trees between the green-trimmed white ranch house and the stables. As he climbed into it, he thought he was acting like a fool. Still, his unease went deep, and hunches had served him in the past. It didn't do to ignore them. They could come back to haunt you. The truck rolled out through the parted white rail gates under the arch with the cutout letters B O H A N N O N on top of it, onto the narrow, pot-holed canyon road. He reminded himself sternly that his hunches often as not came to nothing. Still, he kept on driving. Maybe Celia Gilmore would show up.

He parked the pickup down the street, where she wouldn't take alarm from it, and he did not sit on the front steps waiting for her. He went inside. Breaking and entering, Gerard would call it. But then, Gerard didn't need to know about this. Bohannon looked around. He went from neat kitchen to neat dining room to neat living room, just resting his eyes on the good furniture and carpets, the polished tables, sideboards, with their well-chosen nicknacks, the bookshelves, the pictures. Not surprisingly, the Gilmores had kept to separate bedrooms. Even separate bathrooms. He looked into a third bedroom, plainly Chico's before he'd turned into a pariah. His bed was still there, but storage cartons were piled on it. Discarded furniture cluttered the space. Spiders had made themselves at home. Mark Spitz in tiny swim trunks smiled from a poster on the wall. One of its corners had come loose and folded over. The mirror above the dresser was fogged by dust. Bohannon stepped out and closed the door.

He had saved Clay Gilmore's den for last. There were dozens of polished brass trophies, on a mantel piece, and in glass-fronted cabinets, commemorating football, baseball, basketball, soccer, track and swimming victories. Plaques hung next to the chimney. Clay Gilmore had been Dad of the Year in 1992, honored often by the Chamber of Commerce, Athletic Directors of California, the Presbyterian church, a long list. Framed, glassed photos covered the walls, of teams back to twenty-five years ago, coach Gilmore standing massive and proudly smiling among them. Pennants and banners hung here and there, some bright, some faded by time. A remote control lay on a tufted leather couch next to a jazzy plastic bag of sunflower seeds. Bohannon switched on the television set. A sports channel. Clips of baseball home-runs and dust-up slides into second base. Noisy. He switched it off.

And heard a car stop down on the front road.

Heart bumping, he crossed the living room to look out the windows. To see the car well was hard because of the trees and brush. But it looked like a van, and not your ordinary paint job. More like an old-time circus wagon. Now somebody was starting up the hill toward the house. He stepped back from the window and went to the front door and unchained and unbolted it and waited for steps on the front deck. But first a voice called:

"Fletcher? Are you here? It's Zenobia."

Bohannon felt dizzy for a second, and then remembered the children's book he'd found in Chico Gilmore's pack and given T. Hodges to read. *Fletcher & Zenobia*. He'd looked idly at the pictures. They had made him smile. But he hadn't read the story for himself. Footsteps sounded on the stairs up to the deck and he opened the door.

A plump young woman stood there. She wore jeans and a safari jacket with a lot of pockets. Nothing odd about that. What was odd was her hat, a puffy yellow bonnet decorated with daisies. Something you'd find in a very old attic. But odder still was what she held in her hands, a cake, a big one, with raspberry-colored frosting. It bristled with green and blue candles, and it had to be heavy. She stopped and stared at him.

"Where's Chico?" she said.

"He's not home," Bohannon said. If he had to tell her where Chico was, she might drop the cake. He stepped out. "Here. Let me take that for you."

"It's not heavy." She handed it over. It wasn't real. It was *papier mache* and thick paint and something that made it glisten. She eyed him, a little frightened. "Mr. Gilmore? She said you wouldn't be here."

"He's not. My name's Bohannon. I'm—house-sitting." He set the cake among potted geraniums on the deck rail. "Who are you?"

"Lettice Van Van," she said. "I'm Chico's friend from San Francisco. He was staying with me after he got out of the hospital. Before he decided to come home." She looked at the cake, blushed, snatched off the bonnet and held it behind her. "We had a silly game we played. To cheer him up. He has AIDS, you see. He was Fletcher the cat, and I was Zenobia the Victorian doll, and we lived in a tree and we couldn't get down so we had a party with

cake and ice-cream and punch and waltzes on the phonograph."
Her face changed. "I copied the cake from the illustration in the
book. It's not a real cake. I never baked a real cake, but I'm a dab
hand at *papier mache*. I'm a theatre designer you see, sets,
costumes. I copied Zenobia's costume for myself, and Fletcher's
little embroidered jacket. I can sew, of course. I just can't bake.
Anyway, Chico couldn't keep real cake down. But we did have our
pretend parties. All by ourselves. Like loopy six year olds. Sometimes we'd laugh so hard we'd fall down. It was lovely."

"Why did he leave?" Bohannon said.

"He wanted his mother. He was regressing mentally, you know.
That happens. Turning into a little boy. He wrote to her and said
he needed her and wanted to come home but he was afraid of his
father. And she telephoned, saying she was coming to him. But
he said no, it was home he wanted, here, in these woods. He was
born here, and he wanted to die here. He loved this place." She
turned to look. "And I can see why. An enchanted forest by the
sea. No wonder he was pining for it. And his mother. He always
did miss her." She turned back to Bohannon with a frown. "Isn't
she here, either? What's happened? Did she take Chico to the
hospital? Where? Tell me how to get there."

"He's not in the hospital," Bohannon said.

"He was very sick. The plan was that he'd fly down next week,
on the twenty-fifth. But he had a terrible night on Sunday." A
wooden bench was built along the railing of the deck. As if suddenly weary, she sat down on it. "And Monday morning he said
to me, 'Lettice, I have to go home now. If I wait, I'll be too weak.'
I reminded him she'd said she wasn't ready.

" 'If it spoils her surprise party or something, I can't help it,' he
said. He was desperate. But it took all day to get him ready. He
had to keep resting. It was long after dark when I drove him to
the airport and put him on an SWA flight to Fresno." She peered
into Bohannon's face. "He did make it, didn't he?"

Bohannon nodded. "He made it." This was getting damned uncomfortable. "But I need to know something. How was he in touch
with his mother?"

"You aren't a house-sitter. You're a policeman. I can tell by how
you ask questions." She made her voice deep. " 'I need to know

something.'"

Bohannon tried for a smile, "Don't worry. I'm not going to arrest you for impersonating a Victorian doll." He drew a quick breath. "Something's happened, that's all. The plan Chico and his mother had—it didn't work out. That's why I'm here. To find out what went wrong."

Lettice Van Van was poking into the pockets of the safari jacket. She came up with a little black ring binder and held it out to him. "The number where he called her is in there. I kept it for him because he was starting to forget things. Like some old man with Alzheimers."

Bohannon frowned at the book and leafed over the pages. Lettice Van Van wrote in red ink. In calligraphic style. It was like a tiny medieval prayer book. "What name?" he said.

"Morton Lowry," she said.

Bohannon almost dropped the book.

She said, "Some friend of his mother's. She'd ring him up from there, or he would call and if she wasn't there, he'd leave messages for her. They talked every day. But it had to be where his father couldn't overhear. His father's a terrible man. An ex-football player. You can imagine. He hates Chico."

Bohannon found the name and the number. The area code was in the next county. He sat on the bench and copied the number into his dog-eared notebook and handed the missal back to Lettice Van Van. "Thank you," he said. "You've been a big help."

She put the book back into her pocket without taking her eyes off him, searching his face, begging without words. It was too much. He couldn't keep this up. He moved to get to his feet, and she caught his arm and clung to it. She drew a shaky breath, tears came into her eyes. Her words were a quavery little squeak. "He's dead, isn't he?"

Bohannon nodded. "I'm sorry."

"They all die." She dug tissues from another of the pockets of the safari jacket, dried her eyes and blew her nose. "That's the trouble with looking after them. They become precious to you. And then they just die." She was weeping for sure, now, and her words were hard to understand. "Over and over and over again. So many." She got more Kleenex and tried to mop away the tears, but they just kept coming. "You'd think a person would get used to it. Maybe some do, but not me. Poor Fletcher."

She laid her head on Bohannon's chest. He put his arms around her and held her and stroked her while she sobbed. He didn't tell her poor Fletcher had been shot. It wouldn't help.

Shakespeare by the Sea. The sign was gold gothic letters on a black background and hung off the porch of a typical old saltbox house in Monterey. He found parking a little way along, and ambled back to the place and climbed the front steps. In the glass of the front door a sign hung off a string. *Closed.* He put his face to the glass. Bookshelves all around the walls. Tables with books on them. A desk with a telephone, cash register, computer at the center of the room. He knocked on the door, waited, knocked again. Nobody came. He read his watch. 3:35. Middle of the week. Why closed?

There was a combination green-house-flower-shop next door. He stepped into fragrance and color, dampness and dim green daylight, and asked a woman in a rubber apron. The slim hose in her hand had a misting nozzle with a trigger. She was misting a long table of plants in little green plastic pots. "I don't know, and I wish people would stop asking. How do I know where Morton Lowry is?"

"What people?" Bohannon said.

"First that fat girl with the funny hat. Then that woman with the gold Mercedes. If she didn't know who would? She's been in and out of there"—she jerked her head of short-cropped salt-and-pepper hair in the direction of *Shakespeare by the Sea*—"almost every day for weeks. Never bought a book—not that I saw." She sniffed. "Life's full of surprises. Who'd have thought Morton Lowry cared about women?"

Bohannon took out his wallet, let it fall open so it showed her his private investigator's license, closed it quickly, and pocketed it again. "I need to locate him. It's police business."

She stopped misting and blinked hard at him. "You certainly don't look like a police officer."

"Special assignment," he said.

"Try the back door," she said. "Wallace Finn might talk to you."

"Who's he?" Bohannon said.

She jerked her head back. "Why he's the owner. Lowry's just the hired help." She snorted and began misting again. "When he's sober."

Bohannon knocked on the backdoor of *Shakespeare by the Sea*, an aluminum screendoor a little loose in its frame. The solid door inside it stood open. He called, "Mr. Finn? Bohannon, here. San Luis County Sheriff's Department."

"Oh, Lord," an old man's rough voice said. "Is it about Morton?"

"Need to know where he is," Bohannon said. "Can I come in?"

"I don't know where he is. Drunk someplace. Go away."

"Why don't you open your shop? Lots of people in town today."

"They just want to take photos of each other at Cannery Row." Finn appeared dimly. In a wheelchair, a coffee mug in his hand. "I can't run the shop on my own anymore. Doesn't matter. The public's lost interest in books. You watch TV enough, you haven't the brains left for reading."

"Where did he usually go to get drunk?" Bohannon said.

"Not far. That broken-down old car of his won't travel far." Finn grunted. "I don't honestly think it's just a drunk, this time. It's been too long. You'd better check the jails."

"They allow you a phone call," Bohannon said. "He didn't call?"

"He just disappeared," Finn said. "Why don't you try doing that?"

"First tell me where he lives," Bohannon said.

And Finn told him.

It was an old flat-roofed frame hotel, two sagging stories, once yellow, now in need of paint. Not on a street where tourists would see it. The buildings on those streets were tarted up. *John Steinbeck slept here!* But he didn't think about this. He was too startled. Because not only were Monterey County Sheriff's patrol cars parked in front of that bleak hotel—so was a patrol car from San Luis Obispo County. And Lieutenant Phil Gerard stood beside it, looking up at the sun-struck front of the building. Bohannon parked the pickup and jogged across the street.

Gerard stared at him. "I don't believe this."

"What's going on?" Bohannon asked.

"Drowned man was found a couple hours ago, washed up on the beach here. One Morton Lowry. Bookstore clerk and well-known drunk."

"And years ago a teacher at Madrone high school," Bohannon said, "until Clay Gilmore lost him his job. Moral turpitude."

Gerard's eyebrows rose. "Who told you that?"

"If you didn't know it," Bohannon said, "what are you doing here?"

"They found a gun in his pocket," Gerard said, "and they phoned me, because the serial number makes it Celia Gilmore's gun."

"Right. You missed the letter, but there was one. Chico was dying and wanted to come home. She knew Clay would never permit it. He'd despise the boy even more, now that he had AIDS. And Celia remembered Lowry. Clay had ruined his life. Lowry must hate him. She needed his help, and she got it. Such as it was." Bohannon tilted his head toward the deputies coming out of the hotel. "When they find Lowry's old wreck of a car, tell them to look for an oil leak."

"Jesus." Gerard wagged his head in disgust, looked down at his boots, looked up again, grimly. "All right. You obviously know all about it. Tell me."

Bohannon summoned up Lettice Van Van's story. Then he said, "And if you drive over to the local Ramada Inn, right now, you'll find a gold Mercedes in the lot. I spotted it on my way here."

"She's here?" Gerard gaped. "What in God's name for?"

Bohannon shrugged. "She doesn't know Lowry drowned himself. She's waiting for him to sober up and stagger into the bookstore. I expect she'd like her money back. After all, he killed the wrong Gilmore."

Gerard squinted. "She paid him to do it?"

"He wasn't an avenger. He was a drunk. Of course, she had to pay him."

"So it comes down to the kid arriving home a week early. And Lowry sneaks in by that back door in the dark to kill Clay Gilmore. And the kid thinks he's a prowler, and yells and jumps up. And Lowry panics and shoots him."

"You have a better suggestion?" Bohannon said.

"Hell, no." Gerard got into the patrol car and slammed the door. "But if my mind worked like yours," he said, "I'd never sleep."

"It's questions that keep me awake," Bohannon said. "Not answers."

SURF

Lieutenant Ken Barker of the LAPD shared a gray-green office with too many other men, too many gray-green metal desks and file cabinets, too many phones that kept crying for attention like new life in a sad maternity ward. He had a broken nose. Under his eyes were bruises. He wore beard stubble. His teeth were smoky. He scowled across a sprawl of papers and spent styrofoam cups. He said:

"Yes, Robinson was murdered. On the deck of his apartment. In that slum by the sea called Surf. Shot clean through the head. He went over the rail, was dead when he hit the sand. There's nothing wrong with the case. The DA is happy. What do you want to mess it up for?"

"I don't." Dave shed a wet trenchcoat, hung it over a chairback, sat on another chair. "I just want to know why Robinson made Bruce K. Shevel the beneficiary of his life insurance policy. Didn't he have a wife, a mother, a girlfriend?"

"He had a boyfriend, and the boyfriend killed him. Edward Earl Lily, by name. With a deer rifle, a thirty-thirty. Probably Robinson's. He owned one." Barker blinked. "It's weird, Dave. I mean, what have you got—an instinct for this kind of case?"

"Coincidence," Dave said. "What does probably mean—Robinson was 'probably' killed with his own gun."

Barker found a bent cigarette. "Haven't located it."

"Where does Lily say it is?"

"Claims he never saw it." Barker shuffled papers, hunting a match. "But it'll be in the surf someplace along there. Or buried in the sand. We're raking for it." Dave leaned forward and snapped a thin steel lighter. Barker said thanks and asked through smoke, "You don't like it? Why not? What's wrong with it?"

Dave put the lighter away. "Ten years ago, Bruce K. Shevel jacked up his car on one of those trails on Topanga Canyon to change a tire, and the car rolled over on him and cost him the use of his legs. He was insured with us. We paid. We still pay. Total disability. I'd forgotten him. But I remembered him today when I checked Robinson's policy. Shevel looked to me like someone who'd tried self-mutilation to collect on his accident policy."

"Happens, doesn't it?" Barker said.

"People won't do anything for money." Dave's smile was thin. "But they will hack off a foot or a hand for it. I sized Shevel up for one of those. His business was in trouble. The policy was a fat one. I don't think paralysis was in his plans. But it paid better. The son of a bitch grinned at me from that hospital bed. He knew I knew and there was no way to prove it."

"And there still isn't," Barker said. "Otherwise you could stop paying and put him in the slams. And it pisses you off that he took you. And now you see a chance to get him." Barker looked into one of the empty plastic cups, made a face, stood up. "You'd like him to have killed Robinson."

He edged between desks to a coffee urn at the window end of the room, the glass wall end. Dave followed. Through vertical metal sun slats outside, gray rain showed itself like movie grief. "I'd like Robinson to have died peacefully in bed of advanced old age." Dave pulled a cup from a chrome tube bolted to a window strut and held the cup while Barker filled it. "And since he didn't, I'd sure as hell like him to have left his money to someone else."

"We interviewed Shevel." Next to the hot plate that held the coffee urn was cream substitute in a widemouth brown bottle and sugar in little plastic packets. Barker used a yellow plastic spoon to stir some of each into his coffee. "We interviewed everybody in Robinson's little black book." He led the way back to his desk, sat down, twisted out his cigarette in a big glass ashtray glutted with butts. "And Shevel is a wheelchair case."

Dave tasted his coffee. Weak and tepid. "A wheelchair case can shoot a gun."

Barker snorted. "Have you seen where Robinson lived?"

"I'll go look. But first tell me about Lily." Dave sat down, then eyed the desk. "Or do I need to take your time? Shall I just read the file?"

"My time? I'd only waste it sleeping. And I'm out of practice. I wouldn't do it well." Barker glanced sourly at the folders, forms, photographs on his desk, then hung another cigarette from his mouth and leaned forward so Dave could light it. "Lily is a trick Robinson picked up at the Billy Budd. You know the place?"

Dave nodded. "Ocean Front Walk."

"Robinson tended bar there. The kid's a hustler but way out of Robinson's league. A hundred bucks a night and/or a part in your next TV segment, sir. But somehow Robinson managed to keep him. Eight, ten weeks, anyway." The phone on Barker's desk jangled. He lifted the receiver, listened, grunted, cradled the receiver. "Till he was dead. Lily ran, but not far and not clever. He was better at crying. You know the type. Muscles, but a real girl. Kept sobbing that he loved Robinson and why would he kill him?"

"And why would he?" Dave lit a cigarette.

Barker shrugged. "Probably hysteria. Toward the end they were fighting a lot. About money. Robinson had bought him fancy clothes, an Omega watch, a custom surf board. They'd been pricing Porsches and Aston-Martins on the lots. But Robinson was broke. He'd hocked his stereo, camera, projector. He was borrowing from friends."

"What friends?" Dave asked. "Shevel?"

"Among others," Barker said. "Which kind of louses up your theory, doesn't it? Shevel didn't need to shoot anybody for their insurance money. He's loaded."

The boy who opened the door had dressed fast. He still hadn't buttoned his white coverall with *L A Marina* stitched on the pocket. Under the coverall his jockeys were on inside out and backward. Below the nick of navel in his flat brown belly a label read Pilgrim. He was chicano and wore his hair long. He looked confused. "He thought it would be the layouts."

"It isn't," Dave said. "Brandstetter is my name. Death claims investigator, Medallion Life. I'm looking for Bruce K. Shevel. Is he here?"

"Brand what?" the boy said.

At his back a dense jungle of philodendrons climbed a trellis to the ceiling. From beyond it a voice said, "Wait a minute, Manuel." A pair of chrome spoked wheels glittered into view, a pair of wasted legs under a lap robe, a pair of no color eyes that had never forgiven anyone anything. "I remember you. What do you want?"

"Arthur Thomas Robinson is dead," Dave said.

"I've already told the police what I know."

"Not all of it." Wind blew cold rain across the back of Dave's neck. He turned up the trenchcoat collar. "You left out the part that interests me—that you're the beneficiary of his life insurance."

Shevel stared. There was no way for his face to grow any paler. It was parchment. But his jaw dropped. When he shut it, his dentures clicked. "You must be joking. There's got to be some mistake."

"There's not." Dave glanced at the rain. "Can I come in and talk about it?"

Shevel's mouth twitched. "Did you bring the check?"

Dave shook his head. "Murder has a way of slowing down the routine."

"Then there's nothing to talk about." The wheelchair was motorized. It started to turn away.

"Why would he name you?" Dave asked.

Shrug. "We were old friends."

Dave studied the chicano boy who was watching them with something frantic in his eyes. "Friends?"

"Oh, come in, come in," Shevel snarled, and wheeled out of sight. Dave stepped onto deep beige carpeting and the door closed behind him. But when he turned to hand the trenchcoat over, there was no one to take it. Manuel had buttoned up and left. Dave laid the coat over his arm and went around the leafy screen. A long, handsome room stretched to sliding glass doors at its far end that looked down on a marina where little white boats waited row on row like children's coffins in the rain. Shevel rattled ice and glasses at a low bar. "I met Robbie in the hospital," he said, "ten years ago." He came wheeling at Dave, holding out a squat studded glass in which dark whiskey islanded an ice cube. "Just as I met you." His smile was crooked. "He worked there. An orderly."

"And you brought him along to look after you when the hospital let you go." Dave took the drink. "Thanks."

"Robbie had good hands." Shevel aimed the chair at the planter. From under it somewhere he took a small green plastic watering can. He tilted it carefully into the mulch under the climbing vines. "And patience."

"Who took his place?"

"No one. No one could. This apartment is arranged so that I

don't need day to day help." Shevel set the watering can back. "The market sends in food and liquor." He drank from his glass. "I can cook my own meals. I'm able to bathe myself and so on. A cleaning woman comes in twice a week. I have a masseur on call."

"Manuel?" Dave wondered.

"Not Manuel," Shevel said shortly and drank again.

"You publish a lot of magazines," Dave said. "How do you get to your office? Specially equipped car?"

"No car," Shevel said. "Cars are the enemy." He purred past Dave and touched a wall switch. A panel slid back. Beyond gleamed white wet-look furniture, a high gloss white desk stacked with papers, a white electric typewriter, a photocopy machine. Blowup color photos of naked girls muraled the walls. "I don't go to the office. My work comes to me. And there's the telephone." He swallowed more whiskey. "You remember the telephone?" He touched the switch and the panel slid closed.

Dave asked, "When did Robinson quit you?"

"Eight months, two weeks and six days ago," Shevel said. He said it grimly with a kind of inverse satisfaction, like counting notches in a gun butt.

"Did he give a reason?"

"Reason?" Shevel snorted and worked on his drink again. "He felt old age creeping up on him. He was all of thirty-two. He decided he wanted to be the one who was looked after, for a change."

"No quarrels? No hard feelings?"

"Just boredom." Shevel looked at his glass but it was empty. Except for the ice cube. It still looked new. He wheeled abruptly back to the bar and worked the bottle again. Watching him, Dave tried his drink for the first time. Shevel bought good Bourbon with Medallion's money. Shevel asked, "If there'd been hard feelings, would he have come back to borrow money?"

"That might depend on how much he needed it." David said. "Or thought he did. I hear he was desperate."

Shevel's eyes narrowed. "What does that mean?"

"Trying to keep a champagne boy on a beer income."

"Exactly." Shevel's mouth tightened like a drawstring purse. "He never had any common sense."

"So you didn't lend him anything," Dave said.

"I told him not to be a fool. Forty-nine percent of the world's population is male." Shevel's chair buzzed. He steered it back, stopped it, tilted his glass, swallowed half the new drink. He looked toward the windows where the rain was gray. His voice was suddenly bleak. "I'm sorry he's dead. He was life to me for a long time."

"I'll go." Dave walked to the bar, set down his glass, began shrugging into the trenchcoat. "Just two more questions. Manuel. Does he take you deer hunting?"

Shevel looked blank.

Dave said, "Your thirty-thirty. When did you use it last?"

Shevel squinted. "What are you talking about?"

"A deer rifle. Winchester. Remington."

"Sorry." His bony fingers teased his white wig. He simpered like a skid row barroom floozy. "I've always preferred indoor sports." He was suddenly drunk. He looked Dave up and down hungrily. "Next question."

"Those magazines of yours," Dave said. "The new Supreme Court decision on obscenity. You're going to have to do some retooling—right?"

Shevel's eyes got their old hardness back. "It's been on the drawingboards for months. A whole new line. Home crafts. Dune buggies. Hang gliders. Crossword puzzles. And if you're suggesting I shot Robbie with his rifle in order to get the money to finance the change-over, then you don't know much about publishing costs. Ten thousand dollars wouldn't buy the staples."

"But you do know how much the policy paid."

The crooked smile came back. "Naturally. I bought it for him. Years ago." The smile went away. "How typical of him to have forgotten to take my name off it."

"And the thirty-thirty. Did you buy that too?"

"I paid for it, of course. He had no money."

"I'll just bet he didn't," Dave said.

The development may have looked sharp to start with but it had gone shabby fast. It was on the coast road at the north end of Surf, which had gone shabby a long time ago. You couldn't see the development from the coast road. You had to park between angled white lines on the tarmacked shoulder and walk to a cliff where an iron pipe hand-railing tilted, its cement footings too near the crumbling edge.

Below, along a narrow rock and sand curve of shore stood apartment buildings. The tinwork vents on the roofs were rusting. Varnish peeled from rafter ends and wooden decks. The stucco had been laid on thin. It was webbed with cracks. Chunks had broken out at corners showing tarpaper and chickenwire underneath.

Dave saw what Ken Barker had meant. The only access to the place was down cement steps, three long flights against the cliff face. There'd been too much sand in the cement. Edges had crumbled. Today rain washed dirt and pebbles across the treads and made them treacherous. No—no wheelchair case could get down there. He was about to turn back when, the way it will sometimes for a second, the surf stopped booming. It charged and fell heavily today, like a big, tired army under one of those generals that never give up. But it breathed.

And in the sudden silence he heard from below a voice, raised in argument, protest, complaint. He went on down. The iron rail was scabby with corrosion. His hand came away rusty. He left cement for a boardwalk over parts of which sand had drifted, sand now dark and sodden with rain. He passed the backs of buildings, slope-top metal trash modules, the half open doors of laundry rooms. The voice kept on. He turned between two buildings to walk for the beach front.

The voice came from halfway up wooden steps to a second story deck. A small man stood there under a clear plastic umbrella. He was arguing up at the legs of a young black police officer above him on the second story deck. The officer wore a clear plastic slicker.

The little man shouted, "But I'm the God damn owner of the God damn place. A taxpayer. It's not Chief Gates that pays you—it's me. You know what the taxes are here? No—well, I'm not going to tell you because I hate to see a strong man cry. But they got to be paid, friend, if I rent it or don't rent it. And have you looked at it? I was screwed by the contractor. It's falling apart. Nineteen months old and falling apart. I'm suing the son of a bitch but the lawyers are breaking me. Not to mention the mortgage. A storm like this, carpets get soaked, plaster falls down. Could be happening in there right now. Why do you want to make things worse for me?"

Dave climbed the steps. When he'd come up to the little man, the officer said, "Mr. Brandstetter. That makes three. This one. Robinsons' ex-boss. Now you." His grin was very white. "This a real popular spot this morning."

"Turning people away, right?" Dave said. "Because the apartment's sealed, waiting for the DA?" He looked past the little man. Up the beach, a clutch of slickered cops was using a drag with deep teeth on the sand. Plastic wrapped their caps, their shoes. Nothing about them looked happy. It was work for tractors. But there was no way to get tractors down here.

The black officer said, "DA been and gone."

"Yeah." The little man goggled at Dave through big horn rims. "They talk about human rights. What happened to property rights? I own the place but I get treated like a thief. I can't get in till Robinsons' brother comes and collects his stuff." His nose was red. And not from sunburn. There hadn't been any sun this month. "You're not his brother, are you?"

"Not the way you mean," Dave said. And to the officer, "Flag me when he comes, will you?" He went down the stairs and down the rain-runnelled beach. The sergeant he talked to wore plain clothes and no hat. His name was Slocum. Rain plastered strands of pale red hair to his freckled scalp. Dave said, "What about the surf?"

"Running too high. You can't work a launch on it. Not close in where we have to look. Keep washing you up all the time." He glanced bitterly at the muddy sky. "Storm doesn't quit, we'll never find it."

"The storm could be your friend," Dave said. "Ought to wash anything ashore—all that power." And fifty yards off a cop yelled in the rain, bent in the rain, picked something out of the muddy surf, came with it at a trot, waving it above his head, like a movie Apache who'd got the wrong room at Western Costume. "See?" Dave said.

"No wonder you're rich," Slocum said. It was a rifle. The cop offered it. Slocum shook his head. "You've got gloves, I don't. You hold it. Let me just look at it." He just looked at it while the cop turned it over and it dripped. "Thirty-thirty Remington," Slocum said. "Eight years old but like new. Won't act like new—not unless they get the seawater out of it right away."

"Sea water doesn't erase prints," Dave said and turned back toward the apartments because he heard his name called above the slam of surf, the hiss of rain. The black officer was waving an arm from the deck. A bulky man was with him. Dave jogged back. The landlord was yammering to a girt with ragged short hair in a Kobe coat at the foot of the stairs but there wasn't any hope in his voice now. Dave went up the stairs.

"Reverend Merwin Robinson," the black officer said. "Mr. Brandstetter. Insurance."

"Something wrong with the insurance?" The reverend had a hoarse voice. The kind you get from shouting at baseball games or congregations. A thick man, red-faced. A big crooked vein bulged at one temple.

"What's wrong with it is the beneficiary," Dave said.

Robinson stiffened, glared. "I don't understand."

"Not you," Dave said. "Bruce K. Shevel."

Robinson blinked. "You must be mistaken."

"That's what Shevel said," Dave said.

"But I'm Arthur's only living relative. Neither of us has anyone else. And he'd left Shevel. Said he never wanted to see him again."

"He saw him again," Dave said. "Tried to borrow money from him. I gather he saw you too."

The minister's mouth twitched. "Never at my invitation. And years would go by. He knew my stand. On how he lived. The same saintly mother raised us. He knew what the Bible says about him and his kind."

"But lately he tried to borrow money," Dave said.

"He did." The black officer had opened the glass wall panel that was the apartment door. Robinson saw, grunted, went in. Dave followed. The room was white shag carpet, long low fake-fur couches, swag lamps in red and blue pebbled glass. "Of course I refused. My living comes from collection plates. For the glory of

God and His beloved Son. Not to buy fast automobiles for descendents of the brothels of Sodom."

"I don't think they had descendents," Dave said. "Anyway, did you have that kind of money?"

"My church is seventy years old. We've had half a dozen fires from faulty wiring. The neighborhood the church serves is just as old and just as poor." Robinson glanced at a shiny kitchenette where a plaster Michelangelo David stood on a counter with plastic ferns. He went on to an alcove at the room's end, opened and quickly closed again a door to a bathroom papered with color photos of naked men from *Playgirl*, and went into a room where the ceiling was squares of gold-veined mirror above a round, tufted bed.

Dave watched him open drawers, scoop out the contents, dump them on the bed. Not a lot of clothes. A few papers. He slid back closet doors. Little hung inside. He took down what there was, spilling coat hangers, clumsily stooped, pushed the papers into a pocket, then bundled all the clothes into his arms and turned to face Dave. "That ten thousand dollars would have meant a lot to my church—new wiring, shingles, paint, new flooring to replace what's rotted—" He broke off, a man used to having dreams cancelled. He came at the door with his bundle of dead man's clothes and Dave made way for him. "Well, at least these will keep a few needy souls warm for the winter." He lumbered off down the length of the apartment, on to the deck and out of sight.

Dave looked after him. The view was clear from this room to the deck—maybe forty feet. Lily could have stood here with the 30-30. At that distance the bullet hole wouldn't be too messy. Dave went for the door where cold, damp air came in. Also the little man who owned the place. He collided with Dave.

"Your turn," Dave said.

"It rents furnished," the little man said. "A preacher, for God sake! Crookeder than a politician. Did you see? Did he take kitchen stuff? I saw that bundle. Anything could have been in it. All the kitchen stuff stays with the place. Sheets, towels? All that's mine." He rattled open kitchen drawers, cupboards, slammed them shut again, dodged into the bathroom, banged around in there—"Jesus, look what that fag did to the walls!"—shot out of the bathroom and into the bedroom. Merwin Robinson had left the chest of drawers hanging. From the doorway Dave could see their total emptiness. The little man stopped in front of them. His shoulders sagged. In relief or disappointment?

"All okay?" Dave asked.

"What? Oh, yeah. Looks like it." He didn't sound convinced.

Downstairs Dave pressed a buzzer next to a glass panel like the one directly above that had opened into Arthur Thomas Robinson's apartment. While he'd talked to the dead man's brother and the black officer he'd looked past their wet shoes through the slats in the deck and seen the short-haired girl go into this apartment. She came toward him now with *Daily Variety* in her hand, looking as if she didn't want to be bothered. She still wore the Kobe coat but her hair wasn't short any more. She had on a blond wig out of an Arthur Rackham illustration—big and fuzzy. She slid the door. A smell of fresh coffee came out.

"Were you at home when Robinson was killed?" She studied him. Without makeup she looked like a ten year old boy dressed up as the dandelion fairy. "You a cop?"

He told her who he was, gave her a card. "The police like to think Lily killed him because it's easy, it will save the taxpayers money. I'm not so sure."

She tilted her head, "Whose money will that save?"

"Not Medallion's," he said. "I'd just like to see it go to somebody else."

"Than?" She shivered. "Look—come in." He did that and she slid the door to and put the weather outside where it belonged. "Coffee?" Dropping *Variety* on a couch like the ones upstairs, she led him to the kitchenette, talking. "Who did Robbie leave his money to?" She filled pottery mugs from a glass urn. "It's funny, thinking of him having money to leave when he was hitting on me and everybody else for twenty here, twenty there." She came around the counter, pushed a tall, flower-cushioned bar stool at Dave and perched on one herself. "He was really sick."

"Sick?" Dave tried the coffee. Rich and good.

"Over that Eddie. Nothing—beautiful junk. Like this pad. Robbie was nice, a really nice, gentle, sweet, warm human being. Of all things to happen to him!" She took a mouthful of coffee, froze with the cup halfway to the countertop, stared, swallowed. "You don't mean Robbie left Ed Lily that money?"

"That would be too easy," Dave said. "No—he left it to Bruce K. Shevel."

"You're kidding," she said.

Dave twitched an eyebrow, sighed, got out cigarettes. "That's what everybody thinks. Including Shevel." He held the pack for her to take one, took one himself, lit both. He dropped the lighter into his pocket. "Was Shevel ever down here?"

"How? He was a wheelchair case. Robbie told me about him. It was one of the reasons he chose this place. So Shevel couldn't get to him. The stairs. Why would be leave Shevel his money?"

"An oversight, I expect. After all, what was he—thirty-two? At that age, glimmerings of mortality are still dim. Plenty of time to make changes. Or maybe because Shevel had bought him the policy, he thought he owed him something."

"Robbie owed him? That's a laugh. He used him like a slave for ten years. If anything, it was the other way around. Shevel owed him. But he wouldn't shell out a dime when Robbie asked for it."

"So I hear," Dave said. "Tell me about Lily."

She shrugged. "You know the type. Dime a dozen in this town. They drift in on their thumbs, all body, no brains. If they even get as far as a producer, they end up with their face in his pillow. Then it's back to Texas or Tennessee to pump gas for the rest of their lives. Only Eddie was just a little different. Show business he could live without. Hustling was surer and steadier. He always asked for parts in pictures but he settled for cash. A born whore. Loved it.

"I tried to tell Robbie. He wouldn't listen. Couldn't hear. Gone on the little shit, really gone. You want to know something? Eddie hadn't been here a week when he tried to get me into the sack." Her mouth twitched a half grin. "I told him, I don't go to bed with fags. 'I'm not a fag,' was all he said. As if I and every other woman in the place didn't know that. Woman. Man. Everybody—except Robbie." She turned her head to look down the room at the glass front wall, the gray rain beyond it, the deserted beach, the muddy slop of surf. "Poor Robbie! What happens to people?" She turned back for an answer.

"In his case," Dave said, "murder."

"Yeah." She rolled her cigarette morosely against a little black ashtray. "And he never said a wrong word to Eddie. Never. Eddie was all over him all the time—I want this, I want that. You promised to introduce me to so-and-so. Take me here, take me there."

Dave looked at the ceiling. "Soundproofing another thing they cheated the owner on?"

"I got pretty familiar with Robbie's record collection. Sure, I could hear damn near every word. And a lot that wasn't words. The bedroom's right over mine too."

"Was that where the shot came from?" Dave asked.

"I wasn't here. Didn't I tell you? I was on location in Montana. Up to my elbows in flour in a tumble-down ranch house with little kids tugging at my skirts and my hair hanging over one eye. Twenty seconds on film. All that way on Airwest for twenty seconds."

"Too bad," Dave said. "Were you ever up there?"

"Robbie's? Yeah, for drinks. Now and then."

"Ever see a rifle?"

"They found it, didn't they?" She jerked the big fuzzy wig toward the beach. "Talking to Dieterle, I saw the cop fish it out of the kelp and run to you with it. You brought them luck. They were raking for it all day yesterday too."

"But did you ever see it in the apartment?"

She shrugged. "It was probably in a closet." She drank some coffee and frowned. "Wait a minute. I helped Robbie move in. No, I didn't know him. I parked up at the cliff edge and there he was with all this stuff to carry. I just naturally offered to help. And I hung around helping him settle in and we had a drink."

"Easy to know," Dave said.

"A bartender," she said. "Had been since he was a kid, except for that period with Shevel. Easy friendliness is part of a bartender's stock in trade right? Only he didn't fake it. He honestly liked people. Those old aunties Lauder and White fell all over themselves to get him back. Business has doubled since he took over. If he owned his own place he'd make a bundle." She remembered he was dead and sadness happened in her face. "Except for one thing."

Dave worked on his coffee. "Which was?"

"He also trusted people. And that's for losers."

"About the rifle?" he prompted her.

"He didn't own one," she said flatly. "I'd have seen it while we were putting away his stuff. No rifle. But I can tell you one thing. If there'd been one, Eddie could have used it. He used to talk about hunting rabbits when he was a kid back in Oklahoma."

"Thanks." Dave tilted up the mug, drained it, set it on the counter, got off the stool. "And for the coffee." He checked his watch. "But now it's out into the cold rain and the mean streets again."

"Aw," she said.

Climbing the gritty stairs up the cliff face, he still heard the surf. But as he neared the top there was the wet tire sibilance of traffic on the coast road and the whine of a car engine that didn't want to start. At the railing, the little landlord, Dieterle, sat in a faded old MG, swearing. Dave walked over and wondered in a shout if he could help. Dieterle, with a sour twist of his mouth, gave up.

"Ah, it'll catch, it'll catch. Son of a bitch knows I'm in a hurry. Always acts like this." Rain had misted the big round lenses of his glasses. He peered up at Dave through them. "You're some kind of cop, no? I saw you with them on the beach. I heard you tell Bambi O'Mara you didn't think Lily killed Robinson." Dieterle cocked his head. "You think Bambi did it?"

"Why would I think that?"

"Hell, she was in love with Robinson. And I mean, off the deep end. Weird, a smart chick like that. Not to mention her looks. You know she was a *Playboy* centerfold?"

"It's raining and I'm getting wet," Dave said. "Tell me why she'd kill Robinson so I can go get Slocum to put cuffs on her."

Dieterle's mouth fell open. "Ah, now, wait. I didn't mean to get her in trouble. I figured you knew." He blinked anxious through the glasses. "Anybody around here could have told you. She made a spectacle of herself." Maybe the word reminded him. He took off the horn-rims, poked in the dash for a Kleenex, wiped the rain off the lenses. "I mean, what chance did she have?" He dropped

134 / JOSEPH HANSEN

the tissues on the floor and put the glasses back on. "Robinson was
a fag, worked in a fag bar. It didn't faze her. So many chicks like
that—figure one good lay with them and a flit will forget all about
boys. Except Bambi never got the lay. And Robinson got Ed Lily.
And did she hate Lily! Hoo!"

"And so she shot Robinson dead." Dave straightened, looked
away to where rain-glazed cars hissed past against the rain cur-
tained background of another cliff. "Hell hath no fury, et cetera?"

"And framed Lily for it. You follow?"

"Thanks," Dave said. "I'll check her out."

"Any time." Dieterle reached and turned the key and the engine
started with a snarl. "What'd I tell you?" he yelled. The car backed,
scattering wet gravel, swung in a bucking U, and headed down
the highway toward Surf. Fast. Dave watched. Being in a chronic
hurry must be rough on a man who couldn't stop talking.

Nobody ate at The Big Cup because it was an openfront place
and rain was lashing its white Formica. It faced a broad belt of
cement that marked off the seedy shops and scabby apartment
buildings of Venice from the beach where red dune fences leaned.
Dave got coffee in an outsize cup and took it into a phone booth.
After a swallow of coffee, he lit a cigarette and dialled people he
knew in the television business. He didn't learn anything but they'd
be able to tell him later.

He returned the empty mug to the empty counter and hiked a
block among puddles to the Billy Budd whose neon sign buzzed
and sputtered as if rain had leaked into it. He checked his watch.
Twenty minutes ago it had been noon. A yellowed card tacked to
the black door said in faded felt pen that the hours were 12 noon
to 2 A.M. But the door was padlocked. He put on reading glasses
and bent to look for an emergency number on the card and a voice
back of him said:

"Excuse me."

The voice belonged to a bony man, a boy of fifty, in an expensive raincoat and expensive cologne. He was out of breath, pale,
and when he used a key on the padlock, his hands shook. He
pushed open the door and bad air came out—stale cigarette
smoke, last night's spilled whiskey. He kicked a rubber wedge un-

der the door to hold it open and went inside.

Dave followed. The place was dark but he found the bar that had a padded leather bevel for the elbows and padded leather stools that sighed. Somewhere at the back, a door opened and fell shut. Fluorescent tubing winked on behind the bar, slicking mirrors, glinting on rows of bottles, stacks of glasses. A motor whined, fan blades clattered, air began to blow along the room. The man came out without his raincoat, without his suitcoat. The shirt was expensive too. But he'd sweated it.

"Weather, right? What can I get you?"

"Just the answer to a question," Dave said. "What did you want at Arthur Thomas Robinson's apartment in Surf this morning?"

The man narrowed his lovely eyes. "Who are you?"

Dave told him. "There are details the police haven't time for. I've got time. Can I have your answer?"

"Will you leave without it? No—I didn't think so." The man turned away to drop ice into glasses. He tilted in whiskey, edged in water. He set a glass in front of Dave, held one himself. The shaking of his hand made the ice tinkle. The sound wasn't Christmasy. "All right," he said. "Let's see if I can shock you. Ten years ago, Arthur Thomas Robinson and I were lovers."

"You don't shock me," Dave said. "But it's not responsive to my question."

"I wrote him letters. I wanted those letters back before his oh-so-righteous brother got his hands on them. I didn't know how to go about it. I simply drove over to Robbie's. I mean—I never see television. What do I know about police procedure?"

"Ten years ago," Dave said. "Does that mean Robinson left you for Bruce K. Shevel?"

"That evil mummy," the man said.

"Clear up something for me." Dave tried the whiskey. Rich and smooth. They didn't serve this out of the well. "Shevel said he'd met Robinson in the hospital. Robinson was an orderly. A neighbor named Bambi O'Mara says Robinson was a barkeep all his life."

The man nodded. "I taught him all he knew. He was eighteen when he drifted in here." The man's eyes grew wet. He turned away and lit a cigarette. "He'd never had another job in his life.

Orderly? Be serious! He fainted at the sight of blood. No, one sinister night Bruce Shevel walked in here, slumming. And that was the beginning of the end. An old man. He was, even then. He must be all glamour by now."

"You know that Robinson kept your letters?"

"Yes. He was always promising to return them but he didn't get around to it. Now he never will." The man's voice broke and he took a long swallow from his drink. "That damn brother will probably have apoplexy when he reads them. And of course he'll read them. His type are always snooping after sin. Claim it revolts them but they can't get enough. And of course, he hated me. Always claimed I'd perverted his baby brother. We had some pretty ugly dialogs when he found out Robbie and I were sleeping together. I wouldn't put it past him to go to the liquor board with those letters. You've got to have unimpeachable morals to run a bar, you know. It could be the end of me."

"I don't think he's that kind of hater," Dave said. "Are you Lauder?"

"I'm White, Wilbur White. Bob Lauder and I have been partners since we got out of the Army—World War II. We've had bars all over L.A. County. Fifteen years here in Venice."

"Where is he now?"

"Bob? He'll be in at six. Today's my long day. His was yesterday. It's getting exhausting. We haven't replaced Robbie yet." He tried for a wan smile. "Of course we never will. But we'll hire somebody."

"You live in Venice?" Dave asked. "Oh, heavens, no. Malibu."

It was a handsome new place on the beach. Raw cedar planking. An Alfa Romeo stood in the carport. Dave pulled the company car into the empty space beside it. The house door was a slab at the far end of a walk under a flat roof overhang. He worked a bell push. Bob Lauder was a time getting to the door. When he opened it he was in a bathrobe and a bad mood. He was as squat and pudgy as his partner was the opposite. His scant hair was tousled, his eyes had pouches under them. He winced at the daylight, what there was of it.

"Sorry to bother you," Dave said. "But I'm death claims investigator for Medallion Life. Arthur Robinson was insured with us. He worked for you. Can I ask you a few questions?"

"The police asked questions yesterday," Lauder said.

"The police don't care about my company's ten thousand dollars," Dave said. "I do."

"Come in, stay out, I don't give a damn." Lauder flopped a hand and turned away. "All I want is sleep."

It was Dave's day for living rooms facing the Pacific. Lauder dropped onto a couch and leaned forward, head in hands, moaning quietly to himself.

"I've heard," Dave said, "that Robinson was good for business, that you were happy to get him back."

"He was good for business," Lauder droned.

"But you weren't happy to get him back?"

"Wilbur was happy." Lauder looked up, red-eyed. "Wilbur was overjoyed. Wilbur came un-fucking-glued."

"To the extent of letting Robinson take what he wanted from the till?"

"How did you know? We didn't tell the police."

Dave shrugged. "He was hurting for money."

"Yeah. Wilbur tried to cover for him. I let him think it worked. But I knew." He rose and tottered off. "I need some coffee."

Dave went after him, leaned in a kitchen doorway and watched him heat a pottery urn of leftover coffee on a bricked-in burner deck. "How long have you and Wilbur been together?"

"Thirty years"—Lauder reached down a mug from a hook—"since you ask."

"Because you didn't let the Arthur Thomas Robinsons of this world break it up, right? There were others, weren't there?"

"You don't look it, you don't sound it, but you have got to be gay. Nobody straight could guess that." Lauder peered into the mouth of the pot, hoping for steam. "Yes. It wasn't easy but it was worth it. To me. If you met Wilbur, you'd see why."

Dave didn't. "Do you own a hunting rifle? Say a thirty-thirty?"

Lauder turned and squinted. "What does that mean? Look, I was working in the bar when Robbie got it. I did not get jealous and kill him, if that's what you're thinking. Or did I do it to stop him skimming fifty bucks an evening off the take?"

"I'm trying to find out what to think," Dave said.

"Try someplace else." Lauder forgot to wait for the steam. He set the mug down hard and sloshed coffee into it. "Try now. Get out of here."

"If you bought a rifle in the past five-six years," Dave said, "there'll be a Federal registration record."

"We own a little pistol," Lauder said. "We keep it at the bar. Unloaded. To scare unruly trade."

Where Los Santos canyon did a crooked fall out of tree-green hills at the coast road was a cluster of Tudor style buildings whose 1930 stucco fronts looked mushy in the rain. Between a shop that sold snorkles and swim-fins and a hamburger place Dave remembered from his childhood lurked three telephone booths. Two were occupied by women in flowered plastic raincoats and hair curlers, trying to let somebody useful know their cars had stalled. He took the third booth and dialled the television people again.

While he learned that Bambi O'Mara had definitely been in Bear Paw, Montana, at the time a bullet made a clean hole through the skull of the man she loved, Dave noticed a scabby sign across the street above a door with long black iron hinges. L. DIETERLE REAL ESTATE. He glanced along the street for the battered MG. It wasn't in sight but it could be back of the building. He'd see later. Now he phoned Lieutenant Ken Barker.

He was at his desk. Still. Or again. "Dave?"

"Shevel is lying. He wouldn't lie for no reason."

"Your grammar shocks me," Barker said.

"He claims he met Robinson when he was in the hospital. *After* his so-called accident. Says Robinson was an orderly. But at the Sea Shanty they say Shevel *walked* in one night and met Robinson. According to a girlfriend, Robinson was never anything but a bartender. You want to check Junipero Hospital's employment records?"

"For two reasons," Barker said. "First, that rifle didn't have any prints on it and it was bought long before Congress ordered hunting guns registered. Second, an hour ago the Coast Guard rescued a kid in a power boat getting battered on the rocks off Point Placentia. It wasn't his power boat. It's registered to one Bruce K.

Shevel. The kid works at the Marina. My bet is he was heading for Mexico."

"Even money," Dave said. "His name is Manuel—right? Five foot six, a hundred twenty pounds, long hair? Somewhere around twenty?"

"You left out something," Barker said. "He's scared to death. He won't say why, but it's not just about what happened to the boat. I'll call Junipero."

"Thanks," Dave said. "I'll get back to you."

He left the booth and dodged rain-bright bumpers to the opposite curb. He took a worn step up and pushed the real estate office door. Glossy eight by tens of used Los Santos and Surf side street bungalows curled on the walls. A scarred desk was piled with phone directories. They slumped against a finger smeared telephone. A nameplate by the telephone said *L. Dieterle*. But the little man wasn't in the chair back of the desk.

The room wasn't big to start with but a Masonite partition halved it and behind this a typewriter rattled. A lumberyard bargain door was shut at the end of the partition. Tacked to the door was a pasteboard dimestore sign NOTARY and under it a business card. *Verna Marie Casper, Public Stenographer*. He rapped the door and a tin voice told him to come in.

She'd used henna on her hair for a lot of years. Her makeup too was like Raggedy Ann's, including the yarn eyelashes. She was sixty but the dress was off the Young Misses rack at Grant's. Glass diamonds sparked at her ears, her scrawny throat, her wrists, the bony hands that worked a Selectric with a finish like a Negev tank. She wasn't going to, but he said anyway:

"Don't let me interrupt you. I just want to know when Mr. Dieterle will be back."

"Can't say," she said above the fast clatter of the type ball. "He's in and out. A nervous man, very nervous. You didn't miss him by long. He was shaking today. That's a new one."

"He thinks the storm is going to knock down his apartments in Surf," Dave said. "Will you take a message for him?"

"What I write down I get paid for," she said. "He was going through phone books. So frantic he tore pages. Really. Look"— suddenly she stopped typing and stared at Dave—"I just sublet this space. We're not in business together. He looks after his business. I look after mine. I'm self-sufficient."

"Get a lot of work, do you?"

"I'm part of this community," she said and began typing again. "A valued part. They gave me a testimonial dinner at the Chamber of Commerce last fall. Forty years of loyal public service."

"I believe it," Dave said. "Ever do anything for a man named Robinson? Recently, say, the last two weeks or so? Arthur Thomas Robinson?"

She broke off typing again and eyed him fiercely. "Are you a police officer? Are you authorized to have such information?"

"He wanted you to write out an affidavit for him, didn't he?" Dave said. "And to notarize it?"

"Now, see here! You know I can't—"

"I'm not asking what was in it. I think I know. I also think it's what got him killed."

"Killed!" She went white under the circles of rouge. "But he only did it to clear his conscience! He said—" She clapped a hand to her mouth and glared at Dave. "You! You're trying to trick me. Well, it won't work. What I'm told is strictly confidential."

Dave swung away. His knuckles rapped the Masonite as he went out of her cubbyhole. "Not with this partition," he said. "With Dieterle on the other side."

Past batting windshield wipers, he saw the steeple down the block above the dark greenery of old acacia trees. Merwin Robinson had told the truth about the neighborhood. Old one story frame houses with weedy front yards where broken down autos turned to rust. Stray dogs ran cracked sidewalks in the rain. An old woman in man's shoes and hat dragged a coaster wagon through puddles.

CHURCH OF GOD'S ABUNDANCE was what the weathered signboard said. God's neglect was what showed. Dave tried the front doors from which the yellow varnish was peeling. They were loose in their frame but locked. A hollow echo came back from the rattling he gave them. He followed a narrow strip of cement that led along the shingled side of the church to a shingle-sided bungalow at the rear. The paint flaking off it was the same as what flaked off the church, white turning yellow. There was even a cloverleaf of stained glass in the door. *Rev. Merwin Robinson* in time-dimmed ink was in a little brass frame above a bell push.

But the buzz pushing it made at the back of the house brought nobody. A dented gray and blue sedan with fifties tail fins stood at the end of the porch. Its trunk was open. Some of Arthur Thomas Robinson's clothes were getting rained on. Dave tried the tongue latch of the house door and it opened. He put his head inside, called for the preacher. It was dusky in the house. No lights anywhere. Dave stepped inside onto a threadbare carpet held down by overstuffed chairs covered in faded chintz.

"Reverend Robinson?"

No answer. He moved past a room divider of built-in bookcases with diamond-pane glass doors. There was a round golden oak dining room table under a chain-suspended stained-glass light fixture. Robinson evidently used the table as a desk. Books were stacked on it. A loose leaf binder lay open, a page half filled with writing in ballpoint. *Am I my brother's keeper?* Sermon topic. But not for this week. Not for any week now.

Because on the far side of the table, by a kitchen swing door his head had pushed ajar when he fell, Merwin Robinson lay on his back and stared at Dave with the amazed eyes of the dead. One of his hands clutched something white. Dave knelt. It was an envelope, torn open, empty. But the stamp hadn't been cancelled. He put on his glasses, flicked his lighter to read the address. *City Attorney, 200 Spring St., Los Angeles, CA.* Neatly typed on an electric machine with carbon ribbon. Probably the battered IBM in Verna Casper's office.

Which meant there wasn't time to hunt up the rectory phone in the gloom, to report, to explain. It didn't matter. Merwin Robinson wouldn't be any deader an hour from now. But somebody else might be, unless Dave got back to the beach. Fast.

Wind lashed rain across the expensive decks of the apartments facing the Marina. It made the wet trenchcoat clumsy, flapping around his legs. Then he quit running because he saw the door. He took the last yards in careful, soundless steps. The door was shut. That would be reflex even for a man in a chronic hurry—

to shut out the storm. And that man had to be here. The MG was in the lot.

Dave put a hand to the cold, wet brass knob. It turned. He leaned gently against the door. It opened. He edged in and softly shut it. The same yammering voice he'd heard earlier today in Surf above the wash of rain and tide, yammered now someplace beyond the climbing vines.

"—That you got him to help you try to rip off an insurance company—accident and injury. By knocking your car off the jack while one wheel was stripped and your foot was under it. And he told you he was going to spill the whole story unless you paid out."

"I'm supposed to believe it's on that paper?" Shevel's voice came from just the other side of the philodendrons. "That Robbie actually—"

"Yeah, right—he dictated it to the old hag that's a notary public, splits my office space with me. I heard it all. He told her he'd give you twenty-four hours to cop out too, then he'd mail it. But I didn't think it was a clear conscience he was after. He was after money —to buy a sportscar for that hustler he was keeping."

"I'm surprised at Robbie," Shevel said. "He often threatened to do things. He rarely did them."

"He did this. And you knew he would. Only how did you waste him? You can't get out of that chair."

"I had two plans. The other was complicated—a bomb in his car. Happily, the simpler plan worked out. It was a lovely evening. The storm building up off the coast made for a handsome sunset. The sea was calm—long, slow swells. I decided to take an hour's cruise in my launch. I have a young friend who skippers it for me."

"You shot him from out there?"

"The draft is shallow. Manuel was able to steer quite close in. It can't have been a hundred fifty yards. Robbie was on the deck as I'd expected. It was warm, and he adored sunsets with his martinis. Manuel's a fine marksman. Twenty-four months in Viet Nam sharpened his natural skills. And the gun was serviceable."

Shevel's voice went hard. "This gun is not, but you're too close to miss. Hand over that paper. No, don't try anything. I warn you—"

Dave stepped around the screen of vines and chopped at Shevel's wrist. The gun went off with a slapping sound. The rug furrowed at Dieterle's feet. Shevel screamed rage, struggled in the wheel-chair, clawed at Dave's eyes. Dieterle tried to run past. Dave put a foot in his way. Dieterle sprawled. Dave wrenched the .22 out of Shevel's grip, leveled it at them, backed to a white telephone, cranked zero and asked an operator to get him the police.

Ken Barker had managed a shower and a shave. He still looked wearier than this morning. But he worked up a kind of smile. "Neat," he said. "You think like a machine—a machine that gets the company's money back."

"Shevel's solvent but not that solvent," Dave said. "Hell, we paid out a hundred thousand initially. I don't remember what the monthly payments were. We'll be lucky to get half. And we'll have to sue for that." He frowned at a paper in his hands, typing on a police form, signed shakily—*Manuel Sanchez*. It said Shevel had done the shooting. He, Manuel, had only run the boat. "Be sure this kid gets a good lawyer."

"The best in the Public Defender's office."

"No." Dave rose, flapped into the trenchcoat. "Not good enough. Medallion will foot the bill. I'll send Abe Greenglass. Tomorrow morning."

"Jesus." Barker blinked. "Remind me never to cross you."

Dave grinned, worked the coat's wet leather buttons, quit grinning. "I'm sorry about Robinson's brother. If I'd just been a little quicker—"

"It was natural causes," Barker said. "Don't blame yourself. Can't even blame Dieterle—or Wilbur White."

"The bar owner? You mean he was there?"

"Slocum checked him out. He had the letters."

"Yup." Dave fastened the coat belt. "Twenty minutes late to work. Pale, sweaty, shaking. It figures. Hell, he even talked about apoplexy, how the Reverend hated him for perverting his brother."

"The man had horrible blood pressure," Barker said. "We talked to his doctor. He'd warned him. The least excitement and"—Barker snapped his fingers—"cerebral hemorrhage. Told him to retire. Robinson refused. They needed him—the people at that run-down church."

"It figures," Dave said. "He didn't make it easy, but he was the only one in this mess I could like. A little."

"Not Bambi O'Mara?" Barker snagged a topcoat from a rack. "She looked great in those magazine spreads." He took Dave's arm, steered him toward a door. "I want to hear all about her. I'll buy you a drink." But the phone rang and called him back.

And Dave walked alone out of the beautiful, bright glass building into the rain that looked as if it would never stop falling.

SON OF THE MORNING

FIFTY YEARS AGO, when I first set eyes on Eliot Evans, I privately dubbed him Son of the Morning. I'd half forgotten that. But today it came back to me with irony when he was found shot dead —at dawn. A neighbor woman out walking found him, or rather her dog did, Eliot lying on his back in deep ferns, staring blankly up at the sky through the pines that shelter his little house in Settler's Cove. He'd long ago ceased to be, even for me, a Son of the Morning, and become a wrinkled, wild bearded, fierce-eyed old codger.

His short temper had made him a lot of enemies in his last years. The Sheriff must be scratching his head, wondering where to start his inquiries. He needn't worry. I have the answer. But Eliot Evans's murder was not like others. It was the outcome of a lifetime of events, with a subtle logic of their own, where the options kept narrowing until only one remained. To make this understandable, the whole story must be told.

But I'm not a practiced writer, and to keep things in order, I'm afraid I have to start at the beginning. On the first day of a new term, in a corridor of Villablanca College, where like every freshman I was eager and lost. My name is Dennis Colman. As I looked for something more important on a crowded bulletin board, a hand-lettered notice caught my eye. A freshman drama group was forming that afternoon. I'd been in some high school plays and was stage-struck. The little theatre was hard to find, I got there late, and was panting when I pulled open the door.

As I would learn, Eliot had scant use for chairs, and he lay at this moment propped on an elbow, on the apron of the little stage. A trim kid, dark skinned, brown-eyed, he had a startling mop of blond, almost white hair. A shaft of sunlight fell on him from a high window. He was dazzling.

A dozen youngsters sat in the stepped bentwood seats watching him, listening to him. Trying not to be noticed, I sat down in an empty row behind them. In a deep, authoritative voice beyond his years, Eliot was reading aloud from a looseleaf notebook his plans for Stage One.

"That's the name I chose. It's where we are, right?"

"How about 'Chrysalis'?" The suggestion came from a wiry kid in shabby clothes. Curly haired, snub-nosed, with a wonderful grin, this was Jonas Will, who, I would later learn, could always be counted on for the unexpected.

Eliot sat up. A sudden movement. He made a lot of those back then. Restless. Full of life. He let his legs hang off the apron. He frowned, heels gently thumping the stage, mused over the idea for a second, then shook his head.

"Too hard to pronounce."

"We could do 'The Insect Play,' " a girl said.

"We'd have to," someone else laughed.

"Stage One sounds fine to me," I said. "Let's vote."

And it was Stage One, and the play we put on was not "The Insect Play," but "Sherlock Holmes" by William Gillette, which meant that I, tall and thin, pale and long-nosed, won the leading role. Jonas was Watson, and Eliot the wicked Dr. Moriarty. None of which matters to this story. What matters is that during the weeks of rehearsal, Eliot, Jonas, and I became friends for life.

We did pretty much everything outside classroom time together: movies, sports events, the beach, the canyons, Eliot documenting it all with his Leica. The college radio station caught his attention. Its microphones, dials, meters, enchanted him. And he led us into acting there. His glorious voice got him the best roles. Jonas was never far behind. My own voice being colorless, I took bits as they were thrown to me. And wrote an occasional script. I had literary ambitions then.

We were dejected at the idea of being apart when Christmas vacation came, so Eliot arranged for Jonas and me to spend the second week with him. The Evans house was a new rambling redwood place hidden among trees in a quiet foothill suburb. I was captivated by the subdued beauty of that house, its pitched roofs and rough-hewn rafters, its walls of natural redwood panels. But Jonas positively fell in love with it. He came from a poor family. Our first night at Eliot's, as we got ready for bed, he told me:

"Someday I'm going to own this house."

I also fell in love—with Eliot's mother. She had lovely large brown eyes, and dark hair, sleek and abundant. Once, arriving home flushed from a late evening out, she'd worn a red rose in it. I'll never forget that. Elizabeth Alcott had been a silent movie star while still in her teens.

Then her strict family had stepped in and put an end to that by marrying her off to a sensible young banker called Harold Evans. She was of course by now in her forties, but she still seemed glamorous to me, radiantly charming, with a velvety voice, and a gently sardonic sense of humor.

Actually, we didn't see much of her, or of Eliot's father, either, a stodgy, straw-haired man. Eliot had a den with knotty pine walls at the rear of the house. It looked out on a deep backyard of untrimmed trees and brush. We three boys spent most of our days in that room listening to Eliot's collection of records—classics, jazz, Gilbert and Sullivan—or fooling with Eliot's expensive sound equipment. We improvised comic sketches, wasted quantities of costly acetate recording disks, and laughed till we cried at our sophomoric jokes.

Once, while some romantic symphony played in the room behind me, I stood idly at an open window, and through the tangled shrubbery of the backyard was startled to glimpse Elizabeth Evans. Some rough redwood furniture was grouped out there. Wearing what was in those days called a sun-suit, a cotton flower print affair of ample shorts and a voluminous halter, she lay reading on the chaise in dappled sunlight, a tall fruity-looking drink of some sort beside her, from which she would take an occasional sip through a straw. She still had a good figure, trim and smooth. I was ashamed of what I felt that day, standing at the window, staring. Lust was new and unsettling to me—certainly lust for a friend's mother.

From that moment on, I ached for her to look my way, smile at me, speak to me but, to my despair, it was Jonas who won her affection. At dinner. The dining room looked out on a ferny patio where a mossy fountain dripped. A portly, white-haired cook-housekeeper served the meals. These were the only times we had Elizabeth Evans's company, and that of Eliot's father. Save for an occasional grumpy remark about politics—Harold Evans was convinced Roosevelt was underhandedly steering this country into a European war that was none of our affair—he ate in silence.

His wife drew Jonas and me out—asked about our plans, and hopes, and dreams. Shy as I felt in her presence, yet she got me to talk—probably about being a novelist like Thomas Wolfe. Wolfe was my hero just then. She had a lovely knack of listening, her perfect head tilted slightly, eyes intent and glowing, beautiful mouth sometimes smiling, perhaps in amusement but never mocking or unkind, however naive our answers must have seemed. Jonas was going right to the top. To my ears, he sounded childish. But not to hers. Small sympathetic frown lines appeared between her brows as he unfolded his big plans to her, and she nodded gravely and murmured encouragement while Eliot and I smirked at each other, rolled our eyes, and sadly shook our heads.

"She knows he's had a tough life," Eliot told me later. "She was just trying to make him feel good."

"He's a jerk," I grouched. "You don't become a famous actor like you become a—a carpenter."

"Or a plumber?" Eliot wiped a record carefully, and slipped it back into its envelope. "My mother wants to apprentice me to a plumber. He slid the record into place on a shelf. "I worked two summers in my father's bank, and I learned it all. It seemed to come naturally. But—" He made a face. "A lifetime of loans, interest rates, investments, mortgages? I couldn't face it, and I told him so. He was hurt, but he took it. My mother? She was furious. There'd be no college for me. Theatre arts? Forget it, Eliot. Straight to the plumber's shop."

I stared. "But you've got ten times Jonas's talent."

"But Jonas isn't her little boy." Eliot dropped into a wicker barrel chair and lit a cigarette. "I am. And acting is a risky business. Unless you're lucky, you can starve."

"But you did get to college," I said.

"My father insisted," Eliot said, "but it's still on her mind. If I don't keep my grades up, I spend the rest of my life crawling under people's stopped-up sinks. Plumbers never starve. I mustn't take chances. Jonas?" He grinned crookedly, blew away smoke, shrugged. "Why shouldn't he take chances? What's he got to lose?"

Then Jonas came in, towelling his hair after a shower, and the subject changed.

"Dennis?" Elizabeth Evans smiled, and held out her hand to me. It was sunup. The driveway was deep in cool leaf shadow. Eliot was stowing our luggage in the trunk of his dew-damp car. It was time to return to school. I took his mother's hand. She said, "It was lovely to have you. I hope Eliot will bring you again."

Blushing, I mumbled, "Thank you—for everything."

Then she turned to Jonas. Not with a handshake. With a hug, and a kiss on the cheek. "Goodbye, laughing one." She stood him away from her, hands on his shoulders, and her eyes filled with tears, though she was smiling. "May all your dreams come true," she said.

And my heart broke.

A Shakespeare contest came along a few weeks later. I tried out with Pistol's clownish bluster in Henry V, but I didn't qualify. Eliot did—with Shylock's "Hath not a Jew eyes?" speech, voice deep and trembling, British accent complete with rolling Rs. Jonas got one of his farfetched ideas, that this was America, and Shakespeare's lines ought to be spoken as if by a smalltown hardware clerk. He chose the scene where Hamlet debates whether to kill himself or not, and it sounded really strange, but he acted it as if he was living it, and they made him a finalist too.

The finals took place the next week. Eliot sweated from nerves, but his voice made the windows rattle. He gestured to heaven with clawing hands. He writhed on his low stool, rolled his eyes, roared and whined.

Jonas was cool, almost motionless, and so understated he might have been reading want-ads, except that what he was saying made you think and worry.

Me. Not the judges. Eliot got the prize—Shakespeare's complete plays bound in red leather. I grabbed and hugged him. "Congratulations."

"Don't." He pushed me off. "I hate that." He headed for the door. I followed him out under the trees.

"You were wonderful," I said. "I mean professional—really. Go back. People will want to tell you."

"I know they will," he snarled. "I can't stand it."

"You're crazy," I said. "Just smile and say, 'Thank you.' What's so hard about that?"

Eliot shook his head. "They're fools. What do they know?" He started off across the campus. "I need a beer."

He was drunk and passed out before sundown.

But he had to face the problem again at term's end when he became the first freshman ever to win the best actor award in the annual one-act-play contest between the four classes. The senior play won. But Eliot Evans won the best actor trophy, as a creepy cockney in some melodrama whose title and author I've forgotten. I remember that, wearing a rubber cap to make me look bald, I played the host of a slummy pub, and Jonas, in an awful checkered suit, was an innocent young man killed defending a cheap girl who'd told him she loved him. We all stayed in costume until the winners were announced. But when Eliot's name was called, he wasn't there. He'd fled alone into the night.

Peeling off the rubber cap, smearing my face with coldcream to get rid of the drawn-on wrinkles, I asked Jonas, "What's the matter with him? He worked like crazy to get that part right, every word, every detail. He threw up before he went on tonight. Why put yourself through all that when you don't want anyone to notice?"

"He wants them to notice." Jonas tossed aside his shirt with the fake bloodstain on it, and sat down. He had no wrinkles to remove. Only pancake. It came off easily, in broad swaths. "He's the one who doesn't want to notice."

"A paradox," I said. "Been reading Shaw, have we?"

"Freud," Jonas said. "Look—it's only school now, but someday it will be Broadway, won't it, and Hollywood?" Jonas leaned forward to inspect his face in the lighted mirror that was dusty with face powder. His eyes found mine. "And he's already scared to death, Dennis."

"You're kidding." I laughed. "Of being a star?"

"That, too." Jonas scraped back his chair and stood. "But mainly, of how his mother's going to take it."

I gaped up at him. "His mother?"

"The beautiful lady you fell in love with at Christmas." Jonas pulled an old sweater on over his head. "The one whose parents jerked her out of the movies to marry Mr. Conventional, and live miserably ever after."

"Come on," I chided him. "She'll be proud. She loves the theatre. You've heard her talk about it. She glows."

"But she wants Eliot to be a plumber, remember?"

"She doesn't mean that. It's just a threat to make him keep his grades up."

"Maybe." Jonas walked out. From the corridor noisy with actors from the other plays, he shouted back, "Come on. We'd better go find him."

That summer, Jonas took a job pumping gas. A scholarship covered most of his college expenses, but he wanted to help out his parents. They were both old, and his father never seemed able to hold onto a job. I met the man only once. He'd lost his hardware business in the Great Depression, and never got over the shock, I guess. He looked sick to me, worn out, defeated.

Anyway, most of the summer of 1941, I was Eliot's only guest. We went to movies, to concerts at Hollywood Bowl. We drove to the beach, soaked up sun, or wandered the sleazy old amusement piers, eating hotdogs and ice cream cones, now and then trying the creaky rides. Once we drove up into the canyons, stopping at a little hidden lake Eliot knew about, rowing out in a splintery flat-bottom boat, I aimlessly fishing, Eliot as always snapping pictures.

We shopped for records, on the lookout not just for the latest releases but for oddities and rarities as well, especially in jazz. My father was a Buick dealer, we lived comfortably, and I never wanted for pocket money, but I was startled by the quantities of cash Eliot pulled from his wallet and spent without thinking twice.

To my relief, during the last week of vacation, when Jonas joined us, we didn't go shopping. Eliot would blow in one record store more than Jonas earned in a month at that greasy gas station. By that time, Eliot and I had grown a little bored with each other, so we were extra happy to see Jonas climb down with his battered suitcase from the bus, grinning, primed to chatter about the latest books he'd read, full of the excitement words and ideas always roused in him—and with a surprise.

A beat-up old guitar hung across his back, a hand-me-down from his boss. Now, I'm not going to exaggerate and claim that

Jonas had mastered the guitar in one summer, but it was plain that he was well on the way. He hardly fumbled. And that night, when we sat up late in Eliot's room at the rear of that lovely house, listening by soft lamplight to Jonas play and sing, I got my first inkling that maybe I'd been mistaken. Maybe, for all Eliot's looks and star quality, it was Jonas who had the bigger talent. Hell, Eliot couldn't even carry a tune. But then, did he need to?

In the fall term, Eliot began keeping company with Donna Philips, who in a peaches-and-cream way was beautiful as he was, and whose voice was deep and purring. They met while acting in plays at the radio station. Gillian Foley and I met about the same time, in a drafting class. I still dreamed of being a novelist, and was taking drafting only to satisfy my father, whose own father had been an engineer. Tall, athletic Gillian was taking it to help equip her eventually to become an aircraft pilot. Her dream seemed wildly romantic to me, but that only made her more adorable.

And what about Jonas? Who became adorable to him? Eliot and I didn't tumble at first, taken up with our girls, double dating on weekends, football games, movies, dances—enjoying a new phase in the process of growing from boys into men. Reveling in it, dazed at our good luck. Our old exclusively male camaraderie seemed a distant memory, faintly contemptible. But we continued to see Jonas. At least for a time.

Then one rainy November Saturday, we realized he'd drifted away. Some women's event had taken Donna and Gillian out of reach. We were idle. We went looking for Jonas, sloshing through puddles under the dripping trees. He wasn't in his room, wasn't in the library, nowhere in the eerily silent music department. We tried the doors of the little theatre. The only one not locked was the broad, steel-clad service door at the rear. It worked on rollers, and made a racket. It was dark inside, but we knew our way. Rain-damp, we climbed short concrete stairs, and pushed through curtains onto the work-lighted stage.

Jonas was there with a graduate student, Norman Ordway, a theatre intern, handsome, with a slight limp. They stood paces apart, backs turned to each other among scattered folding chairs.

We'd interrupted something, hadn't we? Jonas looked flushed. His smile was forced. He stammered, "Hey, where—where did you guys come from?" He turned with jerky suddenness toward Ordway. "Do you know Norm? These are my buddies, Eliot and Dennis."

"We've met." The man with the game leg nodded, but didn't offer his hand. While he didn't seem upset, he was famous around the theatre department for his charm, and today he didn't even smile, let alone start a conversation.

"What's up?" Jonas said. "You're never around anymore."

"Neither are you," I said.

"So we came looking for you," Eliot said.

"You picked some day for it," Jonas said.

"Who needs fair-weather friends?" I said.

Then the talk died. We stood there smiling feebly for what seemed a long time, then Eliot tugged my sleeve, and we mumbled awkward goodbyes and made a stumbling retreat. When the door slammed behind us, I asked:

"What were they rehearsing? I didn't see any scripts."

"What they were rehearsing doesn't need scripts." Eliot jammed his hands into his pockets and walked off.

Splashing across wet grass, I ran to catch him up. "What do you mean?"

He stopped and stared at me in disgust. "You don't know?" He pushed wet hair off his forehead. "My God, Dennis, how can you be so naive?"

"I'm as sophisticated as you are," I said hotly.

"Good." He ducked his head, and started walking again. "Then you now understand why Jonas wanted us to call ourselves Chrysalis. He was going to become a butterfly."

After the Japanese struck Pearl Harbor, the three of us gathered again at the beautiful Evans house for Christmas vacation. Elizabeth Evans mooned over us as if we'd all soon be lying dead on some battlefield. Harold Evans was grouchy because there would be a rubber shortage, and he couldn't get tires for his Packard. I? I was edgy at having to share sleeping quarters again with Jonas, knowing what we now knew. Eliot thought it was funny.

Jonas? His parents were worried about the war, about losing him—and after only two days he was on a Greyhound headed for home.

The air force sent Eliot to a training base in Texas. I enlisted in the Coast Guard, and was assigned to a teletype machine in rainy Oregon. Jonas was drafted, and from his letters, was finding his own ways to survive. He staged a camp show, for which he wrote the songs. He sent me copies. They were sharp and funny. Meantime, air force medics, in a routine physical, discovered Eliot had a heart murmur, and discarded him. But he soon landed a job that thrilled him—as an announcer at a big Los Angeles radio station, and not long afterward, he and Donna were married.

Jonas's bubbly letters stopped coming. I wrote him once or twice, but got no replies. Then, after a long silence, a letter reached me with the return address of his parents' house. It was far from bubbly. He had gotten into a scrape he didn't describe, been locked up for six months, then given a dishonorable discharge. He didn't know what he was going to do, now. He would write to me when he settled down. He never wrote.

On my next leave, I stopped off at the small, shabby house where I'd once met his parents. But another family was living there, and they knew only that Mr. Will senior had died. They'd never heard of Jonas. I stayed with my parents for a week, then caught a bus for Eliot's. He and Donna were living in a two-bedroom Spanish style cottage in the foothills not far from his parents' place. It was only half furnished, but there was a bed for me, and they'd asked me to spend the last days of my leave with them. We ate supper in a bright little kitchen that smelled of fresh paint. And over dessert, they had surprises for me—first, Donna was pregnant, her eyes bright with pleasure and pride.

"Congratulations," I said, trying to imagine what the offspring of two such gloriously beautiful people would be. A god, or at least a godlet. "That's wonderful."

"Thank you, kind sir," she said, "but any lady who puts her mind to it can make a baby." She beamed at her husband. "Eliot's got the really terrific news."

I blinked at him. "Yes?" I said.

He glowered as he'd done that day when he won the Shake-speare contest. "I did a screen-test for Paramount." That part I heard. Then he ducked his gleaming head and shoveled pie into his mouth, and I couldn't understand the next sentence. Eyebrows raised, I looked at Donna.

"They've offered him a contract," she said. "Isn't it exciting? It's like a dream."

"I always knew it would happen. Congratulations." I stuck out my hand. Eliot grunted and shook it briefly. I said, "I did. I told you so."

"It's only for a year," he said. "To see if I work out. It won't start till I finish my time at KGJ." He shrugged. "It's no big deal, Dennis. It's the war. All their actors have been drafted. Hell, they hand out those contracts like penny candy."

I laughed. "Not quite," I said. "Your mother must be terribly pleased."

He shook his head sharply. "We haven't told her. And don't you let it slip."

I frowned, cocking my head. "Something wrong?"

"She's—uh—not herself, these days," Donna said.

"I'm sorry to hear it," I said. "She's a lovely lady."

Eliot threw down his napkin and stood up quickly. "Let me show you the new speakers I built. Fifteen inch woofers."

"There are a lot of dishes here, Eliot." I started to gather them up. "We better help Donna with those first."

But Eliot had bolted from the kitchen, calling back, "You never heard anything so great."

And Donna took the dessert plates from me, smiling. "I'll manage, Dennis. Thanks." She nodded after Eliot. "Go on. He's dying for you to look and listen." She set the china in the sink. "Don't spoil his playtime."

On my third night, we drove over to the elder Evans's for din-ner. Eliot said his mother had especially asked to see me. And oddly enough, my heart was racing as we turned in at the familiar driveway under the shaggy trees. I laughed at myself—I was in love with Army ferry pilot Gillian Foley, not with Elizabeth Evans. Yet I trembled as we stepped into the long, handsome, paneled living room and, pulling off my sailor hat, I looked around for her in the gentle lamplight. She wasn't there, and the disappointment I felt was keen.

"Where's Mrs. Evans?" I asked.

"She'll be down," Harold Evans said. "For dinner. Nice to see you, Dennis." He pumped my hand. "How's the Coast Guard treating you?" He led me down the room. "What'll you have to drink?"

It took half an hour to get through cocktails and a lot of humdrum talk about the war. It seemed longer to me. But at last Harold Evans rose and led the way to the dining room. She was there. Already seated in her place. And as beautiful as ever. She beamed at me, held out her arms, and said a little too loudly, "Dennis! How lovely to see you." I went to her, and she bent me down into her arms and kissed me. She smelled of gin. She let me straighten up, but clung to my hands. "Oh, I'm so relieved to see you safe and sound." Tears filled her eyes. "This terrible war."

"I'm all right," I said. "It's good to see you again."

"Sit down, sit down," she said, "I'm so happy you could come. Oh, Harold, isn't this wonderful?"

Harold didn't look as if he thought so. Neither did Eliot. Poor Donna didn't know how or where to look. The stout housekeeper as she served the dinner kept a sharp eye on Mrs. Evans, who was flushed, and couldn't seem to stop talking. Once she broke off, laid a hand on my arm, leaned close, and whispered that she and I must have a long chat later. It was important. It was about Eliot, his future. The housekeeper poured wine for the rest of us, but not for the hostess. There wasn't even a glass at her place.

She solved this oversight, if that was what it was, by reaching out and taking my glass. She smiled. "You don't mind, do you, Dennis? You haven't touched this, and I"—she glared at Harold—"seem to have been left out." She drank deeply, tried to set the glass down and tipped it over.

A red stream streaked across the cloth, ran off the table edge, and onto my white trousers. I jumped up and wiped at them with my napkin. That kept me busy for a futile minute or two, and when I sat down and looked around, Elizabeth Evans had disappeared. So had housekeeper and husband. I heard stumbling and murmuring on the distant staircase.

"I'm sorry, Dennis," Eliot said. "Will it wash out?"

"I don't know," I said. "It's not important."

"She really did want to see you," Donna said. "She kept phoning to be sure we wouldn't forget, didn't she, Eliot?"

"She's losing her mind," Eliot said.

"It's all my fault," Donna said glumly, then, seeing my startled look, explained with a rueful smile, "She started drinking at the wedding reception, and she hasn't stopped since. I ruined her life. I stole her beautiful son."

"Bullshit," Eliot said.

Gillian and I were married at my base and honeymooned for two whole nights at the Motel Mildew in Astoria. Then she had to get back and shuttle a new bomber from Seattle to the East Coast, and I returned bleakly to my teletype machine. It was 1944. Was the damned war ever going to end? I doubted it. Early on, I'd use my spare time to try to write a novel, but every sentence came out amateurish. It only made me miserable, and I stopped trying. I read a lot, hoping somehow the knack of writing would seep into me. But reading had its limits. I was dying of boredom. So when, one surprising day, a yeoman handed me a note from, of all people, Jonas Will, I was absurdly happy.

We met for breakfast at a diner, rain weeping down the window we sat next to. Outside it, little birds sheltered in leafy shrubs. Jonas was too thin, but his spirits seemed bright. He was on his way to Portland to play and sing folk songs in some tavern. That was how he had been making his living since the Army kicked him out. A guitar case leaned beside him in the booth. Over eggs, bacon and hashbrowns, we reminisced about Villablanca days. There were extra mugs of coffee, many cigarettes. We laughed, and it felt good. Then Jonas changed the subject. Somberly.

"Have you heard from Eliot?" he said.

"They mailed me an announcement of the baby's birth. Paul. The godlet. Donna sent some snapshots. But Eliot never answers my letters. How's his mother?"

"She had a fall," Jonas said. "Downstairs."

I felt a chill. "Is she all right?"

He studied me. "I'm sorry, Dennis. She died."

"Ah, hell." I set down my mug. "When was this?"

"Just last week," he said. "I was staying with Eliot and Donna, and the phone rang in the middle of the night. It was Mr. Evans, at the hospital. The baby had a cold, Donna was afraid to take him out, so I went with Eliot."

"It didn't kill her instantly," I said.

He shook his head. "She lived long enough to talk to him." His face darkened. "I wish she hadn't."

"What the hell does that mean?" I said.

"She was unconscious when we got there," Jonas said, "then suddenly she opened her eyes and grabbed Eliot's hands. I don't think she saw me in the room, or Mr. Evans either. Only Eliot. She took him by surprise, he dropped off the chair onto his knees beside the bed. And she said, 'Eliot, I want your solemn promise. Promise me.'"

I blinked. "'Promise me' what?"

"That he'd never be an actor, never step on a stage or in front of a movie camera. Acting would ruin his life."

"She was off her head," I said. "That was her parents talking. Ancient history."

Jonas nodded bleakly. "You know that, and I know that, and Donna certainly knows it, but do you think Eliot will admit it? Hell, no. He promised. Under the circumstances, who wouldn't? She was his mother, she was dying."

"But now he thinks he's got to keep it?" I said.

"He made his agent cancel that movie contract," Jonas said, "the very next morning. On the phone. I heard him."

"But why?" I frowned. "He was never religious."

"Neither was she," Jonas said. "It wasn't religion, Dennis, it was melodrama, Elizabeth Alcott's big farewell performance."

I watched the small birds fluttering in the shrubs, restless, but afraid to go out into the rain. "He'll get over it, once the shock has passed."

"Don't bet on it." Jonas lit a fresh cigarette. "It's a heaven-sent excuse. Don't you see—he never has to try, now." He dropped the burnt match into the ashtray. "Never test himself. Never find out if he's got what it takes."

"He knows he has. You said so yourself."

"I also said it scared him."

"But it makes no sense." Brooding, I watched cars swish past on the glossy street. "What the hell is he going to do with those looks, that voice, the way he—?"

"He'll stick with radio, won't he? But not acting, oh, no. Announcing. A mouth for rent." Jonas sipped some coffee. "Wait and see." Then through the rainy glass he saw someone and waved a hand. "Gotta go," he said.

I looked at my watch. "Me too," I said.

He slid out of the booth, stood, picked up the bill. "Sorry for the bad tidings." He shook my hand, then reached for the guitar.

"Can't be helped." I did my best to smile. "It's good to see you, Jonas. Thanks for looking me up. Won't you let me pay that?"

He wouldn't. We stepped out into the gentle rain. At the curb waited a road-weary 1936 Plymouth. The passenger door opened, and the driver stretched out a hand. Not Norman Ordway. Some man I'd never met, young and fair and smiling. Jonas passed him the guitar, which he swung over the seat back into the rear, then Jonas slid into the car, slammed the door, and they drove away together.

Gillian and I returned to Villablanca to finish college on the GI Bill. Eliot continued announcing at KGJ. He and Donna had another child, a girl. His pay got better. They moved to a larger house. Gillian and I visited them there. Eliot took me with him to his job, I suppose figuring the glamor of it would impress me. He certainly had perfect mastery of it. That I admired. But I saw something else—the old can't-sit-still habit of college seemed to have become a tic. He prowled the rambling building, never settling for longer than it took to rattle off the station call letters and a commercial or two. Also he took a kind of savage delight in shouting obscenities right up until the split second when the microphone was turned on. He watched out of the corner of his eye for my shocked reaction. I hope it didn't show. What shocked me was how childish he was.

After working hours we drank at bars where everyone, male and female, seemed to know and love him. As stunningly handsome as ever, among these people he was a god indeed. We ate at a leather-paneled restaurant in an alcoholic haze, and went on drinking until two in the morning. We spent three days like this. It was unsettling, feverish, and I was grateful when the time came for us to leave. So was Gillian. Except for her delight in the godlets, Donna had lost her old merriment. I could see why. Eliot spent almost no time with her, and when he did, she seemed to get on his nerves.

As to Jonas, he'd written me half a dozen letters while the war dragged on, from towns like Boise, Laramie, El Paso. But he must have lost my civilian address, because when the war ended, the letters stopped. In 1949, Gillian and I went to western Massachusetts for a stay with her parents. It had been proposed as a month-long visit. We ended up lingering in that comfortable eighteenth century farmhouse for almost a year. The country around was New England at its loveliest. Even in icy wintertime. But we couldn't batten on the Foleys forever, open-handed and loving as they were to us.

Back in California, I proved a dud at selling Buicks, and my father talked the head of his advertising agency into hiring me. I wanted to write. This was my father's answer. I didn't like it, but it did set a typewriter in front of me, and the agency seemed satisfied. I even got occasional pats on the back for what they took to be a snappy turn of phrase.

Gillian taught high school science, and was a dedicated teacher, but it wasn't long before the workings of the school system co-opted her interest. At PTA meetings she organized parents into committees to deal with problems like crossing guards and playground maintenance. She would stride in, tall and determined, at the head of delegations of teachers to Board of Education meetings where they made their feelings known on such issues as overcrowded classrooms, inadequate supplies, too few textbooks.

She hired on as business representative for the teacher's union local. But city politicians were spineless and slow to act. The State influenced what happened in all schools, and with a union friend, stout, fortyish Bess Rubicoff, she took to visiting Sacramento to see what changes she could effect at that level. Once I went along for the ride. With time on my hands, I drove out into delta country and there, to my utter surprise, stumbled upon Jonas Will.

Shirtless, barefoot, thinner than ever, and burned brown by the sun, he sat on the afterdeck of a rusty metal houseboat. A square of canvas leaned on an easel in front of him, and he was dabbing paint on it. I stepped onto the deck and started toward him. A ragged straw hat shadowed his face, and for a moment I wondered if I'd made a mistake. But then he heard my footsteps, and looked my way, and it was Jonas, all right. The old boyish grin lit up his face.

"Dennis." He dropped his brush, stood up, and threw his arms around me. He smelled of sweat and sunlight. "How the hell are you?"

"I'm eating," I said, "which you don't seem to be."

"I'm all right," he said. "What brings you here?"

I told him. He went inside and came back with cans of cheap beer. I had shed my suit jacket, loosened my tie. He put the straw hat on me, set me in his ratty canvas chair and himself sat cross-legged on the deck. While I told him how I'd left the Coast Guard with the rank of admiral, of my triumph as an auto salesman, the thrill of writing advertising copy, I studied the painting on the easel. It was good, and I remembered the day he'd cropped up at Eliot's, suddenly able to play the guitar. I nodded at the picture— boats on the water, the view from where we sat.

"When did you learn to do this?"

He shrugged bony shoulders. "A friend of mine—Milton Smoot —he owns this boat. He's a painter. I watched him for a few weeks. Then I thought I could probably do it too." He reached for my cigarette, and I gave it to him.

"You sure as hell can," I said. "It's amazing."

"I sell one on the street in town now and then," he said. "Keeps me in pocket money." A teenage boy stepped out onto the deck. In swim trunks. He stretched sleepily, gave us a bored glance, took a few lazy steps, and dropped over the side into the water. Looking after him, Jonas said, "But I'll be moving on soon."

"Why? This seems like a pleasant way of life."

"Milton's tired of me," Jonas said. "He has a new"—he gave me a doubtful squint, and chose a word—"interest?"—to soften his meaning for my middle-class ears.

I reached for my wallet. "May I buy the picture?"

"It's still wet," he said.

I looked around. "Isn't there a dry one someplace?"

He shook his head. "I only paint them when I have to. Keep your money, Dennis. Honest, I'm all right."

"I wanted it to remember this day by," I said.

He got up. "Let's go get some shrimp," he said.

I gave him my address before I headed back to town to pick up Gillian and Bess. But he didn't write. Then in December, 1953, Eliot rang me at the agency. Could I come to the radio station on Saturday night? He wouldn't say why. He wanted it to be a surprise. Keeping up with my clients at work, and with Gillian's activities at home and up north didn't leave me a lot of spare time, but it was a rare thing for Eliot to ask to see me. For reasons I no longer understand—I'm too old, and too much has happened—he was still fascinating to me, handsome, magnetic, larger than life. So I agreed to go.

I pushed open a pair of red doors, and found myself at the top of an aisle sloping in darkness down between rows of red plush theatre seats to a stage. The stage was alight. Crisscrossed by black cables, cluttered with microphones, sound effects equipment, loudspeakers, all manner of radio junk, it looked unready for any sort of production.

But Eliot was there, headphones on his gleaming hair, papers in one hand, stopwatch in the other, facing a standing microphone. And not far from him, on a steel folding chair, guitar on his knees, sat Jonas. He had lost his suntan, but he hadn't gained much weight. He looked strained. A music stand in front of him held scores. A microphone, at the end of a glittering boom, hung close to his face. At the rear of the stage, the long rectangular window of a control booth framed a fat engineer hovering over recording lathes.

The red doors whispered shut behind me, I sat in the back row, and watched my two old friends record a radio program. And I thought as I listened to the smooth-voiced Eliot read the introduction, and to Jonas spin off one folksy old Christmas song after another in his light, easy baritone, that neither of them had come far from the days when we played at this at school, and in that knotty pine room at the rear of the beautiful Evans house years ago. When it was over, I trotted down the aisle out of the darkness.

"Wonderful," I called, and climbed onstage.

"You're late." Eliot took off his headphones. "You missed it. I'll play it back for you."

"I wasn't late. I heard it all." I brushed stage dust off my hands. "You're a magician," I told Jonas. "You looked scared to death, but you made it sound easy."

"It wasn't easy." He laid the guitar in its case, and looked bleakly at Eliot. "If this doesn't make me rich and famous, I'll kill you, Eliot." He gave me a sorry smile. "Unless it kills me first."

"What you need is a drink," Eliot said.

He had in mind one of those evenings drifting from one beloved taproom to another, and I dreaded it. But at our second stop, while Eliot, scotch in hand, was working his way down the long, shadowy bar, laughing with his boozy friends, Jonas said to me, "Dennis, I can't do this. I have to get up at seven tomorrow and go to work."

I stared. "Work? What are you talking about?"

"I've got a family to support," he said.

"Nobody gets a family that fast," I said. "You were a free spirit. A wandering minstrel. Utrillo, peddling his paintings on the street."

"My sister's family. Her husband died. Meningitis. No savings, no pension, no insurance, feckless son of a bitch. She has kids to raise. I'm the breadwinner."

"I didn't even know you had a sister," I said.

"What I haven't got is a car," he said. "I hate to put you out, but I need a ride home." He glanced toward the back of the tavern, where Eliot's hair shone. As always when he drank, his glorious voice was too loud. "He's being a terrific friend, he's giving me this program to try to help me. It's a big break, and I'm really grateful. But he'll want to go on like this for hours."

"I know all about that, and I'm with you." I gave his shoulder a friendly punch. "You're my deliverer, Jonas. I'll be glad to drive you home."

Home was a squat California bungalow on a side street in Hollywood, two or three blocks from the monster film processing plant where Jonas worked. The house was run down, in need of paint and a new roof. The tree in front wanted trimming. The lawn was weeds. On the sagging porch, Jonas dug out his key, and opened the door. The light inside looked harsh, dogs barked, and I heard the high-pitched voices of tired children quarreling. Jonas carried the guitar case inside, gave me a wave, and shut the door. As I drove off, I hoped that radio program would make him rich and famous soon.

It didn't. It aired once a week for two years, and every week he collected the musician's union minimum of twenty-five dollars. The KGJ sales department couldn't find the program a sponsor. And until they did, the network wasn't interested.

"It's too fucking refined," Eliot told me.

He drove around town in his old Chrysler convertible with the sun-cracked red leather seats, hustling the record companies. I seem to remember a flurry of excitement when a young woman producer at Capitol fell in love with what she heard. There was talk of an album with a string quartet backing up Jonas and his guitar. But she had no power. The sales people at Capitol called it cult stuff.

Finally Eliot somehow located a tiny outfit that agreed to issue a ten-inch LP—no money in advance. There was something wrong with the speed. Jonas came out sounding like a boy soprano. His little band of loyal radio fans bought the record anyway, but this didn't add up to much. His sister's squabbling kids still had to be fed, and Jonas went right on typing at the film plant. Then Eliot heeded the siren song of television, and left KGJ, the program was cancelled, and Jonas hung up his guitar.

Gillian's efforts in behalf of California's school children took her more and more often to Sacramento. By 1956, she'd rented a small flat there. Much of her work was voluntary, and her union paycheck was modest, so I hung on at the advertising agency in LA. When she was too busy to come home, I'd fly north on weekends. But paying rent in two places strained our budget and it soon became obvious I'd have to find a job in the Bay Area. I did. In San Francisco. In January of 1958. The next month, Gillian's talents of persuasion caught the attention of a big Sacramento lobbying outfit, who took her under their umbrella. We had enough income, suddenly, to invest in a house.

Meantime, Eliot was working in television.

"At last," Gillian commented, "the great world can see him in all his glory."

As he'd done years ago at the radio station, Eliot took me with him to his workplace. He was excited about his newest job. It was pathetic. On the glaring set, surrounded by massive cameras, seated at a desk where Eliot belonged was some mousy little man in a bad toupee and glasses, reading the day's news in a strangled tenor voice. Eliot's part? Groomed and dressed to kill, and so tense I thought he'd faint—his part was to announce the name of this nonentity as if he were a king, and to utter three antacid commercials.

Luckily it was only a fifteen minute program. I couldn't have taken more. When it was over, Eliot strolled across to me with an exaggerated casualness that showed plainly he was proud of himself. "Well done," I said, but I wanted to explode. What a waste. Did nobody around the place see his potential, not even Eliot himself?

Well, perhaps he did. Gillian was up north so much, the Evanses invited me over fairly often. Loudly affable when he greeted me at the door, wildly humorous and happy through the first drinks, he was good company. But inside, something was eating at him, and he grew surly and scowling by dinner time, when beautiful Donna and the godlets ate with heads bowed in a kind of paralytic dread of what he was going to say and do next. He often sneered at her cooking, but that was scarcely his only target. At last, I was begging off every time Donna, or more rarely Eliot himself, rang to invite me over.

I asked Gillian, "What happens to people?"

She looked up from a legal transcript she was reading. "To Eliot, you mean—your erstwhile Son of the Morning? They're cowards, and ashamed of it."

"Jonas always claimed Eliot was scared," I said.

"So they drink and bully their families."

I closed the novel I'd been reading. "It was that poisonous mother of his."

She cocked an eyebrow. "You loved her once."

I grunted. "I got off easily—she didn't love me."

"I seem to remember you telling me, she loved Jonas."

"Encouraged him to be whatever he wanted," I said.

Gillian took off her glasses, and nibbled musingly at one of the bows. "And Eliot remembered that, didn't he? And when his frustration got to be too much for him, he tried to make Jonas his surrogate."

"Jonas was grateful," I said. "He really threw himself into it. Digging up old songs, memorizing them, arranging them, researching their origins, writing copy about them. Every spare minute. Why didn't it work?"

"Oh, Dennis." She put the glasses on again, and peered at me over them. "You know the answer to that." She picked up the transcript and studied it. "It didn't work because it wasn't what Jonas wanted, it was what Eliot wanted."

"It could have saved Jonas from that damned film plant." I opened my book and closed it again. "What does Jonas want, anyway, Gillian?"

She made a jotting on a page. "Only a chance. And when it comes, he'll jump at it." She laid the papers aside, took off her glasses, and stood up. "Jonas is not afraid of failing." She headed for the kitchen. "Hot chocolate?"

Our place was one of those bay-windowed Victorian row houses that line steep streets and make San Francisco a photographer's delight. We both took pride in it, and as soon as the remodelling was completed, we asked Eliot and Donna to visit. And the godlets, of course. In the event, the godlets remained at home. And what accompanied Eliot and Donna were Harold Evans's ashes. In a metal box sheathed in leather. Harold had died in his sleep in a Chicago hotel room on the last night of a national banker's convention.

Eliot knew that Gillian had never lost interest in flying, and now that we were able to afford it, took up a rented plane almost every Sunday morning from a small bay area field. Eliot's father had wanted his ashes scattered over the ocean, and Eliot took it for granted that Gillian would oblige him on this mission.

"You're the only one I know who flies."

"Then it would appear," Gillian said drily, "that I am elected."

While we waited for the weekend, Eliot helped me shop for and install a new sound system. The process was harrowing from start to finish because he was never sober. Brandy went into his wake-up coffee, vodka into his breakfast orange juice, and during our shopping treks, he kept steering me out of dazzling sunlight into dark barrooms, where his Scotches were always doubles.

Jeeringly sure of his superior knowledge in these matters, he quarrelled with salesmen in the shops. His vocabulary was as obscene as when he'd tried to impress me with it years ago at the radio station. One store owner, a large affable man, finally lost patience, picked him up and sat him down out on the sidewalk. I feared Eliot would jump up and punch him. He didn't. He was too surprised.

But in spite of all this, we at last took possession of the receiver, amplifier, turntable, tape deck, and speakers Eliot judged best for me, and with much cursing and laughing and falling over furniture, they were duly installed. And I have to admit, they sounded glorious. We sat up all night listening by turns to symphonies and jazz, and it was a carryback to those long lost times in Eliot's room at the Evans house when we were young. Eliot insisted on running everything full blast, so I don't think Donna and Gillian, upstairs trying to sleep, felt the same as we did about it.

I didn't want Gillian to fly with Eliot drunk, and on Saturday night as he headed for bed, I caught his arm and said, "No booze tomorrow morning, Eliot, please."

He peered at me glassily. "Are you trying to tell me not to mourn for my father?"

"I'm telling you it'll be a small plane, close quarters, and you could endanger Gillian, as well as yourself."

"Don't worry, old friend." He stumbled down the hall. "Gillian and I—we're two of a kind. Adventurers both, risk takers, death defiers. I was in the air force—remember?"

"You're scared to death of flying," I said.

"True. Which is why you must not ask the impossible of me." And he disappeared into the guestroom.

I was asleep, but later Gillian told me Eliot was already drunk by the time they left for the flying field at seven o'clock Sunday morning. So drunk he forgot the box of ashes, and they had to double back for it. Strapped into his seat in the little plane, he was pale with fear. He clutched the box in his lap, closed his eyes and moaned as the plane took off. When they were out over the glittering ocean, he sat rigid, staring straight ahead, afraid to look down. Gillian began flying wide, slow circles.

"Any time you're ready," she told him. "Eliot?"

"What?" He jerked. "Oh. Yes. Right." He fumbled with the leather sheathing the box. But his hands were shaking so, he got nowhere. Gillian took it from him, slipped the box free, unlatched the lid, handed the box back to him. He took it dumbly. "Now what?" he said.

"Now open the door, lean over, extend your arm out and down and back as far as it will go, and turn the box over."

He had to fight the door. It kept slamming shut. He grew impatient and unfastened his safety belt. He hinged the door out and held it open with his left hand. With his right he thrust the box out through the opening. But the wind velocity surprised him, his arm struck the edge of the opening, and the box jarred open. Ashes and slivers of bone flew into his face. He gave a roar, clutched at his eyes, tried to stand, banged his head, and nearly pitched out the door. Gillian grabbed at him, caught his jacket, and yanked him inside. Too hard. He toppled backward onto her, howling, swearing, pawing at his eyes.

"Operating an aircraft with a hysterical grown man across your knees," Gillian said, "is not covered in the flight training manuals."

"I told him he could get you both killed," I said.

She kissed me. "Not quite," she said. "But we must give him E for effort."

We didn't hear from Eliot again for years. Donna sent Christmas cards, and an occasional brief, cheerful note about the godlets who, as evidenced by abundant snapshots, were now in their teens and beautiful as flowers. But our hero sulked. Occasionally, I would hear his splendid voice on a radio ad for dog shampoo or toilet bowl cleaner. Once on television we caught a shiny-haired vision of him aloft in a gaudy hot air balloon, in honor of some laundry detergent.

"Isn't money wonderful?" Gillian said. "It's cured his fear of heights."

"That's makeup," I said, "thick pancake makeup."

I believe it was the summer of 1963 when a client with an odd sense of humor insisted on lunch at a patio restaurant off Castro street, where all the patrons were gay. I suppose he was simply curious as to how this square, buttoned-up ad executive type would react. Naturally, I didn't react at all. Not to him. To our waiter, yes. It was Jonas.

"Is this a dream?" I said. "What became of the film lab? What happened to your sister and her brats?"

"She met a big, gentle slob who owns auto repair shops," Jonas said, "and he fell hopelessly in love with the whole fam damily, and married them all, dogs and cats included. I was free again." And in a travesty of any and all female movie stars, he flung his head back, and his arms straight up. "Free to be me."

"Oh, boy," I groaned. "This is Sid Howlett. Jonas Will. An old friend."

"I've seen you here often," Howlett told him, after glancing at me in wonderment. "Nice to meet you at last."

"Pity," Jonas said. "It's too late for us. We'll never know how rapturous it could have been. I'm flying south tonight. To fabulous Hollywood." He spun completely around. "Look me over. A living miracle, a waiter who actually got an acting job."

"Congratulations," I said. "It's great to see you, Jonas. You look fine. You needed to put on a few pounds."

"Oh, no." Aghast, he clapped his hands to his hips. Like me, like Eliot, he was forty now, but those hips were still narrow as a boy's. "Does it show? The camera adds to your weight, you know. God, I'll film like Jackie Gleason."

"That'll be the day," I said. "Here's my card. Will you call me? Gillian and I want you to come visit."

He tucked the card into a shirt pocket. "I'll try. But with stardom being thrust upon me, I'm in a whirl." He dropped the affected voice and touched my shoulder. "I promise, Dennis. Meantime, give Gillian a hug for me. Now"—he drew pad and pencil from his back pocket, and went into a gum-chewing Brooklyn waitress mode—"whaddaya wanna eat?"

After finishing his picture, sure enough, he paid us a visit, and it was a sunny time. Then for me, life began to darken. Cancer attacked my father, swiftly and relentlessly, and within weeks he was dead. Filled with gloomy thoughts about the brevity of life and how important we are to one another, I found myself angrily missing Eliot. So he'd made a fool of himself. Did that give him the right to go silent and distant after all our years of friendship? The day after the funeral, on my way back north (busy Gillian had gone by jet) I made a detour to confront Eliot.

No one answered the door. In the back yard, I found fair-haired Paul shoveling dirt from a high mound into an excavation. He was, what, seventeen, now? He plainly wasn't enjoying himself. His motions were sluggish and unwilling. I could understand why. The excavation was immense. It would take a crew of laborers a week to fill it.

"Hello." I closed the gate behind me. "What's this?"

He turned, frowning. "Who are you?" He stuck the shovel into the dirt and scrambled down. "What do you want?"

"Dennis Colman. I'm looking for your father."

"Oh, Mr. Colman, I'm sorry." He smiled, pulled off a work glove, stuck out a hand for me to shake. "It's been so long, I didn't recognize you."

"I was a small boy," I said. "What's all this?"

He turned and looked at the excavation. "It was going to be a swimming pool," he said wistfully. "Then Dad had a fight with the contractor."

"A fight about what?"

"Come look." He led me around the high mounds of earth to the sharp edge of the excavation. He pointed down. "See that?"

The gray dome of a huge boulder stuck up out of the earth. "The contractor hadn't bargained on that. He wanted extra money to dig it out and break it up and haul it away."

"And your dad wouldn't pay extra."

"No way." Paul laughed briefly, sadly, and shook his head. "So . . . we're putting it all back. Shovel full by shovel full. Dad and I."

I looked around. "Not Dad. Not today."

"Today he's working." Paul climbed the mound of earth again, heavy workshoes slipping as he climbed. "Doing narration on a documentary. At Instructart. You can go there if you want." Paul took hold of the shovel again. "He'll be happy to see you. He's always talking about you."

That cheered me up. "How do I get there?"

He told me, and I started off, but before I was out the gate he called, "Mr. Colman—was he always like this?"

I turned back. "Like what?"

"Always angry, always fighting with everybody."

I shrugged. "You've known him seventeen years."

"Yeah, sure." It began to rain. He squinted upward, stuck the shovel into the mound again. He shook his head. "He wasn't— not this bad." He came down to me. "What's happened to him?"

"He's middle-aged." I said. "Life disappoints us."

Paul pulled off the work gloves. Staring at them, he said, "Right, but—" He looked at me. "Could he be—well—losing his mind?"

"Could he?" I said.

"Are you going to see him, now?" Paul asked. I nodded, and he said, "Then maybe you can tell me."

Instructart was in Hollywood, in a rabbit-warren of boxy stucco buildings on a side street not far from the big lab where Jonas used to work. And that wasn't the only reminder of Jonas I was to get on this day. I found an open doorway, stepped inside an unswept hallway, and read a list of small photo labs, sound recordists, film producers, distributors, equipmental rental services, and the like. The listings were framed behind glass in movable white plastic letters stuck into black felt. A good many letters were missing. But I at last discovered INST UCT RT, with a room number beside it.

I probed dark, low-ceilinged hallways, cluttered with mike booms, light stands, stacks of empty film cans. I peered at doors, but there seemed no sequence to the numbers. Here and there a door stood open. I heard telephones ringing, snatches of conversation, laughter, the rattle of typewriters, the whirr of film projectors.

Then I glanced into an office, saw Norman Ordway seated at a desk, and stopped dead in my tracks. Taped to the walls surrounding him were posters for films. BOY CRAZY, THE BOYS NEXT DOOR, BOYS WILL BE BOYS. The photographs on the posters left no doubt what sort of films these were, or what sort of boys. I felt my face flush, and started to move off, but Ordway saw me and spoke:

"Can I help you?" Then he tilted his head and said, "Why, it's Colman, isn't it? Dennis? Weren't we at Villablanca together—the theatre department?"

"That's—that's right," I stammered. "You're Ordway."

He stood up. He looked much the same as twenty years ago, but he'd traded a jacket and slacks for faded jeans, a tie-dyed T-shirt, granny glasses. His hair was in a ponytail. He reached across a desk strewn with scripts and photographs of naked male teenagers, and I shook his hand.

"You were a special friend of Jonas Will's."

"I think you were the special friend," I said.

He grunted, and his face clouded. "Yes, well—the war took care of that, didn't it? Scattered all of us. A whole generation. All those friendships—"

"I've seen him off and on," I said. "He's weathering the years better than most of us. Still young. In looks. In spirit. Taking life as it comes. He was a folksinger for awhile, you know."

"I didn't know." A hot plate stood on a set of shelves behind him. He turned to it and poured mugs of coffee. "The Army threw him out. I saw him briefly after that." He asked me about cream and sugar, then handed me a mug, and moved a stack of film cans out of a chair to make a place for me to sit. He limped back to his chair, tasted the coffee, lit a cigarette, sighed. "I tried to help him, but things weren't the same between us. He was soon on his way."

"He never stays in one place long." I tasted my coffee, looked at the can on the shelf. It was a pricy brand. And it came to me that maybe Ordway's ragged clothes were only a fashion statement, the ratty little office merely a way to avoid unwanted attention, and that he was prospering at his dubious trade. "Last I heard, he'd got an acting job."

Ordway made a face. "It's a tough racket. For every success story, there are a hundred failures."

"I guess so," I said, and remembered Eliot. "Somewhere in this complex is an outfit called Instructart. Room one oh three. Damned if I can find it."

"Instructart?" He tried to suppress a smile. "Very respectable. An uncommon quality in this place." He ran a mocking gaze over me. "I might have guessed." He pointed. "It's in the next annex over."

In a darkened projection room I sat on one of a scattering of steel folding chairs and watched a film about hummingbirds, while Eliot, in headphones, and with a tiny intense light shining on his script, sat at a desk and read commentary into a microphone. There were long pauses. From a control booth at the rear, a pale, schoolteacherish man was giving Eliot his cues. That was what the headphones were for.

After a few retakes, the job was done. "Whew," Eliot said, shedding the headphones. "That's three reels today." He stood, wincing, rubbing his lower back. "George Werner, Dennis Colman." I shook the hand of the schoolteacherish man and learned he had been that before he began producing classroom films, apparently not very successfully. Soon Eliot and I were in the open air—and a sifting rain. Eliot had parked on a deserted school playground. We trudged across the street, I talking about my father's death, and charging Eliot with neglecting me. He wasn't listening.

"There's something wrong with my brain," he said.

I stared. "You aren't serious."

"I began having these—episodes. Fuguing, it's called. Ever hear of it?" We stepped around puddles in the school yard. "No? Well, let me give you an example. You get trapped inside a Dick Tracy comic strip, and you can't get out. You're living that shit. And you're the only one who's real. Everybody else is just a drawing."

He stopped under a stand of ragged old eucalyptus trees to light a cigarette. I waited with him. "Scared me to fucking death. I quit drinking. It didn't help." A skinny old man in a guard's uniform was walking toward us. Eliot eyed him. "So I went to a psychiatrist. He said it wasn't my mind, it was my brain, and I should see a neurologist."

The old man called in a thin voice, "That your car?"

Eliot ignored him. "And sure enough, the neurologist found some disconnected wires here." Eliot touched his temple. "He can try to reconnect them. But if it doesn't work, chances are I'll lose the power of speech."

"Oh, Christ," I said.

"Hey," the old man called again, "is that your car?"

"A welcome prognosis, right?" Eliot's smile was savage. "For a man who earns his living by the power of speech?" He turned away. "Come on." He headed for his car. The old man followed. Eliot unlocked the car.

"You can't park on school property," the old man said.

Eliot got behind the wheel. "The street's parked up. I work over there. Educational films."

"It's not allowed." The old man took a pad and pen from inside his damp khaki jacket. "I'll have to issue you a citation."

"Don't be an asshole," Eliot snarled. "Look. There's room here for a hundred cars."

"Can't help it," the old man said. "It's not allowed."

Eliot leaned across and opened the passenger door. "Get in, Dennis, God damn it." He started the engine. I got in. He released the handbrake.

The old man said, "Hold on. You're not going anywhere." And he made to step in front of the car. Luckily for him he wasn't fast on his feet, or I swear Eliot would have run him down. He was in a rage. As it was, the car grazed the old man, and he sat down on the wet tarmac. Eliot put the throttle to the floor, we ripped across the lot, jounced off a curb into the street, Eliot yanked the wheel around, tires squealed, hubcaps went flying, and we zigzagged northward, half out of control. We'd gone a mile and more before Eliot calmed down enough to look at me and remember:

"Shit. Your car is back there, isn't it?"

"No," I said. "I walked all the way from your house."

He drove me back. When I got out into the rain, I asked, "What if you don't get the operation?"

He reached into the glove compartment for a little druggist's vial and held it up. "These control the fuguing."

"Good," I said. But as I got into my car to follow him home, I reflected grimly that he needed more. He needed a prescription to control his temper.

A few weeks later, I had to go home again, to help my mother sell the Buick dealership and the house. She didn't want to remain alone in the house. Too many memories. She'd move back to Vermont—she still had a sister there. On one of several trips into downtown Los Angeles to look up records and consult county clerks, I ran into Jonas. At lunch in a restaurant that swarmed with attorneys.

"You look prosperous," I said.

"I keep working," he said. A sleek bald lawyer in dark glasses was with him. He introduced us, shifted over in the leather booth, and asked me to join them. I did, and as I ordered beer and a sandwich, I felt him studying me. He asked. "Are you all right?"

"Feeling mortal," I said. "How do you stay so young?"

"Riotous living," he said. "How's Gillian?"

"She'll be governor one day," I said, only half joking. The lawyer perked up. "You mean Gillian Colman?"

"I'm mister Gillian Colman," I said.

"I'll be damned," he said, and shook my hand again.

"Working?" I asked Jonas. "Tell me the pictures. I'd like to see them."

He made a face. "The picture, singular, was a dog. The rest have been TV pilots that didn't get bought. Not to worry. The pay is good." He changed the subject. "Have you seen Eliot lately?"

I told him about that. All of it.

He frowned and ate in silence. At last he said, "It's too perfect. I mean, of all the things to go wrong with Eliot Evans's brain, an operation to cure it has to imperil his speech."

"What are you talking about?"

"Why not his legs, arms, anything—but no, it's his speech.

Someplace inside, he did this to himself, Dennis. And I'll bet he's delighted."

"Delighted?" I feigned shock, but the same odd notion had struck me—that Eliot had been slyly smug about his affliction that day in the rain, that he'd secretly relished his rage at the old security guard, that it was a kind of performance. Still, I said, "Don't talk rubbish."

Jonas asked, "What does Donna say?"

I laughed wryly. "What does she ever say? She's learned the wisdom of keeping her mouth shut."

"And you? What advice did you give him?"

"He didn't ask for my advice."

"He's in trouble, Dennis. He's going mad and loving it—after all, it's the role of a lifetime, isn't it?—and now he's found a medical excuse. He's your friend, for Christ sake. How can you let him do this to himself?"

"Jonas, it's an injury, an illness."

"Then he should get the operation," Jonas said.

"He's your friend too," I said. "You tell him."

Jonas nodded. "I will."

Gillian was elected state supervisor of schools in 1968. I became a partner at the advertising agency. Jonas got steady work on a successful television series starring someone else. And Eliot? Jonas's commonsense entreaties had been no match for Eliot's terror of brain surgery. He might have to learn to talk all over again. He might never learn. He couldn't face that.

But at least we were friends once more. He and Donna came north and stayed with us twice. The first time, Eliot was his old radiant self. There was no drinking, there were no scenes, not even with Donna. We went sailing, and with his hair agleam in the sun, laughing, active, he was like the boy I'd first met.

The second time, a year later, he was drinking again, and on the very first night he flew into a rage when I unwittingly praised a film he despised. He stormed out of the house and didn't return. After a day or two, we regretfully put Donna on a plane to follow him home.

Business, Gillian's and mine, kept me shuttling between San Francisco and Los Angeles, and now and then my schedule and Jonas's meshed. One spring day in 1971, we met at Scandia as we'd agreed, but we didn't eat there. He asked me to follow him to his house in the Hollywood hills, perhaps because it was a smogless day, and the view from his balcony where we lunched was spectacular. It was a big, airy house, white walls, terra cotta floors, white wicker furniture. Brightly jacketed books everywhere. Navajo rugs. Handsome Mexican pots and jars. All of it newly acquired. Of course. He'd been a rolling stone. I envied him a little. Gillian and I hung onto things. Our garage and attic were crammed with business papers, all manner of junk from the past.

I had a three o'clock appointment. As I was leaving, I nodded at a portrait of Jonas over the fireplace. "By your friend, Milton Smoot?"

"He'd be pleased you recognized his style."

"I recognize the starving Jonas of Sacramento."

He laughed. I thanked him for lunch, and started down the long outside stairway that would take me to the steep street and my car, when he called:

"Did you hear about Eliot?"

I halted, turned, peered up at him. "What now?"

"He's retired, sworn off drink forever, sold the house, and moved to a cabin in the pines up on the central coast—a place called Madrone."

I squinted. "You mean by himself?"

"Donna's with him, but I think she's in shock."

"So am I," I said.

Gillian's election campaign, indeed her whole first term had meant hard work for us both, but once she was re-elected, the pressure eased, and with more time at my disposal, I took my next trip to LA by car, and left myself a day to stop off in Madrone. The house was hidden in Settler's Cove, a tangle of hilly trails among dense pine woods. But I finally spotted a mailbox lettered E. EVANS, parked, climbed a path through ferns to an unpainted H-frame cabin, and knocked.

When Eliot opened the door and saw me, he gave a shout of joy, like that of a man marooned who hadn't seen a human face or heard a human voice in ages. He even looked like Robinson Crusoe: he'd grown a bushy beard. He gave me a bear hug, and soon had me sitting drinking coffee with him at the kitchen table.

Since he'd given up liquor, coffee had become an obsession with him. He drove miles to buy fresh beans, roasted them himself, stored them at controlled temperatures, ground them in batches only large enough for a pot or two. It was a wild rigamarole. And he took it deadly seriously.

Other than coffee, I don't remember what we talked about, but we laughed and were as easy together as if we were twenty instead of fifty, and as if the intervening years had been untroubled. Donna arrived with smiles, and sacks of groceries. She prepared a good supper, we spent the evening listening to records, and they put me up for the night on a sleeping loft.

Small as the cabin was, it reminded me, with its wood paneling and exposed rafters, of Eliot's parents' house. As I drifted off to sleep in the silence of a country night, I reflected that, after all, it wasn't Jonas who had got that house he'd meant to own someday, Eliot had got it—or one as near like it as he could manage.

I was backing out the driveway the next morning before I remembered to ask, "Have you seen Jonas's TV show?"

Eliot turned away, and pretended to adjust a log on a stack of firewood. It was Donna who called, "We can't get TV. Cable hasn't reached here, yet."

"He's very good," I said, and waved, and drove off.

"He's a cipher," Eliot scoffed. A year had passed. Cable had come to Settler's Cove. A television set stood in the living room of the H-frame, and he had seen Jonas on it. "He's got that boyish smile, and that's all he's got."

Gillian didn't take vacations. But after six years of the battering her position attracted, she'd been looking tired. Then a demented woman shot at her in the street. Gillian acted unmoved, but she did buy a gun, a .38 caliber revolver, which showed me she was shaken—and I insisted we take a break together on the central coast among the pines beside the ocean. To my relief, she agreed. She'd soured on Eliot, but she still liked Donna, and wanted to renew their friendship. We were at breakfast in the sunny kitchen.

"Oh, come on, Eliot," Gillian said, "he's good and you know it. He won't stay in supporting roles forever."

"Gillian, he's fifty," I reminded her.

"And effeminate," Eliot said. "An old auntie."

But Jonas's success awakened suppressed yearnings in Eliot. On a drive south, when I stopped off in Madrone to deliver Christmas gifts, I found my old friend flushed with excitement. In the driveway, he was loading up his ancient convertible with coils of cable, an amplifier, tape deck, all manner of gear. It was a damp, cold day. Rain sifted down. Fog hung in the pines. He wore leather gloves, a mackinaw, a cap with ear flaps. I got out of my car.

"What's happening?"

"Little theatre," he said. "'A Christmas Carol.'"

I grinned. "Type casting. Scrooge, right?"

He looked at me in contempt. "Not acting," he said. "I'm in charge of the sound." He headed for the back door. "Come on. You can help me load the speakers."

I carried the Christmas presents indoors, then helped him load the speakers, and unload them again when we reached the theatre —on the highway, behind a cutesy tourist-trap tavern called the Coach and Four. We parked out back, where massive old eucalyptus trees dripped. The theatre itself was tiny, though it had a real stage. We spent hours stringing wires, installing and testing the tape deck and amplifier in Eliot's command post, a closet at the rear of the auditorium. He raged and swore at every little thing that went wrong. But he was plainly having the time of his life.

In 1976, Gillian won a seat in Congress. We spent the next eight years based in Washington. But the frustration of fighting entrenched inertia to get anything meaningful done, the cost of living, the social whirl, the endless campaigning and fund-raising, the constant commutes to California (by 1980 I had bought out my partners at the agency) left us both exhausted. So when the voters allowed us to come home to San Francisco, where we belonged, put our feet up, and draw a deep breath, I was relieved. But Gillian was depressed. I tried to cheer her up with the gift of a twin engine Cessna.

"I was in at the finish," Jonas said.

It was 1985, and we were lunching on the deck of his house—this one in Malibu. On the beach. It had almost been washed away by a huge winter storm two years before and, according to Jonas, its sobered owners had let it go cheap, the only way he could have afforded it. Too busy to watch anything but the news on television, I'd lost track of his career, but he had a talented black woman cooking in the kitchen, and a handsome, white-coated Filipino houseboy to fetch and carry, so I doubted he was hurting for money. At sixty-two, curly hair gone gray, he was still slim, carried himself lithely, and time had not dimmed that fetching grin. We were discussing Eliot—as we always seemed to do.

"'The finish?'" I said. "What do you mean?"

He wrinkled his brow. "Last year, the year before? On my way to San Francisco, I stopped off to say hi. And the next thing I know, I'm his assistant. What are we doing? Trying to tape a fanfare off some record. A sound effect for the next play at the little theatre, okay?"

I smiled and shook my head. "Like old times."

"Talk about hard to please. It took us an hour to get that fanfare the way he wanted it." Jonas had finished his chilled lobster, pushed the plate aside, wiped mayonnaise off his chin and fingers with his napkin. "I guess I wasn't exactly the handiest helper he ever had—but you should have heard the way he talked to me. You know how he barks that laugh afterwards, hoping you won't notice he's just called you five different kinds of fucking incompetent shit-head?"

"Wasn't it you who told me he enjoys his madness?"

Jonas frowned. "Yes, I did—but—"

"Well, now you've had a taste of it first hand."

"And I was wrong. The laugh is only a sound, Dennis—his eyes still hate you. He thought because we were old friends he could abuse me the way he does Donna." Jonas turned in his chair, looking through open French doors into the house, and waved an arm. "I hope he treats you and Gillian with a little civility."

"When he's sober," I said. The houseboy came and took away the wreckage of the lobsters. I said, "He wasn't drinking?"

Jonas smiled wanly. "He was never that awful when he drank. Not to me, anyway."

He watched surfers in a dazzle of sunlight on water, trying to make something of hopelessly placid waves. The boy brought key lime pie and coffee. I tasted the pie. Ambrosia. I laid down the fork, busied myself with my coffee. Then I looked at Jonas.

"It didn't occur to you that he's jealous?"

Jonas laughed. "Of me? You're kidding. Over what?"

"You're an actor, you're a success."

Jonas made a marveling sound, and tucked into his dessert. Between sips of coffee, he finished off the pie before he spoke again. "He could have been an actor if he wanted. We both know that. And a success. Not my kind. He could have been a star. He didn't want it, Dennis. So how can he be jealous of me?"

"Sometimes we have second thoughts," I said. "Usually when it's too late." I drank some coffee. "What did you mean—'in at the finish'?"

"We took the tape down to the theatre," Jonas said. "He sulked all the way. Barely said a word to me. And we've hardly walked into the place with the reel of tape, when he starts raving at the director, who also owns the theatre. What's his name?"

"Russell," I said. "Raving at him about what?"

"Russell greeted him with the news that the technical rehearsal was off. The actors didn't want to be bothered. Sound and lighting could be done at the dress rehearsal."

"And cheat Eliot of the chance to order everybody around all evening long? Oh, boy."

"You better believe it." Jonas laughed. "So with this big ox bumbling after him, wringing his hands, begging, practically crying— grim old Eliot yanks loose every wire, every piece of sound equipment in the place, and with me as his deaf-mute tote-boy carries it out of there, dumps it in the old Chrysler, slams the door and drives off in a rage. If I heard the word 'unprofessional' once on the ride home I heard it twenty times."

"Did you remind him it's an amateur group?"

Jonas nodded. "Didn't faze him."

"And so ends Eliot Evans's last flirtation with the wicked stage." Feeling melancholy, I watched gulls circling against a china blue sky, wings half transparent in the sunlight. "He was a fool, Jonas. In his apoplectic way, he was enjoying himself there."

"Enjoying himself?" Jonas pretended shock. "In the theatre? What would mother say?"

Writing this has been tiring, and I have made myself try to sleep for a few hours before putting the grim finish to it. I slept badly, woke and heated up yesterday's coffee, and by early morning light, I've just read these pages over. What they tell me is shocking. When I met him Eliot Evans was a handsome, personable college boy with a deep speaking voice—that was all. Why had I seen him as talented, dazzling, a Son of the Morning? Stranger still, why had I continued, against all evidence, to think of him that way for fifty long years? Most mystifying of all, when Gillian flew off on a political errand for the governor one foggy February morning in 1990, and her Cessna was lost at sea, and I was left alone in the world, why was the only place I could think of to go in my aloneness Settler's Cove—to be near my oldest, dearest friend, Eliot Evans? I have no answer. But that is what I did. I bought a place just over the ridge from the Evans H-frame, and settled in.

As about so many things, Gillian proved right about Jonas Will. He did not remain a supporting player forever. At age sixty-seven he was cast in a television series as a kindly priest who solved the day-to-day problems of his troubled inner-city parishioners. Dealing simplistically week after week with issues calculated to stir up controversy and headlines—street drugs, teenage pregnancy, abortion, gangs, racial strife—it was an instant hit. Jonas Will was a star at last.

"Still with that goddamned smile." Eliot threw down the new copy of *Time* I'd brought over, with Jonas's picture on the cover. By now, his series was in its third year. And Jonas had just won another Emmy. Eliot glowered at me. "How could this happen? He was nobody from nowhere—no background, no breeding, no anything."

"You believed in him once," I said.

Eliot snorted. "And what good did it do? A bad bet. Everybody makes mistakes."

"It wasn't a mistake," Donna said gently. "It was an act of friendship—a kind and caring gesture."

"The lightning just wasn't ready to strike," I said.

"I mean"—Eliot struggled up out of his old red leather easy chair, and paced, waving his arms—"what's there, for Christ's sake? He hits his marks, looks the other actors in the eye, and delivers the lines. That's talent? That makes you the hottest thing on TV?"

"He's very nice," Donna said. "Sweet and gentle. He always was. And funny. And loving. Those qualities shine through, Eliot. People sense them."

Eliot growled. "The hypocrisy of it. A jaded old queen as a role-model priest. How does he get away with it?"

"Eliot," I said, "he's an actor. Actors get paid for pretending to be what they're not."

"You're evading the point," Eliot said. "There are serious issues at stake here. Moral issues. The whole country worships him." He gave the magazine a savage kick. It landed at my feet. "They're being lied to and cheated."

"It's only make-believe." I picked up the magazine and tried to straighten its crumpled pages. "They know that."

He bent over me, eyes glittering. "How do you think they'd react if they found out what he really is?"

"Who's going to tell them?" I said.

Not long afterward, Eliot's aged convertible creaked to a halt at my back door. It was a sunny morning. I was eating breakfast at the kitchen table, reading the L.A. *Times*. As Mr. Gillian Colman, I'd needed to stay on top of the news. I couldn't break the habit. Eliot as usual came in without knocking. I looked up, and took off my reading glasses. He was agitated.

"Jonas is coming." He helped himself to coffee, sat down at the table, pulled a letter from a shirt pocket, tossed it across to me. "Random House is going to publish his autobiography. He needs old pictures." He grimaced and drank some coffee. "Photos I took at Villablanca."

"Well, God knows, that camera of yours went with us everyplace. There must be hundreds."

If so, they were in my house. When Eliot bought his place in Settler's Cove it was too small to hold much, and he'd put the remnants of the past he couldn't bear to part with into storage in San Luis. When, after moving here, I learned about this, I said, why waste money, I'd store them for him. This is a three bedroom place, with only me in it. So along with Gillian's papers and mine, Eliot's stuff in aging cardboard cartons is heaped in a north bedroom made gloomy by the pines that crowd around it. I put my glasses back on and read the letter. It was on the stationery of some Hollywood production company and typed by a secretary.

"He says he'll do the searching," I said. "He doesn't want to cause you any inconvenience."

Eliot snorted, got up and went to stare out the door while he drank his coffee. Jays squawked in the trees.

"You kept the pictures, didn't you?" I asked.

"Every last one," he said.

I folded up the letter. "It'll be nice to see him."

Eliot turned back. "You think this is a social visit? Do you think he'll talk to us mere mortals? Be serious. He'll barge in here with a staff of faggots, throw all our memories around, and be gone in an hour."

I shook my head. "He's not like that."

Eliot growled, "Who needs him anyway? Pervert."

I grinned. "If you didn't want to see him, you'd have written him you didn't keep the pictures."

"Bullshit." He filled his coffee mug again, back to me as he tilted the glass pot. "No, you're right." He set the pot down and turned. He was smiling, and there was something about that smile that turned me cold. "I do want to see him. I'm going to have a surprise for him, Dennis. The surprise of his life."

At age sixty-five I'd sold out to my young staff, and no longer worked actively for the agency, but I was on call, and a day or two later, an emergency summoned me to San Francisco. When I returned home, after forty-eight hectic hours of bargaining to keep a lucrative and recalcitrant client from leaving the fold—I found Eliot in that north room, seated on a dusty step-stool, digging through his old photographs, peering at color transparencies against the feeble window light, holding close to his eyes the faded handwriting on envelopes of negatives. And I realized Jonas would be along that night.

"These are the best ones," Eliot said.

"I'm back," I said.

"Welcome," he said. "Carry these, will you?" He loaded my arms with yellow boxes. "Out to the Chrysler." He busied himself restoring the stuff he didn't want to its cartons. Mutely, I went out and stacked the boxes on the cluttered rear seat of the old car. In the kitchen I set about making coffee. Eliot came in and turned off the burner on the stove. "There's no time for that," he said. "I want to show you Jonas's surprise."

"Eliot, I'm exhausted," I said.

He took my arm. "This will make you forget all that." And he hustled me out to the car.

He was trembling with excitement, and drove the crooked trails erratically, humming and chuckling to himself. With his sudden brakings, the yellow boxes kept slipping off the seat. He scarcely noticed. When we banged up the driveway to the back door of the H-frame, he was impatient with my overweight old man's climb out of the convertible, impatient with me as I gathered up the boxes of snapshots. He bustled to unlock the door, and stood there motioning for me to hurry. Once inside, I looked around for Donna.

Eliot said, "She's in Ventura. She and her brothers are moving Grandma Philips to another nursing home. She's ninety-five, you know. Impossible."

He set me down where I faced the television set. On the coffee table lay a box for a videotape. I picked it up. BOY HOWDY PROD'S, read the hastily stuck-on label. The address was that of the seedy little office where I'd met Norman Ordway that rainy day after my father's funeral. In the same building where Eliot did voice-overs for classroom films. On a strip of adhesive along the side of the box "Pretty Boy Lost" was lettered in marking pen.

Eliot pushed buttons on his VCR, a faint humming began, then twangy banjo music, and on the television screen the figure of a hitchhiking boy appeared. While the title and credits rolled, the boy waited wistfully with his thumb out on the shoulder of a desert road. He wore ragged Levis, a torn T-shirt, tennis shoes, and carried a small cheap suitcase. There was no mistaking him. It was Jonas Will. So this was how Norman Ordway had helped him when he'd shown up after being sacked by the army. By casting him in one of his edifying films. I stood up.

"That's all right," I said, "I don't need to see it."

"Wait, wait," Eliot said, "here comes his first ride. You'd be amazed how fast the action develops."

I went to the door. "I'm going home," I said.

Eliot switched off the VCR. "Won't Jonas be surprised?"

I had the door open. I turned back. "Don't do this, Eliot," I said. "What do you want to destroy him for?"

"Shit," Eliot said, with that savage grin of his. "He did that himself. He said that about me, you know, when I wouldn't risk brain surgery. Said I was determined to destroy myself, that I'd been doing it with booze for years. Wasting my talent. Afraid to face the world. Using my promise to my dying mother as an excuse to fail. Well, now we'll see how he faces the world, won't we? We'll see how much good success does him."

Speechless, I stared at him standing by the TV set, chuckling, nodding, scratching his beard, rubbing his hands together. Then, with a heavy heart, I turned and left.

Its mortal outcome never crossed my mind, or I'd have prevented their meeting that night. In hindsight, what happened is easy to reconstruct from the evidence. Eliot lying dead under the pines, no trace of Jonas Will. No trace of the videotape either, of course. Jonas would have taken that with him. Sad as the fact makes me, the Sheriff needn't puzzle over this killing. I'll print these pages out while I shave and shower, and then drive them across the highway to the Madrone substation.

The crisply uniformed deputy at my back door is a Lieutenant Gerard, fiftyish, growing bald. In his hand is the manila envelope containing the pages I left for him twenty-four hours ago. He holds it up. "Interesting," he says. "Nobody ever gave me this kind of help before."

"Is Donna at home—Mrs. Evans?" I say. "I ought to go over there."

"We'd better talk," he says. "May I come in?"

I step backward. He comes in. "Coffee?" I say.

He shakes his head, lays the envelope on the table and looks at me. "Mr. Will says you're wrong."

"Of course," I say.

"He went to Mr. Evans's house. They'd agreed to meet at eight o'clock. Mr. Evans's car was in the driveway, but he wasn't home. No one was. Mr. Will waited in his car for half an hour. Then he drove over here. You weren't home, either. He went and got something to eat at Shep's on the highway, then drove back to Evans's. He knocked and called, but nobody came."

"And you believe him?"

"Medical examiner says Mr. Evans was dead by seven o'clock," Gerard answers. "Those yellow Kodak boxes were in his house, all right, waiting for Mr. Will to look at them, but there was no videotape—not like you describe."

"Of course not," I say. "Jonas took it after he killed him. Didn't you find it in his car?"

"He doesn't have it. But someone does. I had the LAPD pay Norman Ordway a visit. The picture was made way back in 1944, but he still had a master print, and he copied it for a customer just the other day."

I smile. "Eliot Evans, right?"

"That's what Ordway said." Gerard goes to stand looking out the back. I hear the door of the patrol car slam. "But there was a hitch." Gerard turns around to look at me. "LAPD asked him to describe Evans."

I stare, feeling sick. "Yes? And?"

"He forgot the beard. It's not a beard you'd forget." A young woman in Sheriff's tans comes in. Gerard looks at me. "Ordway had been told the whole thing was to be a joke on an old friend. He didn't know it was going to come to murder." He glances at the young woman. She comes toward me, unfastening handcuffs from her belt. "When he heard that, he told us who really bought that video."

"I was in San Francisco," I say.

"At your agency?" Gerard says. "No one there saw you." He watched the young woman put the cuffs on my wrists. "Get him a jacket," he tells her, and leads me toward the door, telling me I am under arrest for the murder of Eliot Evans, and reciting the Miranda rules. "You know, Mr. Colman," . . . we start across the deck—"most of the time, in situations like yours, it's better to say nothing."

"I said nothing that would lead to this."

"You said"—Gerard supports me as we descend the steps—"that your papers and your wife's were stored in this house along with Eliot Evans's stuff. And when we went over the Evans's house looking for evidence, we found some of those papers. Hidden where apparently you couldn't find them. And you did try, didn't you? Desperately, from the look of the place."

He opens the door of the patrol car, and being careful that I didn't bump my head, helps me into the rear seat. He stands outside the open door and goes on:

"I wondered what those papers meant. I couldn't make anything of them. But I had an expert check them. A private detective down in Santa Barbara who specializes in accounting procedures, straight and crooked. It seems you handled the advertising for your wife's political campaigns."

"Never," I say. "That would have been unethical."

"Not through your own agency," Gerard says. "You set up a dummy company, a money laundry. You made half a million dollars off campaign contributions, Mr. Colman, and no one knew it. Then Mr. Evans—not on the day you describe, but earlier—happened to look into the wrong carton in that storage room and his eye lit on those records. He'd worked for his father, remember? He had a gift for banking. He saw in a moment what you'd done. And he confronted you with it. I knew Eliot Evans. He was always pestering me about his neighbors breaking some fiddling law or other, unleashed dogs, wrong-way parking. He'd have been shocked."

"Self-righteous bastard," I say.

"Another thing—Jonas Will doesn't own a gun. You do—a .38 caliber revolver. It was a .38 that killed Eliot Evans. Your wife's gun, right?"

"Gillian Colman was a wonderful woman. Millions of people adored her. The financial rigging was my doing. She knew nothing about it. But I couldn't prove that. And it would have sullied her name, her memory, all she worked for. I had to kill him. I had no choice."

"You had a choice not to try to frame Jonas Will by writing it all out for us." The young woman deputy comes with a jacket for me. Gerard leans in, drapes it over my shoulders, tells me one final thing. "As a motive for Mr. Will to murder your old friend, the porno movie was no good. You see—that book about his life Mr. Will has written?—the whole story is in there, Mr. Colman. He isn't covering up anything. The public has been good to him. They have a right to the truth. He says gay celebrities have to start being open about it."

The young woman gets into the rear seat with me. Gerard closes the door, goes around and gets in behind the wheel. It takes five minutes to reach the station. When we walk inside, I see Jonas in an office with glass panels. Seated at a desk, surrounded by deputies and clerks, he is signing autographs. He looks up and for a moment our eyes meet. Always before, whenever that happened, he gave me that marvelous grin of his.

Not this time. Not this time.